BOUNDARIES

JESSICA AIKEN-HALL

**MOONLIT MADNESS
PRESS**

ISBN-13: 978-0-9993656-1-8 (paper)

ISBN-13: 978-0-9993656-2-5 (e-book)

Library of Congress Control Number: 2020906694

Moonlit Madness Press

Cover Design © Victoria Cooper Art

Editor: Proofreading by the Page

*Warning- Contains sensitive subject matter including, but not limited to childhood sexual abuse, domestic violence, and suicide.

jessicaaikenhall.com

BOUNDARIES

ALSO BY JESSICA AIKEN-HALL

The Monster That Ate My Mommy- A Memoir

For my Gram, who loved a good mystery

CHAPTER ONE

I broke a nail trying to unlock my office door. I already knew it was going to be *one of those days*. My coffee spilled as the door jarred open. Thankfully, it only hit my shoes and luckily, I hadn't broken out my new Birkenstocks yet. The clock on the wall reminded me I was twenty minutes late, again.

The phone rang as I tossed my tattered, purple tote bag and shook the coffee off my foot. "Good morning, Lawrenceville Regional Hospital, social services department, this is Valerie Williamson. How may I help you?" I hated they made me say all that stuff. It took a full minute before I could even hear the other person speak.

"Val, it's Jeanine, don't you ever look at the caller ID to know who's calling?" She let a heavy sigh escape. "I need to talk with you about something."

"I'm sorry I was late...again. It's just..."

"Save it, Val, you're not in trouble. Just get up here as soon as you can." The phone clicked down on the receiver before I had the chance to redeem myself. I had worked for Jeanine for five years, and going to her office only meant one thing... more work for me. I pulled out my teal compact and quickly looked at my teeth. I hadn't had enough time to brush them before running out the door.

I wasn't sure what was going on with me, but I couldn't leave my apartment on time if my life depended on it. I couldn't sleep, either. There were too many thoughts racing through my head. Gabriel was the only one I talked to outside of work. He's the only one I can trust.

It was hopeless, there was no way I was going to make myself presentable enough for Jeanine. She doesn't understand me. No one does. I tucked my compact back into my tote bag, locked the door to my office and made my way to the stairs. Jeanine's office was on the third floor, mine was in the basement. Four flights of stairs were better than taking the chance of sharing an elevator that long with someone else.

Everyone at work teased me. They called me the "antisocial social worker." They were not too far from the truth. My office, just two doors away from the morgue, is where I spend most of my time. They said I spent more time with the dead than the living. I liked it that way. Death was a big part of my job. Maybe, my favorite.

When I reached Jeanine's office, the smell of orange and lavender overpowered me. She said it was the perfect combination to bring peace and harmony and disinfect the air at the same time. It was a hospital, after all. God forbid we catch what our patients are in here for. When I knocked on Jeanine's door, I saw her round head poke up from behind the computer. Her tight, dark brown curls were moist with hair gel to make sure they didn't move. She had to be in control of everything, even her hair. The reflection from some website glared on her cat-eye glasses. She pushed up her tan cardigan sleeve and looked at her knock-off Rolex. "What took you so long? You took the stairs, didn't you?"

I took that as my cue to go in. I shut the door behind me as I heard her mouse clicking. I pulled up a stiff, black, pleather chair and sat in front of her desk. I could feel her topaz brown eyes judging me as I sat across from her. Jeanine and I were nothing alike. Nothing.

She shook her mouse around on the mouse pad and sighed as she feverishly clicked. "Just a minute. It's here somewhere." She didn't take her eyes from the screen as she continued to look. "Oh... here it is." She pressed print and pointed to her printer across the room and nudged her head for me to go retrieve it.

I stood with my back to her and rolled my eyes as many times as I could while I waited for the paper to spit out of the machine. *She's so lazy.* I picked up the paper and walked it back over to her. Still saying nothing. The longer I stayed quiet, the less of a chance she could talk me into doing something else. I already worked close to fifty hours a week and barely got paid for forty. A nonprofit hospital with no money for anything.

She pushed the paper back at me. "Take a look at what they are proposing."

I took the papers and quickly scanned them. They were always looking for ways to get more grant funding. This time, they wanted to start a weekly trauma support group. "No." There was no way I was getting roped into this. I cleared my throat. "This is not something in my scope of practice. I'm not comfortable with any of this." I could feel the heat radiate off my face as I attempted to hand the papers back to her.

"Val." Her voice softened as she went on. "You are more than capable of doing this. That's why I'm asking you."

I shook my head. "No, Jeanine. No, I'm not." The anxiety bounced around inside my stomach, reminding me I hadn't eaten breakfast yet. "You know I don't excel at public speaking. There is no way I can do this."

"I'm not asking you to give a speech. I'm asking, no, I'm telling you to start a support group. It probably won't be many people anyway."

"I'll do anything else you need." I stood up, ran my fingers through my messy, blonde hair, and fought back tears as I looked at her.

"I'm sorry, Val, there is no one else to ask. The hospital needs this funding. The group needs to be up and running by the end of the month."

"Are you kidding me? That's next week. This is cra..."

"Thanks, Val. I knew I could count on you." Her eyes left mine and went back to her computer screen. "Please close the door on your way out."

I took the papers with me and slammed her door behind me. I knew I should have started looking for a new job long ago, but there was something about Jeanine. I just couldn't disappoint her. She made me furious, but she always won. She always got her way. I wish I could learn to stand up for myself.

I stopped by the cafeteria to grab something to bring back to my office so I could start researching trauma groups. There was no way I was going to be able to concentrate with an empty stomach. Vanilla yogurt, strawberries and granola. It was what I got when I forgot to have breakfast, which lately was every day.

I carried my tray back down the stairs, past the morgue to my office, and remembered I had locked the door before I went to Jeanine's office. Frustration grew as I searched my sweater pocket and fished out the keys. I felt the tray start to slip out of my hands as I fumbled with the doorknob and key. When were they going to fix this thing? Every other door had keyless entry. But down here, in the hallway of death, no one ever stayed long enough to fix anything. That might have been my least favorite part of my job, until about ten minutes ago.

I sat at my desk and began to search for information about support groups. I had never run one before, I hadn't even attended one. The more information I found, the more inadequate I felt. How was I going to lead a group, when I couldn't even get myself to work on time?

Where would we have it? We couldn't ask people to come down here. That in itself would be traumatic. I was the only one not creeped out by having an office down here. That's why I was given the job of Deceased Patient Coordinator.

The more I fought it, the more I knew I would hate it. I had to talk myself into this thing. There wouldn't be any time to advertise it, so maybe no one would show up. Maybe it wouldn't be so bad after all.

CHAPTER TWO

After hours of researching support groups and trauma, I was drawn into the cause. The more I looked, the more I found. One click led to another. Trauma affected far more people than I had ever imagined. Sexual abuse, sexual assault, physical abuse, emotional abuse, psychological abuse, neglect, domestic violence, the death of a loved one; the list was endless. The more information I found, the more I wanted. This assignment awoke something in me, it made me feel things I had not felt in a long time.

As my thoughts took me down memory lane, a knock at my door made me leap out of my chair, my heart pounded fast and steady in my ears. *Jesus Christ.* "Just a minute, I'll be right there." I always kept my door locked; I didn't like to be surprised when people entered unannounced. With no windows, I got to escape from the outside world for a little while. I liked it that way.

Jeanine was on the other side of the door, impatiently waiting for me to open it. Her arms were crossed as she peered in at me. "I was beginning to think you weren't in there."

"I've been doing research. You told me I have a group to start. Next week. By the way, thanks for the notice."

"Ha. Ha." Her arms were still crossed as she walked through the door. "My God, it stinks in here. Do you ever take out your trash?"

"That's not in my scope of practice," I smirked as she sighed. "Is this what you came down here for? To insult my housekeeping skills?"

"You mean lack of housekeeping skills?" She took the files from the chair and placed them on the desk before sitting down. "No, Val, I have a job for you."

"Another one? Jesus, Jeanine, what do you think I am?"

"Funny, Val." She looked directly into my eyes. I hated it when she did that. I know it's serious when she makes eye contact. "I need you to go up to the emergency department, room three. There was an... accident."

"Accident? What kind of accident?" Jeanine knew I didn't go to patient rooms. I strictly worked with families after patients died. I worked in the conference room on the first floor and the morgue. That was it.

"Well, it's unclear." She bit her bottom lip. "She's young... only nineteen." She shook her head as she closed her eyes.

"You know I don't work with the living."

"I know." Her eyes shot open. "We lost her shortly after they brought her in. They said she did it to herself, but I'm not buying it."

"What do you mean?" I brushed the hair out of my face as I leaned closer to her.

"I think her boyfriend did it. He's in there now, with her body. Her mom is, too. I need you to go in there and tell me what you think."

"Me? How about the police?" Rage began to boil inside me. I didn't understand why just hearing about this had me so upset.

"They have been called, but her mom needs you. And I want to see what you think. Size him up."

"Ahh, shit. What's her name? Her mom's name?"

"Carmen. Her mom is Jane."

I stood up and put my hair up in a bun. Jeanine followed me out the door, she put her hand on my shoulder. I usually push her off of me, but this time, I accepted the warmth of the gesture. Jeanine went for the elevator, as I headed for the stairs. I needed the extra time to think before reaching her room.

At the door of room three, my body sprouted goose-bumps. I took a deep breath before I knocked on the door. "Social Services, this is Valerie." When I opened the door, I was not prepared for what I saw. I let out a gasp as I got closer to her. Her t-shirt was covered in blood, and her wrists were both wrapped in gauze. Her petite frame was being cradled by her mother as she sang her a lullaby. And he just stood there watching, hovering over them. I could feel the anger pouring off of him. He did not act like he just lost someone he loved. Not in the least.

My desire to hurt him overpowered the devastation of witnessing a mother's pain as she mourned her child. I wanted to slap him across the face to see if he would even feel it. I wanted to cause him the pain he obviously caused this beautiful, young girl. Her blonde hair framing the sadness on her face.

I asked him to leave and he refused. "I'm not going anywhere. You can't make me.

"Sir, I just need a few minutes with Jane. Why don't you go get yourself some air?"

"I said, I'm not leaving."

"Do I need to call security? Or are you going to step outside for a few minutes?"

He sputtered under his breath, "stupid bitch," as he left the room. He had to be at least ten years older than Carmen, and the smell of vodka oozed off of him. I did notice the blood on his white t-shirt, as well as his faded blue jeans.

I made my way over to her mother and put my hand on her back. I began to rub up and down. "I'm so sorry for your loss, Jane. Is there anything I can help you with right now?" She let go of Carmen and grabbed hold of me and began to sob.

"Bring my baby back to me, bring her back. Please, God, bring her back."

I didn't know what to say to her. I couldn't bring her baby back, no matter how desperately I wanted to. I just held her as she sobbed, stroking her hair, and slowly swayed her back and forth as we stood together. "Oh, Jane, I don't know what to say." I sucked back the tears.

I took a step back so I could look at Jane's face. "Do you know what happened to Carmen?"

"He said she did this to herself. I don't believe it. My baby was happy, she wouldn't have done this."

"Did she ever tell you she felt unsafe with him?"

"No, never. Don't you think I would have protected my baby if she asked me for help?"

"Yes, of course. I just wanted to see if we could figure out what happened to your beautiful girl."

"He's just upset, he's not a bad guy." She looked down at Carmen, "He loves her, I know he does."

The door to the room opened and he walked back in, with a Mountain Dew in his hand. He paced the room as Jane and I watched him. "I gotta get outta here. Come on, man, we gotta go." He scratched his greasy, ash blonde hair.

"I'm not leaving her. I can't... not yet."

His agitation increased with the volume of his voice. "We need to get the fuck out of here now."

"Sir, I'm going to have to ask you to keep your voice down. Jane's not ready to leave yet, be patient with her."

"She's fucken dead. Let's go."

Jane's sobbing filled the room as she fell to her knees and rested her head on the side of Carmen's bed. "Noooo."

"Get out." I walked to the door and held it open for him to leave. A nurse in the hall stood and watched.

"Val, you need me to call security?"

"No, thanks, he's leaving. Right?"

He blew past us and ran to the elevator, pushing buttons and banging on the doors, waiting for it to open. I couldn't tell what was wrong with him. I had seen grief look many different ways, but never like this. He was hiding something, that was obvious. I needed to know what. I had worked with countless families who had lost loved ones before and never had they hit me like this one did. Never did anger get to me like this. Never had I wanted revenge.

CHAPTER THREE

When the police showed up, I slipped out of Carmen's room and headed for my office. I didn't want to be in the way, and Jane had already forgotten about me when the officers arrived. My heart broke for her. I'll be haunted by what I saw for the rest of my life, I can't imagine how painful this must be for her. Things like this are one reason I keep to myself. You just never know who you can trust.

With all the excitement from the day, the time had flown by. I was working on another ten-hour day. I promised Gabriel I would be home early tonight; I hoped he would forgive me. I am not sure he misses me as much as I miss him, but I hate to break promises.

By the time I made it home, Gabriel was waiting for me by the door. I could hear him yowling as my key pushed into the lock. He was the one thing I could depend on. After a hard day, he always gave me love and listened to the events from the day. Well, after he had his dinner. He was pretty easy to satisfy, unlike the other people in my life. All he wanted was a can of Fancy Feast, and endless hours of getting his shiny, black fur stroked. I don't know what I would do without him.

The sight of Carmen in her bed, in her mother's arms, made me miss my own mom. We hadn't spoken in years. I don't even know where she lives or if she is still alive. Some things can never be forgiven, but I still longed to have a mother at times. There was no way I would ever be able to trust her again. The few nostalgic moments that came every so often were not worth the trouble of getting hurt again.

I pushed the thought of my mom and Carmen out of my head as I made myself a cup of noodles. Gabriel ate better than I did, but I was too exhausted from the day to think about cooking. I hadn't eaten a real meal in ages. Life was just too hectic, remembering to eat was not on my list of priorities.

"Gabe, how was your day?" He jumped up on my lap as I turned on the TV. His yowling had mellowed into heavy purring. "A rough life you have here." I scratched behind his ears as he nuzzled his head against mine. "I know, I know, I missed you, too. I need to find a job with fewer hours, less responsibility and more pay. Today was one of those days I wished we could trade places. You go to work for me, and I lounge around all day, licking myself."

Gabriel curled himself into a ball on my lap as I flipped through the channels. I needed to find some mindless show to watch, so I could unwind enough to get some rest. Sleep was so hard to catch lately; I knew it was going to be next to impossible to clear my head enough to sleep tonight.

"You'll never guess what Jeanine wants me to do now." I

ignored his snoring and continued. "She wants me to start a support group." I giggled. "Yeah, I know how ridiculous it sounds. I hate people. Maybe if it was a support group for cats." I snorted and woke Gabriel up from his nap. "Sorry, buddy." Scratching his head, I continued to vent. "I just don't know how I'm going to pull this off. An hour a week, with a group of people." As the words left my mouth, I realized how small a task it really was. It was just an hour a week. One hour. Why was I letting an hour destroy me like this? I could do this. And, now with Carmen, I had even more reasons to. If I could help one girl, it would be worth my time and the anxiety it caused.

"Thanks for the talk Gabe, I can always count on you to set me straight." I stretched out on the couch while I felt Gabe's chest rise and fall against mine. I closed my eyes as I listened to a rerun of Law and Order in the background.

The cries from a baby filled the room. I looked everywhere, but I couldn't find him. I picked up the soft, blue blanket from the stark white bed, but he wasn't under it. I checked the crib, but there was no trace of him. I followed the cries, looking in each room, but they were all dark and vacant. I ran down each hallway searching for him. The cries became louder, echoing off the walls, but still, I couldn't find him. No one was there to help me look. I was the only one there, and I couldn't find him. I couldn't save him. I was his only hope. The feeling of emptiness crushed me as I gasped for air.

Gabriel's cries pulled me out of the dream and back into reality. My heart raced and my eyes stung. I reached for my necklace, half of a heart —a broken heart, to make sure it was still there. It was. Life was just as it always was. This wasn't the first time this dream had woken me up, and I knew it wouldn't be the last.

CHAPTER FOUR

Today's the day for the first trauma support group. I never came up with a clever name, partly because I didn't want to entice people to come. I did make Jeanine give me some money to buy snacks for the group. She tried to force hospital food on me, but I refused. I think she knew she pushed me to my limit.

While I was at the store, I picked up a box of soft tissues, not the kind the hospital buys in bulk that rips the skin right off your nose, but the kind with the pretty, flowery box with lotion on them. If I was going to sit with a group of people and talk about trauma, I wanted to make it as comfortable as possible. For me and them.

I loaded the belt at the register with the bags of assorted chocolates, boxes of brownies, pre-sliced sharp cheddar cheese, crackers, a bag of baby carrots, and the tissues when the headline of *The Village News* caught my attention, "Death of Local Woman Deemed Suicide."

I felt my face flush as my body began to tremble. I

couldn't read any more of the article or even look at the picture of the beautiful young woman smiling back at me. That feeling of revenge returned and filled every part of my body. I tossed a copy of the paper onto the belt, face down, so I didn't have to look at Carmen just yet. I needed to get her out of my head in time for the group today.

Something in me told me that Carmen hadn't killed herself. I knew this was another situation where the local police department couldn't put the needed hours into the case, so the easiest route was taken. Overworked and under-paid police let Carmen's case be closed, without any concern as to what really happened to her. I had seen this happen before, and it was infuriating to even think about. I totally get being overworked and underpaid, but when you work with people, for people, sometimes that just has to go out the window in order to do the right thing. I like the police officers in Lawrenceville; they are good people. That's why it was so hard to see cases like this happen. I had to believe they did what they felt was right. How could they live with them-selves if they didn't?

After I paid for the items, I carried the paper bag out to my tan Toyota Corolla, tossed them on the front seat and headed for the hospital. The group was still a few hours away, so I brought the paper back to my office, folded it in half and put it in the bottom drawer of my desk so I could read it later. I didn't want my mind in a bad space before the group.

I went to the conference room where the group was going to be and placed a few chairs around in a circle. I rearranged the chairs a few times, trying to get the feel right. I didn't know what feel I was looking for, but I wanted the room to look inviting. I didn't have a lot to work with. The hospital was in desperate need of remodeling, but there was never any money for that. It looked like the original paint from 1950 was still on the walls, and the carpet was so stained, I wasn't sure what color it was supposed to be.

A stale, musty odor hung in the air of the conference room. It wasn't overpowering but was strong enough to stay on your clothes long after you left. I found some cinnamon air freshener on the table in the corner of the room. I know there are regulations about using this type of thing, but I gave it a few sprays and placed it back where I found it. The cinnamon helped but was unable to make the room smell welcoming.

I placed the flowery box of tissues on top of one of the cloth-covered blue chairs. I took a step back to see how it looked. I still wasn't satisfied with the setup, but it would have to do. I put the snacks out on some paper plates, took a couple of Hersey kisses with me, and went back to my office to wait for the group to start. I had plenty of work to do.

The red light on my phone flashed, alerting me there was a message waiting. I used the phone a lot in my job, but I dreaded the unknown. A red light could mean more work for me, leaving me even further behind. I knew one thing; it would never be a personal call. Gabriel hadn't yet mastered how to pick up the phone.

I dialed my passcode into the phone and waited for the message to play. It was Jane. She did not leave any details, only her name and phone number. What could she possibly want? We hadn't talked since the day Carmen died. The urge to vomit came over me as I hung up the phone. This is not what I had planned today. Of all days. I needed today to be low-key, stress-free.

I am not sure why I was getting myself so worked up. I didn't even know what she wanted. Maybe it was as simple as getting Carmen's death certificate. As the thoughts of what it could be filled my head, I calmed down a bit. Deciding if I should call her before or after the group was what was weighing on me now. I wanted to know what she wanted, but I didn't want to get into something deep. I wanted to be my best self before the group. I wasn't sure which would help me achieve that.

I picked up the black phone and started to dial the number Jane left in the message. Before I hit the last number, there was a knock at my door. Startled by the noise, I slammed down the phone. My heart pounded in my throat. "Who is it?"

The knock came again, this time louder. "Val, just open the damn door."

I recognized the voice behind my door. I wasn't sure I wanted to answer it, but it was too late, I already asked who it was. There was no way out of it now. I wish I had a peephole, so I could decide if I wanted to deal with the person on the other side of the door or not. There was enough technology in this world to make that happen. Maybe that is the next thing I ask Jeanine for. As I made my way to the door, I took a deep breath and exhaled before I opened it. My hand on the knob, I pushed my hair out of my face with the other hand and pulled my black sweater down.

"Jesus, Val, I thought you died in here." His laugh was more abrasive than he was.

"Ha-ha, you're hysterical Tim."

"That's Detective Tim to you." His hands were in his front pants pockets as he stood looking at me.

"Really? You think you deserve that kind of respect from me?" A nervous chuckle escaped from my pursed lips.

"Well, are you going to invite me in or not?"

"Or not. That sounds like the option I want." I smiled as I opened the door wider to let him in.

"It reeks in here, Val. Are you keeping your work in here now? Bypassing the morgue?"

"You really are gruesome. And rude." My stomach began to ache as he found a place to sit. I didn't notice an odor in here. I don't know why everyone else was complaining. I guess it might be time to clean the office.

"I'm just teasing Val, you know that. Just relax." He sat in the chair in front of my desk, his hands folded behind his head as he leaned back and crossed his legs. His caramel eyes twinkled as I looked at him. He was wearing a suit so I knew he was on duty. He was one of the detectives that came to the hospital when there were questions about an untimely death.

A homicide detective and a deceased patient coordinator; what a love story that could be. We were meant for each other, except we weren't. We had gone out for coffee a few times. When we talked shop, we got along great. Heckling each other with quick-witted remarks. When we took it a step further, it seemed we had nothing in common. He wanted more from me than I was willing to give away and he didn't want to work for it.

"What brings you down here? There aren't any open cases that I am aware of." I sat at my desk; my arms crossed as

I waited for his response. I licked my lips as I focused on his dimples.

He smirked, "Does there need to be an open case to come say hello?"

"Yes. We agreed, strictly business." I uncrossed my arms and pulled my cardigan closed tight.

"Calm down, Val. Don't get all worked up. Rest assured, I'm here on business. And maybe a little pleasure?" He tilted his head back as his laugh rumbled through my office.

I pushed the smile off my face. "What's the business?"

"Do you remember the family who was here a few days ago? The one with the girl who killed herself?"

"Carmen?" Memories of the beautiful blonde girl in her bed flashed in my mind.

"Yeah, that's the one. We just finished up the investigation, and when I talked with her mom, she had a lot of... what's the word I'm looking for... emotion?"

"Well, that makes sense. Her daughter is dead. Did you see her? The girl? The blood? The sweet face? That's something I won't soon forget."

"I saw the pictures." He paused, closed his eyes, and shook his head from side to side as though he was trying to shake the image out of his head. "Her mom needs someone to talk to... to process it all."

"I have a list of therapists I can mail her."

"Well, she said she doesn't have insurance and no money."

"Tim... I don't like where this is headed. You know I don't do that sort of thing. It's out of my scope of practice..."

"Really, Miss trauma support group leader?"

"How do you even know about that?" Thoughts raced

through my head. If Tim knew about this group, who else knew? How many people were going to show up? My throat went dry as I tried to swallow.

"Val, it's in the paper, on fliers around the hospital, at the domestic violence shelter... word is out. I didn't know it was a secret."

"In the paper? Really? Jeanine didn't tell me she advertised it so well." I stood up from my desk, straightened my cardigan and looked at my watch. "Speaking of the group, it starts in fifteen minutes, I've got to go."

"Okay, okay, I can tell when I'm not wanted." He stood up and put his large hand on my shoulder. Instinctively, I leaned into the warmth of his skin. As I realized what I was doing, I pulled myself out from under his grip. "Just give the mom a call. For me?"

I took a step toward the door and a smile spread across my face. The scent of his Old Spice hit my nose and brought me back to one of our coffee *dates*. "She already left me a message. I'll call her after the group."

"Thanks, Val. It was nice to see you, even if I have to come down here, to the tunnel of death to do it."

"It was nice to see you, too, Tim." I shut the door behind us and locked it. "Taking the stairs?"

"No, I don't trust myself alone with you." He smiled as he walked to the elevator.

CHAPTER FIVE

A lady pacing the hall in front of the conference room met me when I arrived. Her salt and pepper hair was cut short and sticking up in all directions. Her long blue dress sat just above her white high-top sneakers and she clutched her brown leather purse. "Is this the trauma support group?" Her hazel eyes darted away from mine as soon as she made eye contact.

"Yes." The fear of failure began to creep up inside of me. I had no business leading this group. What if I'm not what these people need? What if I say or do the wrong thing? It was too late now; I had to figure a way to get through the next hour. I flipped on the lights and held the door open for the woman. "You can come in if you want."

She walked past me and sat down in the chair closest to the exit. She kept a tight hold of her purse as she sat up straight and looked around the room. I walked over to the table where I had arranged the snacks earlier and shuffled them around. Everything was already set up, but I needed the distraction while I tried to calm my nerves. I shut my eyes tight before I turned around to face the woman. When I opened them, I noticed another woman at the door. "Are you here for the group?" *Of course, she was.* What a stupid question. My heart thumped against my chest so loud, I was positive they could hear it, too.

"Yeah." Her voice was louder than mine, and she looked as if she was on her lunch break. Her black blazer matched her dress pants perfectly, not as if she had just thrown it together in the moonlight like I sometimes do. Her auburn hair was in a perfect braid down her back, and her black pumps were just as flawless. Her presence alone was intimidating.

"Come on in." I choked on my words and cleared my throat. "Find a seat where you're comfortable." She walked in, placing herself as far away from the other lady as she could. She pulled out her iPhone and scrolled through while she avoided interaction. I didn't blame her, I wished I had something to focus my attention on.

I walked out into the hallway to see if I could spot anyone else who might be joining us. I lifted the sleeve on my left arm to look at my pink Avon watch, a gift from Jeanine last Christmas, nothing I would have bought myself. Still five minutes until 1:00 pm. The second hand moved like a turtle as I waited for the time to pass.

At the registration desk, a woman who looked like she was in her seventies was nodding her head while the volunteer greeter pointed to me. I forced a smile and shot my hand up in a quick wave, and just as quickly put my hands together in front of me. My cheeks flushed as I tried to take back how uncool that move was. Maybe they weren't even pointing at me. I looked behind me to check, no one else was in the hall. I hated that I was so awkward. Human interaction was exhausting.

The older woman smiled as she walked toward me. I waited in the hall as she approached the conference room. Her tight silver curls bounced with each step. The navy-blue cardigan she had on over a white t-shirt with chickadees was the same one I wore just the other day. The swish of her blue corduroys became louder with each step closer.

"Are you here for the group?" Another stupid question. So much for first impressions.

"Yes, dear, I am." Her smile pushed her round cheeks up under her glasses and her blue eyes sparkled. She brought the sense of calm I had been searching for earlier.

"Great. Go on in and find a seat, we will get started shortly."

As she made her way into the room, I scanned the hall one last time. There was no one else who looked like they may be joining us. I walked back into the room and closed the door behind me. "Is everyone okay with the door being closed?" They all nodded their heads in agreement. I made my way to my seat, the one I had placed the box of tissues on earlier. Before I sat down, I cleared my throat, "Welcome everyone, my name is Valerie, but please call me Val."

When I sat down, I noticed that the woman with the iPhone was still scrolling through apps. I had the other two women's complete attention. I sat up straight on the edge of my chair. "There are snacks and a water cooler over there. Please help yourself, feel free to get up and move around anytime you need to. The first thing I'd like to do today is introduce ourselves." I scanned the room, three people and only four eyes on me. I could deal with this. "Who would like to start?" No one jumped at the offer. "I can begin if you'd like." The older woman's smile warmed me enough to continue.

"I'm Val. I work here at the hospital, in social services. This is Lawrenceville Regional Hospital's first group of this kind. I am glad you decided to come. If there is anything you need to make this more comfortable, let me know and I'll do my best." The iPhone was now out of sight. "Would you like to go next?" I smiled at the older woman.

"Sure, dear. My name is Norma, I'm retired, and well, thought this kind of thing might help me enjoy my free time a little more. When you're as old as I am, you've seen a lot of things, been through a lot of..." She paused before she went on. "Stuff."

"Thank you, Norma, for sharing." I nodded to the woman on her right. "Will you go next?"

She fidgeted in her seat as she looked at her feet. "I'm Maggie. My therapist said this would help me. I'm not sure how I feel about being here." The grip on her purse tightened as she adjusted herself in the seat.

"Thanks, Maggie. I think new things like this are hard for a lot of us." Norma nodded in agreement.

The last woman leaned back against her chair and crossed her right leg over her left. "Guess you saved the best for last." She looked around the circle to see if anyone reacted. We sat quietly as she went on. "No, but really, I'm Sonya. I found out about this group when I was at the domestic violence shelter a couple of days ago. I just want to get to the bottom of all this and get back to normal."

"Thanks, Sonya. Thank you, everyone, for the introductions. This group will be held weekly, in this room, at this same time. There aren't many rules, but a couple of the most important ones are that what we say in this room stays in this room, and we all need to be respectful of each other. If we feel we need to make more as we go along, we can."

Maggie raised her hand before I finished. "We don't need to raise our hands in here, we can just talk when we have something to say."

Her hand went to her face. "Do we have to talk when we are in here?"

"No, of course not. Only do what feels comfortable."

"None of this is comfortable. What if he finds out I'm here?" Her voice trailed off as she finished.

"Maggie, can I ask who you are referring to?" I paused for her to answer.

"I'd rather not say... not today."

"That's fair enough, we only share what we feel safe sharing." I noticed her knuckles turned white from the grip on her purse. "Can I ask you if you are safe at home, Maggie?"

"I'm not sure. I don't know if he knows where I live." I didn't know Maggie enough to know if her fears were valid, or if she was paranoid.

Sonya let out a heavy sigh, turning my attention to her. "Is everything alright, Sonya?" I was thankful the group was small enough that I was able to remember everyone's name.

"I don't understand why she's here if she's not going to

talk. I mean... I don't really want to be here, either, but I'm ready to be fixed. I want life to go back to normal."

The strain from not rolling my eyes induced a migraine. I rubbed the bridge of my nose to try to push it away before it settled. "Please be respectful of her. Of each other. We all just met, none of us know why the other is here." A tinge of annoyance danced off my words. "Have you ever heard the saying, 'Be kind to people, because you never know what kind of battle they're facing?' This group, this room, is a place for all of us to be kinder than we usually are. This is our safe space. We need to be patient as we get to know each other."

"Sorry. You're right, when I'm nervous I tend to lash out. I'll try harder." Her head turned toward Maggie and she forced a smile. "Sorry, Mags."

Maggie nodded her head, her eyes fixated on her purse. The anxiety in the room made mine increase. What had I gotten myself into? The real question was, where was Jeanine? It was her fault I had to be the referee to a group of troubled women. Hell, who am I kidding? I need this group, maybe more than they do.

"Norma, how are you doing over there?" Her calmness kept the energy in the room tolerable, but that was supposed to be my job.

"I'm fine, dear." I could tell her smile was forced this time. She wasn't fine. If she were, why was she here?

When I looked up from Norma, I saw a face peering in the small, rectangular window in the door. It was Jeanine. Maybe she was coming to rescue me after all. I motioned for her to come in. As the door opened, the women in the group turned around to greet her. She was not alone.

A familiar woman stood at her side. I searched my memory to place who this woman was. I knew I had seen her before. I see a lot of people here at work, it was not uncommon for me to draw a blank, but this time, it was different. I felt connected to this woman, so much so that the other ladies faded from my vision.

"Sorry to interrupt ladies, but I have a new member for your group." Jeanine smiled as she patted the woman on the back. "This is Jane, she will be joining you."

Jane. I couldn't get rid of her if I wanted to. Jane looked at me, smiled, and sat between Norma and Sonya. Seeing Jane brought the images of Carmen back to me, just as the newspaper headline had done only hours before.

"Thanks, Jeanine, will you be joining us as well?" I knew the answer before I asked but wanted to put her on the spot.

"No, not today. I've got a meeting to run to." At the door, she waved to the five of us and shut it behind her.

"Welcome, Jane. Glad you are joining us today." The other women nodded, as though in agreement with me. "We were just getting to know each other a little bit, this is our first meeting."

"Thanks." She pushed her straw-like brown hair behind her ear. "I'm here because of my baby, Carmen." Her words pierced my chest as they left her mouth, like an arrow into a target. "I just found out that... that... she killed herself." She took a crumpled-up tissue out of her jeans pocket and dabbed at her eyes. They were both dry, maybe she wanted to stop the tears before they escaped.

"Oh, dear. I'm sorry, honey." Norma reached her hand out to Jane. She accepted the offer and bowed her head. We all sat in silence while we waited for Jane to continue. I fought the tears back as I watched the others come together for this stranger. I wanted some of this sympathy, but who was I in the big picture? In anyone's big picture? I wanted what Jane and Carmen had —but now she didn't even have it. Guilt washed over me as I took relief in that. *She* knows the pain I carry. I didn't want the joy this brought me.

I could not shake the feeling that Carmen was murdered. This was not the time or place to question Jane about it. There may never be a *right* time to question the authorities' decision. And who am I to question them? A whirlwind of thoughts raced through my mind. I closed my eyes and shook my head to get them out.

"Jane. I'm so sorry. This news must be tough for you." She lifted her head up and nodded.

"It really is. It feels like I didn't even know her. Carmen wasn't like that. She wouldn't... she would never have..." Her eyes closed again as her head dropped back down. Norma's eyes glistened with tears; their hands still attached. I looked around the room, Sonya and Maggie both had moisture in their eyes. This was a rough turn of events for day one of a trauma support group. This is not at all what I had imagined. I didn't know what to expect, but having Jane join us was the furthest thing from my imagination.

CHAPTER SIX

G abriel was waiting for me in his usual spot, ready to greet me after a long day. His love was just what I needed after today. I prepared his dinner, and then heated up some left-over Chinese; egg rolls and lo mein. I placed his bowl on his mat by the kitchen table, and pulled out the *Village News* from my tote bag, put it on the table, and retrieved my leftovers. I wasn't sure I was ready to read this, but I *needed* to.

When Gabriel was done with his dinner, he jumped up on my lap so I could pet him. He purred as my hand ruffled up his fur. "Should I do this, Gabe? Or let it go?" He continued to purr as his green eyes looked up at me. "You're right. I just need to get it over with." I pushed my soggy egg rolls over and unfolded the paper. A sigh built up since morning escaped as I was faced with Carmen's beautiful smile.

Nineteen-year-old Carmen Davidson's death came as a surprise to her family. She was a happy girl, on her way to her second year of college, without a worry in the world, ... or so her mother, Jane Cater thought. After she claimed her daughter would have never harmed herself, she was the one to find the suicide note Davidson left behind. Relationship troubles are said to be the cause of her unhappiness. Her death has now been ruled a suicide.

"I don't buy it, Gabe. This seems fishy...like a big ole' can of tuna fish." I expected more to the front-page story. I waited all day to read this, afraid of what it might say, and then... nothing. Jane found her suicide note, but never mentioned a word about it today. My mind tried to recreate the note. I wondered what it said. I tried to picture Carmen, so depressed with life that she sat down with a piece of paper and a pen...or a computer...and wrote her good-bye letter to those she loved most. Why had it been so hard to find before? Did the shock of finding her covered in her own blood blind Jane before? Or did someone plant the note to make it look like a suicide?

A hundred different scenarios played out in my head. I found a notebook and began to write down the thoughts as they came. What would I ever do with this? Not like I would give it to Jane, or Detective Phillips. My connection to this girl is borderline crazy. Maybe because she was nineteen. Such a loss, and so young.

I folded the paper back up and carried Gabriel to the couch. "Snuggle time, buddy." Gabriel's warmth was just the right amount of comfort needed after a day like today. I flipped on the TV for my nightly veg session. *Snapped* was on next. Tim told me about this show before. We joked about him watching it. He said it was to help him figure out how deranged people think. He told me if I ever needed some ideas, this was the show to watch. Guess it was time to see what he was talking about.

"I wonder if Tim is watching this tonight, too. Think we should invite him to join us?" I scratched behind his ears as he hummed against my chest. "Don't worry, buddy, you're the only guy I want to share my evenings with. There's no room for him on this couch." When the show came back on, it caught my interest. The voice of the host had me hooked by the first commercial break. There was no way I'm falling asleep on the couch tonight. "This is pretty good; don't you think, Gabe?" It hadn't kept him from sleeping, but napping was his favorite thing to do with a full belly.

A hitman hired by an unfaithful wife. What could possibly go wrong with that? I couldn't believe how stupid people can be. Did she really think she would get away with it? Collect the insurance money and start a new life with a new guy? People like her made me sick. Were these the kind of people Tim had to deal with all the time? Or was this Hollywood? Either way, I was intrigued. Maybe I was in the wrong business. I already worked with the dead, perhaps it's time I started working with the reason they were dead. That just seemed too risky. I enjoyed flying under the radar. Some days I didn't want to deal with people and just lock my door and spend my time doing paperwork. I bet homicide detectives didn't have enough paperwork to stay away from people as long as I needed.

Another episode came on. "Looks like it's our lucky night." I placed Gabriel's sleeping body onto the sofa so I could go to the bathroom and get a cup of tea. Peppermint tea always reminded me of my grandma and helped settle my stomach when I forgot how awful Chinese made me feel. I ran the water, put the kettle on the back burner and went to the bathroom. I left the door open so I wouldn't miss anything. It was just Gabriel and I, so who cared if I shut it? When I did close it, he laid by the door, stuck his paws under and meowed, forcing me to talk to him while I'm trying to be civilized. Thank goodness we never have company.

After washing my hands, I put the tea bag into my favorite blue ceramic mug and poured the hot water over it. When the scalding water hit the teabag, the scent of peppermint tickled my nose. The heat of the cup in my hands warmed my frigid fingers. Cold hands, warm heart, they say... but I don't remember the last time I felt warmth in my heart.

I took the fleece throw off the back of the couch, covered up with it and placed Gabriel back on my chest as I waited for the tea to cool enough to drink. Lost in the show, I forgot about my tea until Gabriel woke up, stretched and jumped off me. These shows helped me get into the mind of killers. Murderers are normal people until they snap. These shows reiterated my point that you never know who someone is. They are never who they seem. That has been my experience anyway.

It was already eleven when another show came on. I didn't want to miss what might happen, but I also needed to get up for work tomorrow. Most likely, sleep will elude me, like all other nights, but I had to at least try. I made my nightly rounds to make sure the front door and all of the windows were locked, turned on the flashlight on my nightstand to make sure it worked, brushed my teeth, and opened up my nightstand to make sure my can of pepper spray was still in there.

Tim offered to teach me how to use a gun when he found out about my pepper spray. I told him I didn't dare. If I was worried, I would hurt myself or someone else, I wasn't sure. It just seemed like too much power for me. I wanted to be able to protect myself but didn't want to kill anyone. Being able to take care of myself is important to me; there was no one else out there to do it. Gabriel might try, but what could he really do? It's my job to take care of us.

Once in bed, I pulled the lavender cotton sheet and white down comforter up over my shoulders and tucked them under my chin as I shimmied my body into a comfortable position. Gabriel rested above my head as I turned off my lamp. The four women from the group were on my mind. I wanted to know their stories. Why had they come to the group? Maggie said her therapist suggested she come, but what about Sonya? Or Norma? What could have possibly happened to them to make them think it was a good idea to sit with strangers to discuss things that had hurt them? That was not something I would have done. But here I am, forced to run a group I wouldn't even attend.

"Gabe, I didn't tell you what Jeanine did today," I grunted my disgust. "She had the nerve to interrupt my group to bring Jane in. She didn't even tell me she was coming, or that I should expect her. She didn't even stay for the group." A heavy sigh filled the room. "Guess that's why she's the boss and I'm not. I'd never make anyone do half the stuff she makes me do.

"But you were right, the group wasn't that bad...well...

actually, it was pretty awful, but there were only four people, all ladies, so it could have been a lot worse. Can you imagine what it would have been like if some jackass showed up?" A laugh escaped. "Well, one did." I looked over at Gabriel, the moonlight glowed on his face just enough to make out his silhouette. "Tim stopped by before the group to ask me to call Jane." I paused before continuing. "Yeah, I know, Jane is everywhere today. I can't shake that lady. If it's not her, it's Carmen."

I rolled over to try to block out the light coming in from the window. "Must be a full moon out there. Good night, buddy." I closed my eyes and tried to push out all the thoughts. I might need to ask one of the doctors for something to help me sleep if this continues. I don't even remember how long it had been since I was able to get a solid night's sleep. Maybe, twenty years.

CHAPTER SEVEN

The light flashed red on my phone; it was the first thing I noticed when I put my tote bag down. After the group yesterday, I hadn't even checked my messages. I put my coffee down, got a pen, picked up the receiver, and dialed the passcode. Three messages. A hangup, Jeanine, and Tim. Jeanine demanded I go see her as soon as I get in, and Tim just invited me to coffee. Either he wants to talk shop, or he wants to try to convince me to go on a date with him. I'd love to pick his brain and let him know I found a new favorite show.

As I powered up my computer, the phone rang. I just needed to check my email, but if I don't answer another message. . . A vicious cycle; some call it work. Looking over at the caller ID display, I saw that it was Jeanine. Rolling my eyes, I picked up the phone. "I was just on my way up there."

"Well, I am impressed you used the phone's features. But unimpressed that you're late... again."

"The traffic was a killer."

"Really, Val? What? A herd of cows escape?"

"No, not this morning. A family of opossums was crossing the road. I tried to catch one, you know, for granny's stew, but they were just too gawd darn fast fur me."

"Funny this morning, aren't we? I just have a couple of things to run by you. Get settled in, wash the damn opossum off your hands, and come on up."

Surprised at how well Jeanine reacted to my joke, I didn't take my usual time to get up to her office. It's always better to get things over with, worrying about them takes so much of my time. I couldn't think of anything she might be upset with me about, maybe she found someone else to run the group. At Jeanine's door, the smell of tangerine drifted through the entrance. I wondered what she was trying to cure today. "Hey."

"Oh, hi, Val, that was fast." Her eyes went to her wrist. "Come on in, have a seat, shut the door behind you."

"Uh oh...this doesn't sound good. Don't fire me...my cat will starve."

"Oh, stop it, Val, why would I fire my star employee?"

I raised my right eyebrow at her. "Cut the crap Jeanine, what's up?"

"Tim has asked me to have you spend some time with Jane. He thinks you would be able to help her through her grief."

"Since when does Tim get to decide what my job is? We already talked. I told him I'd call her, but she came to the group... you know, the one you abandoned. You didn't even stick around for a piece of cheese."

"Well, I just think if Tim's asking, there must be a good

reason, so we should just follow his command."

"His command. What is this, the 1940s? I'll give Jane a call, because you asked me to, not because Tim told you to ask me."

"Jesus, Val, I don't care why you call her, just do it." Her sense of humor had drifted away with the scent of tangerine. As I stood up to head back down to my office, she continued. "Thank you for stepping outside your comfort zone with that group. It looked like you did a great job."

"Yeah, that's why I am your number one morgue dweller." I laughed as I opened the door. I think she meant it. She was hard to read, but I felt the genuineness behind her words.

Walking back to my office, my head dropped with disappointment. What if this was the only reason Tim had left that message? I keep pushing him away, but it's still nice to be sought after. I like to feel wanted, at least sometimes. The echoing of my footsteps tapping down the cement stairs to the basement put me into a trance. My eyes glossed over as I reached the door. Damn it, Val, suck it up. A deep breath filled my lungs before I exited the stairwell.

Fumbling in my pocket, I found my key. As it unlocked and turned in my hand, I felt a tap on my shoulder. Startled, I jumped a foot off the floor and looked around. No one. What in the hell? As I turned back around, I heard snickering. "You're so easy, Val."

"Jesus Christ, Tim, you scared the shit outta me. Be careful, next time I might shoot."

"I'm not too scared...you don't like guns. You think I don't listen, but I'm not like other guys. I'm just having some fun."

"Real funny. If you actually knew me, you'd know that I don't like..." I caught myself before I continued.

"Don't like what?" "Oh, never mind. Why are you here, anyway? I got your message, is it your policy to

follow up every unanswered phone call with an office visit?" Opening my door, I didn't wait for his answer.

"Only for you." His smile made me forget how obnoxious he was. "I just wanted to touch base, and I was in the area."

"Tim, everything in Lawrenceville is in the area." The past couple of years, it was easy to push him away, but he wouldn't give up. His persistence was breaking me.

"Okay, you got me. Is it a crime to want to see you? And, we do have a case to talk about."

"A case? I thought it was closed. That was yesterday's headline in the *Village News*."

"Well, that part is closed. I just worry about Jane. She is so upset; I thought your sweet nature would help her out." He smirked as his eyes met mine.

I caught myself nibbling on my bottom lip as I stared back. "Was that a compliment?"

"An attempt at one anyway."

"Jane came to the group yesterday, but she didn't stick around to talk. I can call her if you think that would help, but I'd rather wait until next week to see how things go for her."

"You know what's best, I trust your judgment." The electricity between us was too intense to ignore. The sparkle in his eyes awoke parts of me I tried to put to rest long ago.

Too much time had passed and the silence became awkward as our gazes held each other. "I've been watching your show. It's pretty good. It makes you think about—"

"My show?" He laughed. "Do tell me what my show is before you go on."

The heat from embarrassment stained my cheeks red. "Snapped. Didn't you say I should watch it?" I wrapped a strand of my hair around my finger as I looked at him.

"Oh...that show." He paused and his face went straight. "Should I be worried?" He raised one eyebrow.

"Maybe." Scrunching my nose, my lips turned up. "Us ladies are nothing to mess with."

"Don't I know it! Such a complicated creature."

"Anyway, I think I'm hooked. I watched a marathon the other night with Gabriel."

"You're watching my show with another man? I'm hurt." His rugged hand went to his heart.

"Calm down, the only man I share my time with is my cat. I'm hurt you don't remember that."

"Oh, yes, that's right, Gabriel. I might have remembered him if you ever let me meet him."

"Maybe someday."

"Whoa, someday is better than never." He nodded his head and smirked.

Something was happening inside me. I longed for the connection of another person. It gets so hard, being lonely. How long would I be able to keep everyone from getting close? It used to be safer that way, but maybe Tim could keep me safe. A shiver went down my spine as I imagined the touch of his hands on my skin. Maybe he was one of the good ones. There was only one way to find out.

"How about tonight?" My boldness surprised even me. "I mean, if you're not busy and maybe it's not even on." The vulnerability of the moment took my breath away. *Why did I just say that? What if I misread the whole thing?*

Tim's deep voice took me out of my negative filled head. "Tonight sounds great, even if it's not on, I'm sure we can find something else to watch."

I cleared my throat before I could speak. "Do you need directions to my place?"

"Don't be silly, I'm a detective, I'll just look you up."

"You can do *that*?"

"No. Well, yes, but it's a small town, I know where everyone lives. What apartment number?"

"Three. See you at 7:00?"

"I've been waiting *forever* for you to invite me over." He winked as he stood up to walk to the door. "See you later, Val."

"See ya." Nausea swept over me as I thought about what just happened. I couldn't believe I wasn't strong enough to stand up to temptation, but it was time. I had been alone for too long. Maybe having Tim in my life would help with the anxiety and fear that keeps me locked up away from the world. He'd been trying so hard to reach me; it must mean something. There was still time to cancel. Still time to push him away. It's just all so confusing.

I wasn't always this skittish. There was a time in my life where I had friends, even a boyfriend. But once you've been hurt the way I was, it was hard to trust people. The people I should have been able to trust the most were the ones who let me down. Not everyone is out to harm me. I couldn't be that cursed. Could I?

CHAPTER EIGHT

"**G**abriel, we're going to have company tonight." I hurried around my tiny apartment, tidying up the messes that take so little effort to accumulate.

"We're slobs. Don't you think you could help out while I'm at work?" I joked as I scurried around straightening piles and pushing things into drawers. The sink was full of dishes, but there was no time to wash them before Tim arrived. A quick glance around the kitchen, I gathered the dirty plates and silverware and shoved them into the stove.

"Don't judge me, and don't tell." Picking him up off the floor, I pressed my nose against his cold, wet, black nose. The comfort from his purring calmed some of my nerves.

"I'm so nervous, Gabe. I don't know why I thought it was a good idea to invite him over. He's just so irresistible, I guess. I'll deny that if you say anything." I took a deep breath as I lowered him to the floor. My eyes drifted to my messy bed. There was no way he was going in there tonight. I closed the door, but before it latched shut, I went in and pulled up the top sheet and comforter.

"Just want to make sure you have a place to hide, buddy." That was the story I was going with, at least. I wasn't sure what I wanted to come out of this meeting. I didn't dare call it a date, we were just two friends, with loads of sexual tension. It would be helpful if he wasn't so gorgeous and charismatic.

"Oh, Gabe, I should just tell him not to come." I bit my thumbnail as I paced the living room. Grabbing my phone to find his number, the knock at the door reminded me that I lost track of time. Everything will be fine; I am in control. *I am in control.*

I blew out the deep breath I was holding and opened the door. "Well, aren't you punctual?"

"Early, in fact. I didn't want to give you time to change your mind." The sparkle in his deep brown eyes was brighter than the bouquet he was holding. Pink, red, and white roses in a ceramic blue vase.

An unfamiliar, warm sensation flooded me as he handed the flowers to me. "What do you think this will get you?"

"I was hoping for an invitation in." He ruffled up his hair as his eyes darted to his feet.

"Of course, come on in. I'm just messing with you, you know that, right?"

Nervous laughter spilled out. "I never know with you, Val."

"Thanks for the flowers." I stuck my nose in the bouquet and inhaled the delightful fragrance. "They're beautiful. It's been ages since anyone did something like this for me." I set the vase down on the center of my kitchen table and pushed my hands into my back pockets. "You wanna see if *your* show is on?"

"Can I get a hug first? I mean, it's the least you can do for those beautiful flowers." He walked over to me and held his arms out.

"I knew there had to be a price." I knocked down my wall and let him embrace me. As my head rested against his chest, I closed my eyes and inhaled his masculine scent. "What are you wearing?"

"Clothes, Val."

"Ha-ha, smartass. I mean, what is that smell?"

"You like? It's the old standby, Gravity."

"Yeah, I like. It mixes well with the smell of your skin."

"Whoa. I feel violated." A smirk pushed up his cheeks.

My face blushed as I realized how forward I was. I needed to control myself and not let things like his scent get to me, or how great the warmth of his arms around me felt. I needed to bring it back to what it actually was; two friends watching TV together. Nothing more. Not yet. I couldn't deal with anything more yet. "Sorry."

"No, no, Val, it's fine. Please don't be sorry. I like that you like it. Let's go see what's on TV." He took my hand and led me to the couch, where Gabriel was sitting. He had been watching Tim since he arrived.

"Gabriel, this is my friend Tim. Tim, this is Gabriel. Don't mess with me, he's got my back. Isn't that right, buddy?" Gabriel's green eyes focused on Tim as he put his hand out to pet him. Surprisingly, Gabriel let Tim scratch him behind his left ear, and I do believe I heard him purr. "Oh, well, it looks like he likes you. Guess you can stay."

I picked Gabe up and sat down, placing him between us. I handed Tim the remote. "Go ahead and see what's on."

Tim turned on the TV and started scrolling through the channels. He landed on *Investigation Discovery* channel. "If *Snapped* isn't on, something similar will be."

"Do you want a drink or anything to eat?" As soon as I asked, I regretted it. I hadn't gone shopping in a few weeks and didn't have anything to offer him, except tea and water.

"Nah, I'm good. Thanks, though." Relief found me with his answer. I needed to make a point to get to the grocery store. It would be good for me to eat healthy meals once in a while and learn how to entertain. A good hostess would have snacks and drinks already out.

Tim's voice pulled me out of my head. "This is nice. You don't know how long I have waited to see the inside of your place." His arm reached over and he draped it over my shoulder. I leaned into it, causing Gabe to jump down. I pushed myself closer to him as we settled in to watch TV.

"It is nice. You don't know how long it has been since I shared my time with anyone other than Gabriel."

"Why is that, Val? I never understood why you despise people so much."

"It's not so much as I despise them, it's more that I don't trust them. I despise what they do." The comfort of his body next to mine opened me up, more than I had planned on. He felt safe. Why had I pushed him away for so long? At thirty-four, I spent more than half of my life alone. I didn't think I could continue living in isolation after knowing what this feels like.

Tim turned his head to look at me. "Why don't you trust

people? Who hurt you that caused you to feel that way?" He rubbed my shoulder where his hand rested as he waited for my answer.

"I don't know. A lot of people. People I should have been able to trust. People I loved."

"I won't hurt you, Val. I promise you that." There was something in the way he spoke that made me believe him. After so many years of not believing anyone, I believed him. Tears formed in the corner of my eyes as I scrunched up my nose to push the emotion back in. His thumb touched the moisture, and we held each other's gaze. "I mean it, Val. I won't hurt you, and I won't let anyone else hurt you again."

With the sleeve of my cardigan, I wiped away my tears. "Thanks, Tim. I hope that's true." There was so much more I wanted to say but couldn't. There were some things I hadn't told anyone, not even Gabriel. For almost two decades, I've held these secrets close. I wanted more than anything to find someone I trusted enough to tell. Maybe I could trust Tim with them, but it was too soon to tell.

CHAPTER NINE

The week flew by, and it was time for the trauma support group to meet again. I wasn't as nervous this time, I might have even been looking forward to it. I still had plenty of snacks from last week, so I didn't even need to inconvenience Jeanine for any money. The room we used last week was still set up how we had left it. Not a whole lot happens at Lawrenceville Regional Hospital, we couldn't even deliver babies here. It was a pathetic excuse for a hospital, but I guess that was why I fit in so well.

Norma was the first to arrive. I was relieved to see her. Her calmness kept me grounded. "Hi dear, how was your week?"

"Busy, but I guess that keeps me out of trouble."

"Oh, honey, I don't see you having that problem. You remind me of me when I was your age. I should've gotten into trouble; it might have spiced things up a little."

"I lead a pretty boring life. Work and home to my cat."

"Sounds like you need some trouble." She chuckled.

"Honey, don't forget to have a little fun. Before you know it, you'll be an old lady like me, and no one will want to include you in any fun. Live now, while you can. That's the advice I wished someone had told me at your age."

"Thank you, Norma. That is wise advice. I'll do my best to live a little."

"That's a good start, honey."

Maggie waited at the door, looking in at us. "Can I come in? Or is this a private meeting?"

"Hi, Maggie, please come in and join us." Sonya was right behind her and pushed Maggie in as she entered.

"Hi, Sonya, glad to see you again."

As Sonya and Maggie found their seats, I looked up at the clock. There were still two minutes before the start of the group. Jane wasn't here yet, and I regretted not calling her last week to check in with her. Norma and Sonya were talking, while Maggie sat still, her eyes focused on her feet. As I sat and watched the ladies, I wondered if I had what they needed. I felt like a phony, not able to work through my own trauma and offering them support to work through theirs. But this group wasn't about me, it was about them. They are the ones that need help, not me. I must remember that.

I stood up to shut the door. "Alright, ladies, we can get started now. Looks like it's just the four of us." I looked around the small circle to see if it looked like anyone was anxious to start. Norma sat with a soft smile, Maggie's eyes were still focused on her feet, and Sonya's sighs were on instant replay. It was apparent I didn't know how to read people as well as I thought. "How was everyone's week? Anything come to mind that you want to talk about?"

With her head still down, Maggie began to speak. "I'm worried he'll find me. I'm scared to die." Her words silenced the room. Norma's smile faded, and Sonya sat on the edge of her chair.

"Who? Who are you afraid of? Maggie, look at me. Who?" Sonya's voice was high and fast. Her energy was unable to be contained as she waited for the answer. "Why are you so afraid? Is that why you're so weird?"

"Sonya, stop. Leave her alone. Maggie, only answer what you feel comfortable with."

Maggie's eyes lifted from her shoes and met mine.

"My husband, Hank. He's hurt me before. Me and our girls. He promised he would kill me and take the girls. I know he will. I just know it." Maggie's eyes stayed wide open as she continued to look at me.

"Wow, that's messed up." Sonya shook her head as she looked at Maggie, but Maggie did not take her eyes off me.

"Sonya, please. Let's try to be supportive of Maggie." She let out another sigh. "Maggie, have you gone to the police?"

"Yes, the girls and I have a protection order to keep him away from us." She paused. "But it's just a piece of paper. How will that save us?"

"Do you have a gun? If I were you, I'd blow his brains out."

"Sonya. Please, stop."

"For heaven's sake." Norma closed her eyes as she shook her head. "Maggie, honey, do you have family or friends you could stay with?"

Maggie turned to look at Norma and took her hand that had been extended to her. "No. Hank kept me away from all of my friends during our marriage, and my family all lives in Texas. Hank and I moved here twenty years ago, and I lost touch with most of my family. I didn't have the money to visit them, and he wouldn't let me call them. I didn't even get to go to my mom's funeral, Hank wouldn't let me."

"Oh, honey, I'm so sorry. What can we do to help you and your girls?"

I handed the box of soft tissues to Maggie as she began to cry. "I don't know." She blew her nose into the tissue. "I don't know."

"We can take today to work on a plan to help you find ways to stay safe if you'd like."

"That's a great idea." Norma's grip tightened on Maggie's hand.

"If she blew his brains out, she'd be safe. Just saying." Sonya crossed her arms and tapped her foot as it dangled off her left leg.

"Sonya, that's not very helpful."

Maggie blew her nose again." She's right, though. I've thought about it before. I just don't have what it takes to kill someone. Not even him."

"We probably shouldn't openly discuss murder in here. Sometimes it feels nice to think about hurting the people who have hurt us but to be helpful to Maggie, we should talk about things we can actually do."

"Yes, dear, that is the best plan. Do you have any paper? So can we brainstorm?"

I picked the legal pad of yellow lined paper and Bic pen up off the floor. "I can take notes if you'd like, Maggie. Or you can." I held the pad of paper up for her to take.

She shook her head. "No, can you do it for me?"

"Sure, I'd be happy to." Adrenaline raced through my body as I related to feeling unsafe and alone. My hand trembled as I rested it on the paper. "Do you think Hank knows where you are staying?"

"I'm not sure. The girls and I moved half an hour from our old place. The victim's advocate helped pay for the rent. I've asked the girls to stay off social media and not post any pictures of themselves online that might give away where we are."

I wrote down what she said, not sure what it would amount to, but it gave me a job to keep my mind off the memories brewing inside of me. "How old are your girls?"

"Sammy is fourteen, and Lexi is sixteen. They had to change schools and are struggling to make friends. They are just as scared as I am. Sammy sees my counselor, but Lexi refuses."

"Do they know you come here?"

"No, only my counselor knows."

Sonya couldn't stay quiet. "What did Hank do to make you so afraid?"

Maggie closed her eyes and rocked back and forth in her chair.

"Maggie, you don't need to share any more than you're comfortable with."

"She kind of does. How can we help her stay safe if we don't know the details?"

"Details aren't an important part of the plan right now."

Maggie let out a deep breath. "He hurt us all. First, it was just me. Sometimes he would hit me, slap me across the face, and then he..." Her body began to tremble as she continued. "He spit in my face, kicked me, choked me...you name it, he did it." She reached for the tissues that I placed on the floor next to her feet and dabbed her eyes. "I could deal with all that. What was I worth anyway? I didn't earn money, or even have access to the check..."

"You are worth so much, Maggie. You're a mom, a house-wife, a person. You didn't deserve anything that asshole did to you." The anger in Norma's words caught me off guard.

"Norma is right. You didn't deserve any of that."

"But you don't know the rest." Maggie began to sob. "I'm not a good person. I'm a bad mom."

"Oh, Maggie, that's not true." Tears ran down Norma's cheeks.

"It is. You don't know all of it yet." In between gasps, she continued. "I...I... let my babies down. He...hurt them, too...because I wasn't strong enough to protect them."

Sonya piped up, "It's on him. He's the one that hurt them, not you. I never want to hear you say that again. Do you understand me?" The harshness of her voice stung.

"Sonya, I know you want to be helpful and supportive, but try to be gentle." A deep breath escaped after the last word.

"I'm sorry, I just hate how these low life pieces of shit make us feel like it's our fault when it's not."

Maggie blew her nose into the tissue she was holding. "I didn't tell you the worst part...the part that kills me." She closed her eyes and began to rock back and forth in her chair. "He made the girls his personal sex toys. The only reason I found out was when I took Lexi to the doctor. She hadn't been feeling good, sick for days, so I took her to the doctor to see what was wrong. They ran a bunch of tests and couldn't find anything. Until the pregnancy test results came back positive."

Her words hit me hard. I felt the bottom of my stomach drop out. I wasn't sure how much more I could listen to. The room went dark, and the only thing I could hear was my racing thoughts. My chest tightened and reminded me to breathe. I took a deep breath and reached for my necklace. The warmth of the metal against my skin brought me back to the group. My face was flush, and I hoped no one noticed I had zoned out for a little while. This was not about me. This was about Maggie. She needed me to be present with her and not lost in my head.

As I glanced around the room, I noticed I had not created the disruption I imagined. I hadn't lost as much time as I thought, so I was able to pick back up where we left off. "Oh, Maggie." The anguish in Maggie's voice ate away at me.

"What happened next? Did someone beat the shit out of him?" Sonya was on the edge of her seat, bent over as far as she could without falling off. She bit her left index fingernail as she squirmed in her chair, waiting for a response.

Maggie's pain was contagious; all of us were dabbing at tears. Norma had pulled her chair closer to Maggie and wrapped her in a maternal hug, rubbing her back. "Hush, Sonya. Violence doesn't always fix everything."

"It sure as hell does. Tell me where that piece of shit is, and I'll teach him a thing or two."

"Sonya, that's enough for now. I don't disagree with you, I want to hurt him, too, but right now, Maggie needs us." My honesty surprised me as much as it did them. The candor brought a smile to Sonya's face, and she extended her right hand up for me to give her a high-five. As our hands joined, I felt a connection I hadn't known I was missing. The four of us made our circle in the room so small that we were all touching. My hand went to Maggie's shoulder, and Sonya's followed. Maggie was still in Norma's warm embrace as she sobbed.

"All for one, and one for all, or something like that." Sonya chuckled as she removed her hand and patted Norma's knee. Big things were happening in that stale conference room at Lawrenceville Regional Hospital. I stopped feeling nervous about failing these ladies and realized all I needed to do was be authentic. That was not something I had been in a long time, but trying didn't seem so scary anymore. There were people who needed what I could give them, and they had what I needed, too. It wasn't complicated, it was just remembering all of that when things got difficult.

Maggie lifted her head off Norma's shoulder, her eyes met mine, and I handed her a fresh tissue. She blew her nose and started where she left off. "Lexi was ten weeks pregnant when we found out. At that point, I didn't understand it was *his*, or the full extent of what had been happening." She moved away from Norma to get comfortable in her chair, still holding her hand, and continued. "When we got to the car, I questioned Lexi about a boyfriend. She swore to me she didn't have one, and that she was a virgin. I made a snide comment about Mother Teresa and reminded her how much I can't stand liars. And then she blurted it out. 'It's Dad's!' I had to pull the car over after that because I believed her. I always felt that he was touching the girls, but I never had proof. I never saw anything, but I couldn't shake that feeling. Mother's intuition?" She paused as she shook her head.

"So, on the side of the road, as cars passed by us, my world fell apart. I'd just been yelling at my daughter, who I failed to protect, and then everything I feared was coming true. And there was a baby to worry about. I mean, what do you even do?"

"Holy shit, Maggie, I'm so sorry." Sonya took a tissue from the box and dabbed her eyes, keeping her black mascara from running. "What did you do?"

"I asked her if she was scared of him, she said yes, so I turned the car around and went to Sammy's school and signed her out early, then I drove us back to the doctor's office. I didn't know what to do or where to go. They gave us a room and called an advocate from the domestic violence center to come talk with us. As we waited for her to arrive, Sammy tells me he's been raping her, too." She took a long breath and closed her eyes. "I asked them to test her, too. Waiting for them to come back with the results was tortuous. I kept thinking, what if she's pregnant, too? When the nurse came back in the room, she wasn't smiling, so my heart kind of dropped. But she said it was negative. I guess, even with a negative test, there was nothing to smile about. Both of my girls had been violated in unspeakable ways."

Norma tightened her grip on Maggie's hand as I handed her a cup of water. With her free hand, she took a sip. "When the advocate came, Lexi and Sammy both shared some of the hideous things he did to them. It had been happening for years. He videotaped them doing all kinds of things, and it was my job to try to find the tapes, but that's for a different day. Anyway, before long, the police showed up, and the girls had to tell their stories all over again. They heard enough from the girls that they went straight to Stop and Shop and arrested him."

"Thank goodness they have you for a mom." I wiped away my tears as our eyes met. My heart danced in my chest as memories flooded my mind.

"No, that's not true. Any other mom would have protected her kids. I failed them both."

"It might feel that way, but do you know how many moms would have hidden the whole thing and pretended not to know anything?"

"No mother would ever do such a thing. That's absurd. You're just trying to make me feel better."

"No, I'm serious, Maggie. I worked with a family where the mom knew her daughter was being molested, but she didn't tell anyone, she just let him keep doing it." My throat tightened as I tried to push the memories out of my head. "Some moms don't deserve their kids, but you do, Maggie. Your girls have you, and that's important."

"She's right, honey, your girls are lucky to have you."

"That's hard to believe. Lexi had to have an abortion. I mean, how could I let her have his baby? Either way was cruel. We don't believe in abortions, but what other option did we have? We had to kill a baby because of him."

"Don't look at it that way, you saved a baby with the abortion." For once, Sonya offered some helpful advice. "You gave Lexi her life back with that abortion."

"I guess you're right. I didn't look at it that way."

"But, wait a minute...he was arrested? So, isn't he still in jail?"

"I think so."

"So why are you so freaked out that he knows where you live?"

"Sonya." Her helpfulness wore off as quickly as it came.

"What? It's a valid question."

"I don't know where he is, I just don't want him to find us. If he gets out, he'll kill us. He only got ten years. And what if he escapes?"

"As long as the court has your information, they will let you know if he gets released, or if he escapes. It's hard to trust, but all of you need this time to gather your strength. Let's work on that together, okay?" I looked around to the others to get their encouragement.

"That's a good idea, dear. We're here to help each other." Norma nodded her head.

The door to the room opened and Jane walked in. I had forgotten about her while we were listening to Maggie. I had no idea how to make her fit into our group now. It was only our second meeting, but so much happened in this last hour. It didn't feel like we were strangers anymore, it felt like family. The clock on the wall said we had already overstayed our hour by ten minutes. "Ladies, we lost track of time, we have gone over our hour. You're welcome to stay if you want to keep talking."

"Sorry, I'm late. I'd like to stay." Still standing at the door, it felt like Jane needed more than I could give her today.

Sonya pulled her phone out of her bag, sent a quick text

message, and slipped it back into her purse. "I can stay for a while longer."

"All I have is time." Norma smiled as she looked around the room. "Come have a seat, dear. Sorry, I forget your name."

"It's Jane."

"We were supporting Maggie today. She had a lot to share with us, that's what you walked into."

"Sorry to interrupt. I lost track of time."

"It's OK, so did we. Maggie, are you OK with Jane joining us now?"

"Yeah, it's fine, we all know what it's like to hurt."

"Do you have more you want to share today, Maggie?"

"I don't think I have anything left in me right now." She blew her nose into her tissue and straightened her back against her chair.

"How was your week Jane?"

"How do you think? It was awful and lonely, and, well, it just sucked. I'm so angry at Carmen for leaving such a mess behind."

"It's normal to be angry. Have you been able to sleep?"

"Only if I take something. A couple shots of Jack Daniels and an Ambien usually do the trick."

"Do you have friends or family that you can lean on?"

"Nope. I don't have any family to speak of, and all my friends are either dead, or I wish they were." A laugh that didn't match her words escaped. "I'm just kidding. Humor is the only thing taking the sting out of the pain right now."

"Do you have a therapist, dear?" Norma held her hand out for Jane to take, but she didn't accept the gesture.

"No, I don't have insurance or extra money." Her gaze held mine, and guilt flooded me.

"Why don't you stick around after group, and we can work on setting something up for you?"

"Alright. Detective Philips said you were going to call me."

There it was. I wasn't sure he had told her I would call, but of course, he did. Why wouldn't he? If things got uncomfortable, Tim wanted to fix them. I guess I can't fault him for that.

Another forty-five minutes passed before we decided we had enough for one day. Norma suggested they all exchange phone numbers, in case they wanted to check in before next week. When it came time to share my number, I handed them each a business card with my contact information. Part of me wanted to give them my cell phone number, but I didn't want to cross that boundary. We had to keep this professional. It was the only way I was able to last in this position for as long as I had. Boundaries are what keep me from burning out.

When Norma, Maggie, and Sonya left, I watched them walk down the hall as friends. My heart felt full as I witnessed the friendship blossom. There was so much room for potential for them, and me.

Jane and I set a time for the following day for her to come in and talk. It went against everything inside of me, but I had to do this for her. I couldn't let her struggle alone just because she didn't have the money. This would be my gift to Carmen —for the beautiful girl with so much pain.

CHAPTER TEN

Back at my office, there was something white peeking out from under my door. My hands were too full to pick it up before entering. After unlocking the door and setting the armload of stuff on my desk, I went back to pick it up. A white piece of computer paper folded in half. *Call me* was all that was written on it. My mind went blank. Who would leave such a vague note? I crumpled it up and threw it in the trash, I had too much on my mind after that group to worry about something so insignificant.

I needed to talk to Tim. He was the first person I thought of as all the memories came flooding back. I picked up the phone and began to dial his number when a knock on the door froze me in my tracks. I wasn't in the mood to deal with anyone else. I just wanted to go home and sit on the couch with Gabriel and Tim. I quietly placed the phone back on the receiver and stood up. *Shit. What if I didn't lock the door?* Another knock, this time I saw the handle turn. Unsure what to do, my eyes stayed on the door as I stood in place. My heart raced during the seconds that passed.

The door didn't open. My heart rate returned to normal when I realized I remembered to lock it. A piece of paper slid under the door. I tiptoed over to it, bent down, and picked it up. *Will you be my girl? Check yes or no* was all that was written on the white piece of paper. My heart fluttered in my chest as I read the words. I opened the door to see if Tim was still in sight. He had his back to me, waiting at the elevator. As the door chimed to open, I blurted out, "Yes."

Tim's head turned as he heard my voice. "Where in the hell did you come from?" A smile pushed up his cheeks. "Were you in there the whole time?"

"Yeah...I was about to call you when I heard the knock on my door. I just didn't want to deal with anyone except you after the group we just had."

He took a step toward me and grabbed me in his arms. The warmth of his embrace and the musky smell of his skin washed away the anxiety I carried inside me from the day. "I can read your mind, Val. I knew you needed me; I could just feel it."

The thought scared me, there were too many things he couldn't know, not yet, but it also put me at ease. Someone knew I needed them. That was still new to me. I worked hard to not need anyone, but Tim was different. There was nothing left in me to keep from *needing* him, and he knew it. "I'm glad you're here. Do you have plans for tonight?"

"I hope to. What do you have in mind?"

"Want to come over, get some take out and watch some more criminals in action?"

"Sure, that sounds fun. Is this a date?" He smirked as our eyes locked.

"Well, I did say yes to being your girl." The words made my body stiffen as they left my lips. *Relax, Val, go with it.*

"What do you want for dinner?"

"You said you can read my mind, let's see how good you are. I'm leaving soon, can you come right over?"

"The pressure's on. Maybe I shouldn't have opened my big mouth." A nervous laugh danced off his lips.

"I am confident that you'll do just fine."

He reached down and kissed my cheek. The warmth of his lips made my body tingle. I grabbed onto his hand and squeezed. "See you soon."

Back in my office, I noticed the crumpled-up paper that had waited for me under my office door, picked it out of the trash, and compared the writing. Tim had left that one, too. Mystery solved. I grabbed my bag, turned off the lights and headed for the door. Excitement with lingering anxiety made my heart skip a beat.

Gabriel was at the door waiting for me when I arrived home. His dinner was late, something he was used to, but it still made me feel guilty. "Hey Gabe, you'll never guess who's coming over. I know, I know, it's not that hard to guess, since he's the only company we've had, but Tim is coming over again. And, this time, it's a date." Gabriel brushed up against my legs as I prepared his dish. "He asked me to be his girl, can you even imagine? I think Tim is going to be around for a while. I like him a lot. Do you know what's funny? I miss him when he's not here. Crazy, I know. But don't you worry, Gabe, you will always be my number one guy."

I checked my bedroom to find the bed a mess and in need of fresh sheets. Changing them would indicate that I was ready for something I knew I wasn't, and leaving them as they were would only keep us out of here. Just having Tim next to me after today was what I craved. I felt safe with Tim. That was all I wanted, especially after the memories that came back to me today. I just wanted to shower and try to get it all off of me, but I knew it was deeper than that. I knew I had a lot of work to do, and a simple shower wouldn't cleanse the toxic memories off of me. I knew and yet, I still wished it were that simple.

A knock on the door took me out of my head. The smile left my face when I answered the door. "What...how did you find me?"

"Ever hear of Google?"

I stared back at her, hoping she would just disappear.

"I need to talk to you, you said *anytime*."

"Jane, I meant at the office. *Call* me anytime at the office."

"Well, since I'm here now, aren't you going to let me in?"

"No, I'm sorry, I have company on the way. We have an appointment tomorrow. I won't be of any help to you today, I'm exhausted."

"I knew you wouldn't understand." She turned to walk away.

Her words cut like a knife. I prided myself on under-standing. That was my livelihood. "Jane, wait. I'm sorry, you just caught me off guard. I was expecting someone else."

Turning back around, she dabbed her eyes with her sleeve. "No, I get it, you don't have time for me. You can forget about tomorrow."

"No, Jane. Please come in. Tell me what's wrong."

She accepted my invitation without any further luring and made herself comfortable on the couch. Gabriel jumped down as she went to pet him. A tickle in my throat kept me from speaking. I sat on my desk chair as I attempted to clear my throat. "What can I help you with, Jane?"

"I don't know. I just knew I needed to talk to someone, and you were the last one there with Carmen and me."

Of course, this day could not end without more uncomfortableness. "OK." No other words would follow.

"And, I've been thinking about that note I found." My heart dropped as she reached into her purse. Disappointment filled the void in my chest as she blew her nose on the tissue she retrieved. "I don't think she wrote it. What if she didn't write it?"

"What are you saying, Jane?"

"That she didn't kill herself. Someone else did."

"Who do you think would have killed her?"

"That's the thing I don't know."

"What makes you think Carmen didn't write the note?"

"It didn't look like her writing. I hadn't noticed before. I was too...emotional."

"Do you have a copy of the note?"

"No. I gave it to the cops."

"Do you remember the name?"

"No, they're all the same."

"What do you mean?"

"Oh, you know. They are all out to get you."

"I don't think that's true, Jane. I think they want to help."

A knock on the door got both of our attention. I had

forgotten Tim was on his way with our dinner. Apprehension held me to the chair with the weight of a thousand pounds. What if he's still in uniform? What is she recognizes him?

"Well, aren't you gonna get that?"

"Yes, and I think we should pick up where we left off tomorrow at the hospital. OK?"

She didn't budge as I got up to get the door. "Hi Tim, Jane is here, but she's just leaving, right, Jane?"

Both of his hands were full, a bag of Chinese, a six-pack of Sam Adams and a dozen red roses. His right eyebrow arched up as he took in my words. "Ah...do you want me to come back?"

"No, don't be ridiculous, come in." I turned to hold the door open and watch Jane for a reaction. She didn't seem to recognize Tim. Thankfully he had changed into jeans and a sweatshirt, and his baseball hat hid some of his face. Jane reluctantly stood up and started for the door.

"I'll see you tomorrow, Jane. Try to get some rest."

"Thanks a lot." She sighed as she walked out the door, shutting it harder than she should have as she left.

"What in the hell was that about? How does she know where you live?"

"Hello to you, too."

He pulled me into a hug and the tension lifted. "Sorry, Val. That just caught me off guard. How are you doing?"

"A little freaked out. She said she found me on Google. In all my years as a social worker, no one has ever done that before. I didn't know I was so easy to find."

"Well, it is a small town, don't you know what they say?

Everyone knows everyone." He laughed as he picked up the flowers and handed them to me.

"More flowers? What did I do to deserve that?"

"Just being you." He smiled as I put them in a tall glass cup.

"You're the only one who thinks so."

"Yeah, me and Jane." He leaned up against the counter and chuckled.

"Knock it off, that's not even funny." I playfully pushed his chest.

"I hope you like Chinese and beer. My ability to read your mind only comes and goes."

"I love Chinese and beer. I'm a little worried about how well you already know me."

"I'd love to know you better." He winked at me as he twisted the cap off his beer.

"Oh? How so?"

"You know." He smiled as he waited for my reaction.

"Wow, aren't you forward?"

"Hey, a guy's gotta start somewhere."

"So, anyway, where do you want to eat? At the table or in there?"

"Let's get cozy in there." He picked up the bag of takeout and took it into the living room with the six-pack. I brought the plates and forks.

As he opened the boxes, I noticed pork lo mein and orange chicken. "Wow. You *really* do know me. This is getting scary."

"This is my go-to order. My favorites, and I just hoped you'd like them."

"Mine, too. This is literally my order when I go."

"So, I remember something about you missing me."

My body temperature increased, my face not allowing me to hide my embarrassment. "Yeah, well, that's true. I did miss you. I mean, I do miss you. I mean, well, you know what I mean."

"Go on."

"Today's group was a tough one. Some stuff came out for one of the ladies, and it got to me. The only thing I could think about was you. I'm so glad you were able to come over tonight. You don't know how badly I needed this."

"I never thought I'd live to see the day where you wanted me around." He reached over and took my hand. "I think about this a lot, too. There is something about you, Val, that I find irresistible. Your dark sense of humor, your desire to be alone, your kind heart, it's all just the perfect combination. You're me, but a girl."

"So, you love yourself so much that you want to date someone like you?"

"Haha, very funny. More that it feels like you *get* me. It's hard to explain it."

"No, I understand. It's hard to find people who get me or people I *want* to get me. I'm pretty closed off."

"You don't have to tell me that again."

"Funny, Tim. It's just that I have a hard time trusting people. It's easier to be alone than be hurt. But, something about you makes me feel like you are worth the risk."

"I'm honored, and like I told you before, I won't hurt you. I promise."

"Thanks, Tim, now let's eat, I'm starving. I forgot to eat lunch today, and probably breakfast."

My unwillingness to go further left an uneasiness in the air between us. I needed to talk to Tim more than I had ever needed to speak to anyone, and I really thought he would understand, but what if I wasn't ready to go back to the pain? What if it was too soon and he leaves? What if he thought I was too much work or had too much baggage? All of my thoughts took me further away; in the wrong direction. I wanted to be close to Tim, but now it felt like we were miles apart. Why did it always have to be a war inside my head? Why couldn't it ever just be easy?

"How's the grub?" Tim's voice brought me back to the room.

"It's perfect, thanks for bringing it."

"My pleasure. Now, how about you tell me where you just went?"

"What do you mean?"

"Val, I'm a detective for Christ's sake, it's my job to notice things. You were in your head there for a while. What's up? Hard day at the office?" His sympathetic eyes were believable enough to trust his concern was sincere.

"Yeah, it was a rough one. Obviously, to have Jane show up is eerie, I mean, if she knows how to find me, who else is going to show up?" As the words hit my ears, I thought about the magnitude of what I just said. The fear the words brought jolted me to start talking.

CHAPTER ELEVEN

"There's a lot about me, about my past that I have never told anyone. I've always been too afraid to talk about it, ashamed, embarrassed, angry, I don't really know what I feel." My gaze left his as I thought of where to start.

"Val, you can tell me anything and I will understand. There is nothing you can say that will scare me off. Try me."

"There's just so much. Today's group triggered me, it made me remember stuff that I have tried to bury away. One of the ladies talked about how her husband raped her daughters, and he got one pregnant." I paused to see his reaction. There was none, he was still just listening. "Hearing that made me sick. It paralyzed me for a minute, like a hard punch to the gut. I was sure the ladies would see how upset I was, but thankfully I was wrong. They focused their attention on her, as they should have. I didn't know what to say or how to act. It was just so..."

"Wow, Val, I can see why that was hard. I think I'd kill anyone who did that to my kid."

"Wait, you have a kid?"

"No, my hypothetical kid. But, just for the record, I do want kids. Anyway, enough about me, go on. Only if you want to."

"Well, hearing her say that brought me back to being fifteen again. When I was raped." I looked up to see if he was scared yet. His face was stoic but hinted red. "I told my mom, but she didn't believe me; she just thought I was a whore. A great word for a mom to call her daughter, right? Anyway, she made my life hell when I needed her the most. Turned against me, sent me away to a home for pregnant teens." I felt the color drain from my face as I realized what I had just said. I didn't want to tell him that part, not yet.

"Jesus, Val, I don't know what to say." He put his hand on my knee and looked into my eyes. My pain was resting in him now.

"I didn't mean to say that last part. You must think I'm..."

"I think you are remarkably strong. And I admire you so much more now."

"The place she sent me to was nice, I made some friends while I was there with some of the other girls. I wasn't the only one that rape sent there. When I was there, I didn't have to do it alone. When it was time for the baby to come, I had a great team with me. I forgot about what an awful situation I was in. Until. . ." My throat closed as my eyes watered as I remembered. When I was able to swallow, I continued. "Until they took my baby."

"Oh, Val." Tim's eyes were wet with tears as he listened.

"My mom told them that I wanted to give my baby up for adoption. She told them that I knew it was going to happen but asked them not to talk with me about it. The adoption agency worked with my mom and had everything signed, and a family picked out. All done behind my back. When he was born, they weren't going to let me hold him, they said it would be too hard for me. They were right, but I am glad I had the chance to meet him.

"One of the girls I was friends with told me I should write him a letter and give it to the adoptive family. I asked her to go to the gift shop for me and get something I could give him. She came back with this." I lifted my necklace with half a heart to show him. "I kept this part and sent the other half with the letter to the family."

Tim shook his head as he wiped away the tears from his cheek. "I can't even imagine being fifteen and having to think like that. Do you know where he is?"

"No, it was a closed adoption. My mom wanted to make sure I would never be able to find him. I never got pictures, updates, or anything. I don't even know his name."

"Did you name him?"

"Gabriel."

Tim smiled as he caught the connection. "That's a nice name, Val."

"I hope you don't think I'm a tramp now."

"Don't be ridiculous, Val. You are not a tramp. You were raped and robbed."

"As soon as I turned eighteen, I left home and never looked back. I don't talk to my mom or any of my family. I left everything behind because I didn't want her to be able to find me."

"Ah, so now I know why having Jane find you was so upsetting, well, aside from the creep factor of it."

I nodded my head and wiped the tears off my face. "Thanks for listening and not judging me. Can we please keep this between us? I don't want anyone else knowing about any of this."

"Val, you can trust me. Your secret is safe with me. Have you ever thought about looking for your son? Now that you're older? How old is he now?"

"He turned nineteen on April 5th. I haven't looked for him. I think about him every day, I've worn our necklace every day since he was born. I just didn't want to disappoint him, and honestly, I am not strong enough to take the rejection if he doesn't want me in his life."

"I can help you find him if you ever want to."

"The perks of having a detective for a boyfriend?"

"One of many." His smile eased some of my grief. He moved closer to me and pulled me into him. "I only want to make you happy."

"I think I'm ready for that."

Tim leaned down and kissed me. He took my face in his hands and gently kissed my lips. I loved the way he made me feel. His warmth calmed me. Years of angst floated away when I was in his arms. I knew he meant what he said about protecting me. I had never felt safer in all my life.

CHAPTER TWELVE

W hen I arrived at work, I had an hour before Jane was scheduled. I wasn't sure what she was going to want. There was nothing I could do to help her get Carmen's case re-opened. Once a case was closed, it was rare the detectives ever admitted they might have been wrong. I didn't know what she expected of me.

Ten minutes before nine, my phone rang. "Val, your nine o'clock is here, would you like me to ask her to wait?"

"No, I'll be right up." Ten minutes early, but at least she showed up. I grabbed a notebook and pen and headed for the stairs. Counseling the living was not my favorite part of the job, but Jane intrigued me, or maybe what tugged at me more was that Carmen was the same age as Gabriel. I could relate to the pain of losing a child.

Jane sat up straight in a chair pushed into the long conference room table, a legal pad of yellow paper in front of her, with her pen capped, at the side. Under the pad of paper was a large manila envelope. She seemed more approachable than she had been last night. "Hi Jane, how are you doing this morning?"

A heavy sigh escaped as she took a deep breath. "I'm really sorry about last night."

"It's okay, I..."

"No, it's not. I know I should have never shown up at your place like that. I was just desperate and had a little too much to drink. That's a deadly combination." Her choice of words made her close her eyes as she dropped her head. "I sometimes drink to make the pain go away. To make it all go away. I know how bad it is for me, I just don't have it in me to stop."

"I get it, Jane. The pain you're feeling must be overwhelming. A part of you was stolen, and now you question if she did it herself, or if someone did it to her. I can't even imagine what you're feeling." Except, I could, to some extent. I knew that pain all too well. It kept me up some nights, and the pain of not knowing where Gabriel was, or how he was doing ate away at my sanity.

Jane's eyes met mine, and we held each other in a gaze of understanding. It was almost as though she knew what I was thinking. "You know, you're the first person who hasn't said they know how I feel. You don't know how much that pisses me off. No one knows what this feels like."

"You're right. You're the only one who knows your pain. Some people think they're helping when they say that stuff, but it usually makes it worse."

"You've done this a time or two, huh?"

"Just a few, but I've been in a situation where people said

that to me, and I know how much it didn't help, so I try to be aware of what's not helpful."

"Have you?" She paused. "Lost a child?"

"We're not here to talk about me, Jane, we're here for you."

"Yup, just like the rest of you." Her voice rose as frustration bubbled up. "You want to know my business, but I can't know yours."

Caught off guard by her sudden change in mood, shame took over, instead of the normal anger this would have brought. "No, Jane. I haven't lost a child. I'm sorry you feel that way. I don't want to talk about me when we have so little time to talk about your needs." Had I lost a child? I don't even know. I lost him, but is it forever? Is the pain the same?

"I'm sorry to be so short with you. It's just that I've heard this all before. You know? I have to tell my secrets, and any time I have a question, I get shot down. I just want to be real. You know?"

"Yes, I do. I understand it can feel like we are above you, but that's not how I operate, Jane. We are both human, we have both seen and done many things in our lifetimes. Some things hurt, some things are great, but we all know how it feels to be...well, human."

Jane's eyes were damp as she sucked in some air. "Fair enough. Maybe we'll have time later to get to know each other."

"Maybe we will." Not sure how true that was, but I met her with a smile. "What would you like to talk about this morning?"

"I brought the letter." The anticipation of getting to read the note muffled the words that followed. Jane took out a business-size envelope, with the top torn open and handed it to me. "I didn't get to keep the original, that's in evidence, but at least I was smart enough to make a copy before I gave it to them."

My hands trembled as I held the envelope. Carefully, I pulled out the paper, unfolded it, and began to read it.

"Read it aloud."

Dread circled me, I didn't want to follow her command, but I didn't want her to snatch it back from me, so I complied. *"Dear Mommy, I am sorry, I can't take it any longer. I know you will be sad but try to get over it. I am going to a better place. Please don't be upset with me. I love you. Love, Carmen."*

Jane was on the edge of her seat, her body leaned forward onto the table. "See what I mean?"

"No, Jane, I'm sorry, but I didn't know Carmen."

"I mean, is this letter good enough? It's the last words to me, shouldn't she have said more? Told me why?"

"It was pretty short, but maybe she was in too much pain to write more. Is there anything else about it that doesn't sound like her? Did she call you Mommy? Do you know what she might have been upset about?"

"She called me Mommy as a little girl, but not since she was about ten. We weren't that close. She was rebellious. I know she was having boy problems, I mean, before Seth, but I wouldn't think it was bad enough to kill herself."

"How long had she been dating Seth?"

"Oh, a few months maybe. He's a good man."

My memory painted him differently. Just the thought of him increased my heart rate. From my interaction with him, I would not have classified him as a good man or even a man for that matter. "Do you still keep in touch with Seth?"

The question brought a smile to her face. "Yes, he checks up on me."

"Has he seen the note?"

"Yeah, I let him look at it. He told me to drop it and just let the case stay closed. Part of me wants to drop it, but part of me wants to know for sure."

"Do you think he'll be mad if he knows you're talking to me about this?"

"He won't find out. Right?"

Her lack of an answer was good enough for me to know. "Are you afraid of him? If he were to find out?"

"Of course not." Her body stiffened with her response. "I just don't think he needs to know."

"What are you hoping will come of this? If they were to find out that she did not commit suicide?"

"I want whoever did this to my baby to pay. I don't want people thinking that she would have done such a thing. I want her name cleared of all this."

"Where would you like to start?"

"How about with you asking that hunk of yours for some help?"

My cheeks flushed as I cleared my throat. "What do you mean?"

"Oh, don't play stupid with me, I saw that detective at

your place last night. For being *one of them* he is pretty hot, I don't blame you for bumping uglies with him."

"Oh, my goodness, Jane, it's really not what it looks like."

"What? It looks like the two of you are dating. No?"

"Well, I guess so, but..."

"Then you're the perfect person to get him to open the case."

"Oh, Jane, I don't..."

"Jesus Christ." She pushed herself away from the table and stood up. "What do I have to do to make you understand how important this is?"

The desperation of her anger spoke to all the right places in me. If I were in her shoes, I would want someone to help me. I don't even know what I would do or how I would act. "Jane, please sit down. I want to help you."

My words were all it took to change her attitude. "Thank you, Val." As she sat back down, she placed her hand on top of mine. "I knew you'd understand."

"I don't know what I can do, but I will ask Detective Phillips."

"You know it might help if you gave him something for the information."

"What do you mean?"

"You know." She smirked as she winked at me.

"Oh, my goodness, Jane. I don't think I'll be doing that, but I will ask him."

"Well, if that doesn't work, you can pull out the big guns."

"For now, I want to get back to how you are doing. I know you mentioned that you take something to help you sleep, but have you been to see your doctor since all this happened?"

"No, why? It's not like I'm sick. I hate doctors."

"It's just that they might be able to give you something to help deal with some of the...feelings."

"Oh, you mean how I'm so unstable?" She used her fingers to make air quotes for the last word.

"I wouldn't call it unstable."

"Why the hell not? Everyone else does. This is how I've always been. I used to take some stuff, but I haven't had the money to get it, and I don't think I need it. I kind of like being...what's the word...animated?"

"What kind of pills were you taking? Jane, I might be able to help you get your prescriptions."

"I don't know what they're called. A little white one, a blue one. Besides, the only help I want from you is getting me answers. Don't you worry about my medications. I hate taking those things anyway."

"Jane, can I ask you an uncomfortable question?"

"Sure. Let me guess, am I crazy?"

"No, not crazy, but have you been diagnosed with anything?"

"I hate labels." She looked away from me and her eyes went to the door then came back to me. "I've been told I have a personality disorder, but do you really think that's true? I mean, there's nothing wrong with my personality."

Of course, how had I not noticed this before? Jane's moods were so unpredictable. Walking on eggshells doesn't even work with her, because there is no predictability. "There's nothing wrong with your personality, Jane." The only answer I could give without risking her walking out.

"Did they give you a name for it? I know there are so many different types."

"Frank."

The seriousness on her face made me regret asking. "Frank?"

"Jesus, Val, no, not Frank, I can pass anything by you." She chuckled as she stared me dead in the eyes. "Border something, I think, like I said, I don't like titles."

"Fair enough. To be honest, I don't like titles either, but sometimes they help us understand what's happening with people. Did Carmen take any prescriptions?"

"You mean, was she as crazy as her mother? No. She was too perfect for that."

The hint of anger behind her words was hard to ignore and made me question things more than I had before. "Can you tell me a little about Carmen? I remember how beautiful she was, and that sweet lullaby you sang to her, but I don't know that much about her."

Jane closed her eyes and bit her bottom lip as she shook her head. "Ahh, yes, she was beautiful, but so was I. She was even prettier as a little girl, and not as much of a problem then."

"What do you mean? How was she a problem?"

"All the boys she would bring home, all the drinking, all the sex and all the drugs. How would that make a mama proud?"

"That does sound like a handful. What kind of drugs did she do?"

"You name it, she tried it."

"I'm a little confused, Jane. How did that make her perfect?"

"Well, she was perfect. So much better than me." Tears started to build in her eyes.

"Are you okay, Jane? We can stop for today if you want to."

She sucked in tears and ran her hand through her hair. "Yeah, I think we've talked enough. Now it's your turn to do some work for me, right? Talk to that piece of meat of yours and ask him for some private information for me." She winked at me as she stood up.

"I'll talk to Detective Phillips, but, Jane, can you use his name? It makes me uncomfortable when you..."

"Don't get your panties in a bunch, I was just kidding."

"Will I see you at group next week?"

"Won't I see you before then? I can bring dinner."

"To be honest, Jane, I would like to just meet at the hospital. If you need to talk or think of anything, you can call me here, okay?"

"Yeah, sure, I get it, we're not friends."

"No, Jane, it's more that I could get in trouble with my boss if she knew you were coming to my house. I have strict boundaries I must adhere to."

"Yup, whatever. I'll call, or I won't, you'll just have to wait and see."

"See you next week?"

"If you're lucky." She left the door open as she walked down the hall.

Our interaction left me exhausted. My doubts about Carmen's death just became even more cloudy. On the one hand, I wouldn't blame her for trying to escape her mother, but on the other hand, there seemed to be a lot more to the story than Jane was telling me. She did give me a good idea, though. I didn't know why I hadn't thought about talking with Tim about the case to get the inside scoop, the details that the paper didn't give. I bet he'd tell me anything I wanted to know.

The first two meetings of trauma group and its members had taken a lot more of my time than I had imagined they would. Maggie's story hadn't left my head since I heard it. I *knew* what her daughters went through, and that wasn't something I wanted to remember. Now Jane, crossing every boundary I put in place to keep myself distanced from my clients was getting too much for me, but not enough to stop. The first time I saw Carmen, I knew I had to find answers for her. I *knew* there was so much more to her story. There always was.

Norma and Sonya hadn't even shared their stories yet. My curiosity wanted to know, but my heart couldn't take knowing yet. Norma was so sweet; it would pierce my heart to think about anyone hurting her. The group already destroyed all of the walls I spent my entire career building. Not even a brick at a time, but the whole damn thing at once.

Thank goodness for Tim. I wasn't sure how I would handle all of this without him. *Piece of meat.* I still couldn't get over how brash Jane was, well, actually I could. Borderline personality disorder was always the diagnosis that made me cringe when I read it in a chart. I do hate labels, but that label is one that could not be forgotten. The manipulation, behavioral changes, the stolen energy was always so hard to see happening until you were in too deep. Jane did have all the textbook symptoms, and if mixed with alcohol, she'd quickly spiral out of control, taking anyone in her line of sight with her. I just needed to remind myself to not get sucked in. *Poor, sweet Carmen.* Being raised by Jane must have taken its toll on her.

CHAPTER THIRTEEN

The phone rang three times before Tim picked up. "Detective Phillips."

"I know who I called." I regretted my attempt at sarcasm as soon as I finished. "Hey Tim, it's Val."

"I know who it is, I can read." Silence followed his words.

Unsure if he was checkmating my sarcasm, I wasn't sure if I should hang up, or wait and see.

"Hey, Val, what's up?"

Relief. Our relationship made me question so many things. Sarcasm was our language before, but now it felt rude, not fun. "Sorry for being a smartass. Hey, do you have some time to swing by the hospital?"

"Well, that depends, will you be there?"

"Yes, for a few more hours anyway."

"Don't you think it's risky?"

"What's risky?"

"It's a small place, people will talk."

"About what?"

"About me leaving your office with a smile."

"Oh my God, Tim."

"Relax, Val, I'm joking. Remember, it's our thing."

"Ha-ha. Yeah, it's just so...weird now. I don't know how to act. I've worked so long to not like you, now it's hard to untrain myself."

"You were pretty good at it. I'll let it slide. I'll be there in a few."

After he hung up the phone, I thought about what people might say if they knew we were dating. As far as I knew, Jane was the only one who had any idea. That thought was scary enough to give me hives. What would people think? There was no one around the basement. Having him in my life was worth the risk of being found out. There was no harm in dating, nothing to feel guilty about.

To clear my head, I went outside to walk around the parking lot. The coolness in the air was just enough to need my cardigan. I was thankful I didn't leave home without it, regardless of the season. Hospital air conditioning, especially in the basement, was brutal, like the arctic most days. As I rounded the first corner of the driveway, Tim pulled up in his black Crown Victoria. I heard the door unlock and his window roll down.

"You are under arrest for being so smoking hot. Now, get in the car, before I cuff you."

I was thankful my cheeks were already pink from the temperature outside that he couldn't see me blush. "Well, I have been known to put up a fight. I think you better get the cuffs out. You know, just in case."

"Damn. I didn't expect that to work." A smile spread

across his face. "Seriously, though, do you want to talk out here? It's beautiful out today, we should soak up as much sun as possible before the snowflakes start falling."

"You really know how to kill the mood."

"Especially since I've worked so long to create it."

I opened the door and got in, to help alleviate some of the awkwardness we were creating. "Let's park over there, under that oak tree."

"You totally missed the part about soaking up the sun, huh?"

"What can I say, I'm a vampire." My eyes met his as the sexual tension filled the car. "So, Jane came by today."

"Yeah? How did that go?"

"It was...interesting. She showed me a copy of the suicide note."

"How in the hell could she? We have it."

"It was a copy. She made a copy before she gave it over."

"That's not that strange, I guess. She must have known we would keep it."

"She made me read it to her. And then wanted me to tell her that Carmen didn't write it like I knew her. She thinks *someone* killed her, but she won't say who. When I asked about the boyfriend, she got upset, well, not really upset, but she refuses to even answer questions about him. What do you think?"

"I can't say much, Val. It's closed and you know how hard it is to open it back up. Lawrenceville doesn't have enough manpower to give it another look."

"That's awful. What if she were your daughter? I bet you'd find the resources to open it back up."

"Val, it isn't that easy. You're right, I would do everything in my power to get answers for my daughter. *Our daughter*."

"Whoa, that took an uncomfortable turn."

"Why is it uncomfortable? Just something to consider."

"Carmen was nineteen. She was just a baby, the minute I saw her, I knew I had to help her. When I met the boyfriend in the room, I instantly disliked him. He brought rage out in me that I haven't felt in years."

"Are you saying you think he killed her? Wrote the note to make it look like a suicide?"

"I'm not sure what I'm saying, just that I *know* Carmen didn't kill herself."

"What makes you so sure, Jane? Or, something else?"

"Well, Jane is just...odd. I have figured out why, though."

"Oh? Do tell."

"She said she has Borderline Personality Disorder, which is always a challenge to figure out, but it does explain why she thought it was okay to show up at my place last night...and she did recognize you." I smiled as I waited for his questions.

"And?"

I couldn't tell if he was blushing, or if it was just the sun beaming onto his face. "And she wants me to ask my piece of meat for some help."

"Whoa. I'm not sure if I'm flattered or not."

"I know, it kind of threw me off, too."

"What kind of help do you need from this piece of meat?" He chuckled as he put his hand on my knee.

I placed my hand on his as I savored our time together. "She wants you to help get the case opened back up."

"I don't know, Val, that's next to impossible. We're so

short-staffed, and it would make the department look bad... they don't take it lightly when you tell them they were wrong."

"I know, that was sort of what I told her." I looked out the windshield as I thought about how to ask the question I really wanted to ask. "Do you think you could let me look at the evidence? Or the reports?"

"I could probably pull that off...but it'll cost you...this piece of meat doesn't work for free."

"Whatever could I repay you with?"

"How about...you kiss me?" He puckered up his lips as he brought his face closer to mine.

"It would be hard to say no to that face." I leaned in and touched my lips to his. At that moment, I didn't care who could see us, or that I was letting myself fall in love with him. Tim put his hand on my cheek and pulled me closer as we continued to kiss. I didn't want him to let go, or for it to stop. Could he be the man I wanted to spend my life with? Just the thought of that would have made me run before, but now, I could think of nothing more.

"Wow, Val, you're electric. You know how to get me going. Do you think there will be more of that later?"

"I hope so." I also hoped he couldn't tell how hard I'm falling for him.

"Music to my ears. So, I guess I owe you something. Want to stop in the barracks when you get off tonight? Everyone else should be gone by 5:00."

"Banker's hours, huh? No wonder there's no time to open closed cases."

"Yeah, well, we have to have some perks, or no one would

want to join the force. Besides, the state police pick up patrol until morning. We just don't have enough manpower."

"No comment. Thanks for doing this for me. And for the record, I would have kissed you for free."

"Now you tell me." His smile sent a vibration through my body.

"Do you want to come in for coffee? Or lunch?"

"I'd love to, Val, but I have to get back for a meeting. I'm looking forward to seeing you later tonight."

"Yeah, I guess I have work I need to do, too. See you later. Thanks for stopping by." I leaned in to get another kiss.

"My pleasure...literally."

As I walked back into the hospital, I felt my confidence building. It was incredible how being made to feel special could help life not suck so bad. I wasn't sure why I fought it for as long as I did.

Thoughts about what I might find out in Carmen's file helped make my day go by faster. I was no detective, but I knew when people were lying to me, or at least I liked to think I did. That was one of the perks of being a casualty of narcissists.

CHAPTER FOURTEEN

As I pulled up to the Lawrenceville Community Center, I noticed how dilapidated the old building really was. I pulled around back, where Tim's car was and parked next to the back door. The brick building had a tattered blue tarp on the backside of the roof, blowing in the breeze. Plywood covering a window on the second floor was grey from the weather, and many of the bricks were crumbling.

I pulled out my phone to let Tim know I was there, mostly because I had no idea where in the building his office was. In all of our years as friends, he was the one to always come to my office for both business and pleasure, it was about time I visited him at his office...even if it was for selfish reasons.

The backdoor opened and Tim walked over to my car. He arrived at my door in time to open it for me. "What a gentleman."

"Hey, I have a reputation to uphold."

"There is so much I could say, but..."

His lips met mine before I could finish my smart remark. I fell into his arms and let him hold me close. "Are you ready for this?"

Forgetting why I was there for a moment, I smiled. "Of course."

"Don't get upset when you see the file, OK?"

"No promises." He took my hand and led me into the building. The parking lot was dark, only lit by the lone street-light on the other side of the street. Inside the building, Tim opened the second door on the left and motioned for me to enter.

"Where's your office?"

"You're looking at it."

"Impressive."

"Yeah, I know, it's pretty amazing, right?"

"Well, I expected more from someone so amazing."

"I know, I'm too sexy for this place." His smile was bright enough to light up the darkness of the room. He picked up a white cardboard file box and moved it to a long table. "Here, this is from the Davidson case."

The reminder of why I was there took the joy out of the moment. I rested my hand on top of the box as I took a deep breath. My eyes met Tim's as I removed the cover. The box held just two files. "What is this?"

"It's the Davidson case."

I lifted out the two folders and held them up. "This?"

Tim ran his hand through his hair and jammed his hand in his pocket. "Yeah, I told you there wasn't much in there."

"A girl is dead, and this is all there is?"

"Val, it was a suicide. Sometimes there isn't anything."

"We aren't sure about that yet. That's why we're here."

"But we are sure. There isn't anything we can do about this now."

I set the two files down and opened the first one. It held a few photos. There were pictures of what looked like it could have been Carmen's bedroom, taken from different angles. There was a photo of a messy living room, a tiny kitchen with a sink full of dirty dishes. Under these pictures were the photos of Carmen's dead body. The beautiful girl I saw in the hospital bed looked different in the pictures. The sadness was overwhelming. Hers, mine, they became one as I held the photo up. Tears fell onto the open folder on the table as I tried to imagine what would make Carmen want to end her life. What could have been so bad that she would do this to herself?

When I looked down to see what my tears had fallen onto, I saw the pictures of her unbandaged wrists. Deep cuts covered both wrists. The sight was too gruesome to keep looking at. I felt my stomach flip as I put the photos back and shut the file.

"You doing okay?" Tim's voice was a gentle reminder that I wasn't alone.

I wiped the tears off my face with my sleeve. "Yeah, I'm fine. I just...don't understand." His silence gave me time to pull myself together. "Why would she do something like this? Why would anyone want to die like that?"

"I don't know. I've seen this type of thing before and I never understand."

"She was so young, so beautiful. Her mom said she was in

college. Does that sound like someone who would do this to themselves?"

"Val, it's just so hard to understand what someone else is thinking. I don't know why she did it, why anyone does it."

"I still don't think she did it herself. What did she use to cut herself? Why isn't it in this box? That's evidence, right?"

"The knife wasn't found when they went back to the home after Carmen died."

"It wasn't found? Shouldn't it have been on the bed, where the EMT found her?"

"Yeah, it should have been, but it wasn't there when we went back after she died and it became a crime scene."

"It wasn't a crime scene until after she died? Why? Shouldn't it have been searched as soon as the EMT got there?"

"We didn't even get a call about this until Jeanine called us after Carmen died. We might not have even known about Carmen if Jeanine hadn't called with her concerns."

"How is that even possible? How can someone die and you guys don't care?" Frustration turned to anger as I lashed out at Tim.

"Whoa...wait a minute, Val. We do care, but if we don't know about it, how can we do anything?"

"Sorry. This whole thing just makes me angry. A young girl's life is lost and there are no answers." I picked up the other file and pulled out the report. Minimal information filled the three pages. No details. No interviews. No justice. Under the report was the suicide note Jane had shown me. A life was gone, and nothing to show for it. "This is everything?"

"Yeah, I'm sorry, Val. Once the note was turned in, the case was closed. It never really was open anyway."

"But the note doesn't really say anything. Anyone could have written that."

"I know. It's just how they do things here. I don't agree, but what can I do? And now that

Carmen was cremated, there isn't anything we can do."

"Was there at least an autopsy done?"

"I'm not sure, let me look." Tim walked over to the computer and typed some information into the search bar. "Yeah, it looks like there was one completed, but we don't have a copy of it."

"Wait...there was one done, but you guys don't have a copy of it? Are you serious?"

"Yeah...let me see if I can get it." Tim pulled out a form from his desk and started filling it out. "It might take a while to get it and they might not even release it to me since the case has been closed."

"I still can't understand how it could have been closed without that report. I mean, what if she was drugged or something?"

"Wow, Val, you really have been watching *Snapped*."

"Knock it off, Tim, I'm serious. How can this be a closed case without all of the details? You just took her unstable mom's word for it?"

"Well, that note and even her mom told us to close the case. When the Chief heard her say that, he kind of let out a sigh of relief."

"Please tell me you see a problem with this."

"Of course, I do, but I need a job, and if he says case closed, it's closed."

The image of Carmen, dead in her hospital bed, took over my thoughts. How could I help get her justice? What if I was wrong and she actually did take her own life? I guess I might never know. I put the report and note back in the folder and put both files back in the box and handed it to Tim. "Thanks. Sorry for being so upset about all of this. I just felt like I owed this to her. At least I can say I tried."

Tim stood up, took my face in his hands and kissed me. "Val, I love that about you."

I fell into him as I let those words settle in. "You have such a big heart and so much integrity. You don't see that very often. I can't fault you for trying. I can't say I believe the right thing was done, but I will at least try to get the autopsy report to see if there is any reason we might be able to reopen the case."

"Thanks for all of your help. Can I treat you to dinner and *Snapped*?"

"You're so romantic. You know the way to a man's heart; food and murder." His laugh made me realize how bizarre it all sounded, but I was thankful we could find humor in the dark side of life.

"Pizza or Chinese? It's too late to cook anything now."

"Let's grab a pizza and finish that six-pack and get our minds off all of this."

"It might take more than that."

"Oh, I like how you think."

Embarrassed by how that sounded, I wasn't sure I wanted to correct him.

CHAPTER FIFTEEN

I could hear Gabriel crying as I unlocked the door. "Hey, buddy, sorry I'm late. I brought you something to apologize." He rubbed up against my legs, purring and pushing against me as I walked into the kitchen to put the pizza and bags down. I took out a saucer and the can of wet food on it for Gabriel. A peace offering. As Tim took up more of my time, Gabe was getting less of it. That was the hardest part of this relationship, finding a balance between going too fast and not fast enough.

As Gabriel ate his dinner, I heard a light knock on the door, followed by the door slowly opening. My heart dropped as I realized I had forgotten to lock the door behind me. Tim pushed through the door, his backpack on his back, and a brown paper bag in his hand. "Honey, I'm home."

"Oh, thank God, it's you."

"Who else?" He set the paper bag down, pulled out a bag of cat treats and another six-pack of Sam Adams. "You said you might need more, so I wasn't sure if you meant beer...or me...so I brought clothes for a sleepover, too."

"Wow, I don't know what to say. I guess we'll see how the night plays out." I hadn't slept with anyone before. Never. At thirty-four, I had never been in a relationship, not even casual sex. The idea of falling asleep in Tim's arms made everything else fade away. I guess there is always a first for everything. And he even brought a gift for Gabe. How could I turn him away now?

I grabbed some plates and the pizza and headed to the living room. Tim brought the beer and we sat together on the couch. I wasn't sure why this felt so comfortable, after so many years of never wanting anything to do with another person. "I have a confession to make."

"Oh no, is this when you tell me you're into ladies?"

I reached over to tap him on the shoulder. "No, perv. What I was going to say was that I've never been in a relationship before. I've never had sex before...well, consensual sex."

Tim reached over and took my hand. "It's OK, Val, I just want to fall asleep next to you. We can take this as slow as you want."

"I think I'd like that." My body tingled as I felt the warmth of him next to me. "Thank you for understanding and not being a normal guy."

"I think that's a compliment?" He laughed as he opened up a beer and handed it to me.

"Yeah, you know, a pushy, all you want is sex guy. I'm glad you're sweet and sensitive."

"Settle down with the compliments, Val, or I might have a hard time remaining a gentleman."

"No, really, you're one of a kind and I am so happy you tried so hard to get me to change my mind."

"Me, too. You were worth the work."

I turned the TV on to try to take the awkwardness out of the air. I wasn't sure what I was feeling, but I thought it was love. I loved Gabriel, my son and my cat, but I never felt it for anyone else before. I just hoped he didn't turn out to be a mistake. He seemed to understand me and all of the baggage I carried. I just wondered what it would take to push him away.

Snapped happened to be on again, it always seemed to be on whenever Tim was over. The episode was about another cheating husband and an angry wife looking for revenge. That seemed to be the regular theme of the show. So many relationships end because someone can't be trusted. It wasn't the best choice to watch starting a new relationship. Trust was something that eluded me. I had tried to push past those feelings when I was around Tim because he hadn't given me any reason to doubt him, but it just seemed like the inevitable. There was no way I alone would be enough to keep him happy.

"Earth to Val. Where'd you go now?" Tim was so good at reading me, he knew I struggled. I didn't know if that was a good thing or not. There was definitely no hiding around him.

"How do you always know? Are you watching TV or me?"

"You're too beautiful not to look at, sorry, I can't help it."

"I was just thinking about all these shows and how many people cheat on their spouse. I mean, what's the point of being in a relationship? And then, the revenge? I mean, how can you trust anyone? Especially the people you love?"

"Whoa, maybe we should find something else to watch? But, wait...did you just say people you love? Does that mean...that you love me?" He turned the TV off and put his plate down to take my hands.

"I didn't say that." My cheeks burned as I felt my face flush. "I mean, I guess I did. I don't know what I mean anymore."

"Val, I've told you I won't hurt you, and I won't let anyone hurt you. You're safe with me. Please trust me when I say that. I know you have every reason not to believe me, but let me prove it to you."

"I'm trying, I really am. This is why I never let anyone in. I don't know what to do with all of these feelings. The idea that you'll keep me safe feels nice, but the thought that you might hurt me keeps me from really believing it. I want to. I want to be normal."

"I love you the way you are, please don't be normal." His attempt to crack a joke made me smile. "Just give me time to show you, and if you get scared, talk to me. Don't run away in your mind and let all the crap thoughts take over. Promise me you'll talk to me, tell me what you're thinking, what you need."

Tears ran down my cheeks as I looked up at him. "I'm so glad I waited for you. Or you waited for me. Whichever way it is, I'm happy. I've never felt understood before. Not by anyone. Well, other than Gabriel, but you know what I mean."

"I do and I'll try my best to be who you need. Thank you for trusting me enough to let me in."

I snuggled closer to him and turned the TV back on. There was only so much I could handle before I needed to escape. Another episode of *Snapped* was about to begin. "Why are the women always the ones that are doing the crimes in these shows?"

"Because it's called *Snapped*. The women finally snap and commit the crime they have been dreaming of. Don't you ever think about doing something like this? Anyone you want to make pay for something they have done to you?"

"Hmmm, I guess I never thought about that." So many people had hurt me throughout my life. So much so I just stopped thinking about them. When they were out of my mind, they lost their control over me, but maybe that was their control. The thought of taking my power back and making them pay made me consider things I never would have thought of. "I don't know. Do you ever think about doing something like this to anyone?"

"Yeah, sometimes, when we have a messed-up case, I want to make the perp pay for what they did because I know jail won't be enough. I don't think I could kill anyone, but I'd love to see them suffer like they made their victims suffer."

"You've never been hurt by anyone before? No one you'd want to make suffer for what they did to you?"

"No, I guess not. There has been plenty of people that have wronged me, but not enough to want revenge."

"Your life must have been pretty amazing to not have anyone worth murdering in it." I pushed out a laugh to try to take back what I had just said. I wanted revenge not that long ago, when I met Seth. There was something about him I just didn't like, and now there would be no way to help Carmen get her revenge.

"I think murder should be reserved for the select few who have done the unthinkable. You know, harming a child or murdering someone else. Like that old saying, what is it, an eye for an eye?"

"OK, I can go along with that theory. I'd rather take both eyes, though. You know, they take my eye, I want to take both of theirs. I need to one-up with my revenge."

"Whoa Val, I like it when you get feisty." His smile took the seriousness out of the air, but I meant what I said. Maybe that was something I should have kept to myself. I don't think many people would understand the desire to right the wrongs of others. I never knew how much I really wanted to get revenge.

"I'm getting tired, do you want to go to bed?"

"Really? You're really going to let me stay?"

"Yeah, I think it'll be nice to fall asleep in your arms."

"I've dreamed about this." He pulled me into a hug and kissed me. I wasn't sure I was making the right decision, but everything in me was telling me I was. I just hoped he didn't make me regret this.

CHAPTER SIXTEEN

When I arrived at the hospital, I was greeted by Jeanine. For the first time in a long time, I was right on time. The smile on my face must have confused Jeanine because she raised her eyebrows at me before she spoke. "Hey, ahh, have you called Jane yet? She keeps calling me, telling me she hasn't heard from anyone. And, well, that doesn't sound like you."

"Did she tell you about our meeting the other day?"

"You've already met with her?"

"Yes, Jeanine."

"So, she's a little nuts, huh?"

"Yeah, just a little. What did she want, did she say?"

"Oh, just that she had something important to tell you, but she doesn't know how to reach you since you never answer your phone."

"Right. Because I'm dealing with nut jobs like her all day. Tell me again why I love my job?"

"Because you have the best boss." She pushed up her glasses on her nose and took a sip from her teal metal travel mug.

"Yeah, that's true. You're the best. Now, how about that vacation you promised me?"

"I didn't promise you...oh...I see what you did there. Why are you glowing? You're glowing, right? Or am I seeing things?"

I pushed my hair out of my face and looked down at my loafers. "I'm glowing? Nah, I think you're seeing things. Guess I just got a good night's sleep."

"Well, that's good to hear. Everything else going okay? How is the group going? Do you need any help with Jane?"

"Yeah, everything is fine, the group seems to be good, and I think I can handle Jane. I told her I could get in trouble if she came to my apartment again. Not sure that will work, but I just wanted her to know it's not OK for her to just show up at my place. She will be a challenge, but I get it, she just lost her daughter. That's enough to mess anyone up."

"Thank you, Val, for all of your good work."

"Anything for the best boss in the whole world." As we parted ways, I saw the smirk on her face. It was nice knowing she had my back, especially if things got messy with Jane.

The red light was blinking on the phone again, I didn't want to know what awaited me, but didn't want to prove Jane right. I prided myself in returning calls, even the ones I didn't want to. Five messages. Three hang-ups, a message from Jane, and one from Sonya. I was more interested in what Sonya wanted but knew I had to start with Jane.

The return call to Jane ended with a voicemail message. I made a note on my calendar that I attempted to return the call, in case she decided to tell Jeanine I never return her calls again. As much as I didn't want to talk to her, I wanted to know what she wanted. She was exhausting but intriguing, and I was hoping to learn more about Carmen. She was the only way to do that.

Sonya answered the phone right away, which I guessed shouldn't be surprising since she always had her phone in her hand. "Hi Sonya, everything OK?"

"No...not really. Do you have time to meet today? I have some stuff that came up...that I'm not sure what to do with."

"Sure, come by the hospital anytime today."

"Great, I'll be right there."

Sonya was the last person I expected to hear from. She seemed so closed off in the group, I wasn't even sure she would stay. Different scenarios ran through my mind as I waited for her to arrive. I wasn't sure what exactly right there meant, but I hoped it was literal. There was no way I could get any work done without knowing what was going on with her. I thought about what might have sent her to the group in the first place. She mentioned something about a domestic violence group, but that was the only hint she gave. It seemed like domestic violence was the route to everyone's problem in the group, well, except for Jane, but she was a different story.

I went upstairs to wait for Sonya and let the front desk know where she could find me. I got a cup of coffee to help keep the migraine away. As I sat in the dimly lit conference room, scrolling through my phone, Sonya walked in. She shut the door behind her and sat down in the chair next to me. Her left leg bounced as she caught her breath.

"Hey Sonya, what's going on?"

"You remember the last group we had? Where Maggie told us about what her piece of shit husband did to her girls?"

"Yes, that's not easy to forget."

"Well, I literally have not stopped thinking about it since I heard it. I want to kill him and make him pay. Jail isn't enough. Do you know how bad he ruined those girls' lives? Like, that is not something they will ever be able to forget. They'll never be normal again, and all because of him. Like, hearing their story awoke some rage in me that I didn't even know I had. Why does she have to live in fear, when all that fucker gets is a few years in jail? I just don't get it. It's not fair. It's worse than that. I don't even have the words for what it really is. I'm so fucken mad. Like, I can't even think about anything else. I go to bed thinking about this and wake up from nightmares about it. He needs to pay."

I placed my hand on her knee, to try to calm her a little. "I get it, Sonya. It made me angry, too. We can't let it destroy us, though."

"I knew you wouldn't get it. I knew you'd try your social work bullshit with me."

"Now wait a minute. That's not fair. Maggie's story got to me, more than you know."

"Then we have to do something. We can't sit back and wait for justice to be served. We need to make sure he gets what he deserves."

"What are you suggesting?"

"I want to hurt him. I want to cut his dick off and shove it down his throat and watch him bleed to death, and then, when he's almost dead, I want to set him on fire."

"Wow, that's specific. I guess you have been thinking about this a lot."

"That's what I said. I can't get it out of my mind. I can't stop thinking about hurting him."

"What if you get in trouble for taking things into your own hands? Have you thought about that?"

"Yeah, of course, I've thought about it, but don't you think it's worth it? Besides, if I was smart about it, I could probably get away with it."

"I don't know, Sonya, I understand how angry this makes you, but I don't think you going to jail is something Maggie would want. What would that prove? And now you've told me about your plan, someone else knows."

"You'd rat me out? You'd turn me in?"

"Sonya, you've put me in a tough spot. I understand you're angry, but a better way to

help Maggie would be to just be her friend. We haven't even heard all of the story. How do you think her girls would feel if they found out a stranger would risk going to jail to protect them? Maybe they don't want their father to die."

"I don't know why they'd care. You heard what Maggie said. Why should he live?"

"It's complicated, Sonya. I think it's great that you want to help so badly, but I think you need to slow down. Let's get to know each other a little more. Let's see what the other ladies think."

"How are you so calm? How come you don't want to kill the motherfucker?"

"Sonya, I didn't say I didn't want to. I just said we need to slow things down."

"When do we meet again? I don't think I can wait until next week. The weekend leaves me a lot of time to think."

"Want to see if the others can come in tomorrow? Do you think you can wait until then?"

"I guess. I mean, he is in jail; not like I can break in there and kill him in front of the guards." She smiled for the first time since sitting down.

"Do you want to wait while I call the others?"

"Yeah, I want to know if anyone else feels like I do."

I pulled out the other's information from the intake forms they filled out at our first meeting. Norma was the first I called. She was surprised to hear from me but was agreeable to meet the following day. Maggie sounded concerned by the call, and I didn't want to give her too much information, but she agreed to meet with us. When I placed the call to Jane, she still didn't answer, but she hadn't been part of the group when Maggie shared.

Sonya was content with knowing we were all going to get together to discuss her feelings before the weekend came. She was able to pull herself together and said she was going to return to work. I was hopeful the extra meeting would be enough to keep her from doing anything stupid. Although, I'd be lying if I said I hadn't thought about wanting to hurt Maggie's husband. I could relate to Lexi, more than anyone could know, but I couldn't condone Sonya's desires. I couldn't go down for her actions. What a mess that could turn into.

I wasn't sure if I should put a note in the computer about our visit, even a vague one, because I didn't want any trail left behind for anyone to find. I had a strong feeling this wasn't going to be the end of Sonya's desire for revenge. I couldn't say that I blamed her, but I don't want to get linked to any of her crazy ideas. That was the one thing I learned from all those *Snapped* episodes, don't leave any trail behind.

CHAPTER SEVENTEEN

I knew I couldn't tell anyone about the visit from Sonya, especially Tim. It was crazy to think about everything Sonya said, but it did get me thinking. What it takes to make someone snap is different for everyone. I thought about what it would take to make me snap. So much had happened to me, and most of the people I met in my career had their own sad stories. Amazingly, I hadn't snapped already. What did I have inside me that kept me from causing harm to them? When would it be my turn to change the pain into payment? But did I even have it in me to hurt someone else?

When Tim texted me to ask me if I wanted him to come over, I wasn't sure how to respond. I wanted to see him, to get my mind off all of the thoughts Sonya's visit awoke in me, but I also wanted to give them time to play out.

"Gabriel, what do you think I should do?" I scratched his head as he sat in my lap on the couch. "Do you think Tim should come over tonight? Or just the two of us tonight? Yeah, I know he brought you treats, but what do you think?"

His purrs didn't answer my questions, so I had to make up my mind myself. "Is it too soon to tell a little fib? I do think I have a headache coming on, that's not a lie."

I replied with a simple, "I think I'm just going to rest tonight, long day at the office. Talk to you tomorrow." Accompanied by a smiley face emoji. He didn't pester me any further, I was glad he knew how complicated I can be.

I got up to make a cup of peppermint tea and got my iPad. I didn't usually go online at home since I was on the computer so much at work, but I had research to do. Sonya's visit made me want to look into my mom. It had been almost twenty years since I spoke to her, and sixteen years since I last saw her. In the last few years at home, I wouldn't talk to her, not after what she did to Gabriel. I had to live under her roof until I was old enough to leave, but she couldn't make me talk to her.

I logged onto my Facebook account and typed her name in the search bar. Nothing came up and then I remembered I had blocked her years ago, so she couldn't find me. I had a lot of people blocked on there, it seemed like a good idea just to create a new account. I created a new Hotmail address, and then a new Facebook under the name Stephanie Mills. No one I knew, but no one they would suspect as being me.

I typed my mom's name in the search bar again. This time her smiling face popped up in the first search. Just seeing her look so happy fueled the dormant rage that I hosted. How dare she be happy when she stole so much from me? Scrolling through her page, it looked like she was still married to the same jackass. I scrolled through pages of inspirational sayings and happy pictures. This was what was going to make me snap. Seeing that evil woman enjoy her life when she threw her own daughter away. All those sappy sayings meant nothing when there was no truth behind them. How dare she live such a lie. As far as I knew, she had never tried to find me and she never apologized for stealing Gabriel from me. She didn't even understand how much pain it caused. She didn't even care; all that mattered was the image she portrayed to the rest of the world.

Hours went by before I stopped scrolling through her page. I think I looked at every post she ever posted, read every comment. Countless friends wishing her a happy birthday each year. Pictures from girls' getaways and romantic adventures with her sleazy husband. No one knew the woman I knew. I never told anyone what she did to me because it was too painful to talk about. She got away with everything. She always did.

After looking at all I could see on her page, I clicked on his page. Dr. Chad Ross. My skin crawled when his big, round head loaded on my screen. His hair had started thinning and was all gray now. He had grown a full beard and resembled a cheap mall Santa. I imagined he smelled the part, too. He was the only one who knew the truth, and he was equally as evil as my mother.

His page had less on it, probably so his patients couldn't find him. His page was boring in comparison. It looked like they lived at the same place and he worked at the same office. The thought he still had his license was disturbing. I wondered how many girls he had hurt. I thought about the amount of time that had passed and tried to calculate the number of victims he might have had by now. Maybe age slowed him down, but I doubt it. It's the power he was after, not just the sex.

I clicked on each of his friends to see what else I could find out. I didn't recognize many of the names. He never could keep friends, they eventually figured out what an arrogant asshole he really was. "Gabriel, look at this. Chad hasn't changed a bit. I hate everything about him. I think if there is anyone I could kill and not feel bad, it would be him."

Gabriel jumped into my lap and rubbed his head against my chin. "Are you trying to tell me it's time to go to bed?" I glanced down at the clock and saw it was past midnight. I was never going to be able to wake up in the morning. "Good thing I have you to keep track of me." He jumped down and followed me to the bathroom while I got ready for bed.

As I brushed my teeth, I couldn't shake the images of Chad and my mother out of my mind. I wished I hadn't spent my whole night lost in their life. I worked hard not to think about them, and now it was like I opened Pandora's Box. Years of suppressed anger bubbled over. I thought about what life should have been like, and all I missed out on. I thought about the family that I loved that I was forced to leave behind. I wondered if my grandmother was still alive and why she hadn't tried to find me. I wonder what lies my mother told her. I didn't have the chance to say goodbye to her because I knew she wouldn't be able to keep my secret. Mom knew how to manipulate information out of everyone.

Gabriel curled up on my pillow as he waited for me to join him. "Just a minute, Buddy, I need to check something." I went back out to the living room, grabbed the iPad, and entered my gram's name in the search bar. My heart raced as

I waited for the results to populate. I didn't want to find out that she was dead this way. I closed the cover before I could look. It was too late to find out that I'd never get to see her again. Why hadn't I thought about this before now? It's been sixteen years and I never thought about this possibility before. I lost sixteen years of my life when I ran away. I lost any chance at a healthy relationship with my gram, all because I had to escape the Hell my mother created.

"I can't look. I can't do it." I paced the bedroom with my iPad in my hand. "What if she's dead?" I sat on the bed and ran my fingers through Gabriel's fur. "I've got to look, don't I?" I opened the cover to reveal the search results, nothing there. I typed her name again, with the word obituary...still, nothing came up. "Gabe, she's not dead. Maybe there is time to find her and reconnect. Is that crazy? Should I just give this up?" Gabriel was already asleep, not listening to anything I was saying. I turned off the light and got into bed to try to get some sleep for the big meeting tomorrow.

CHAPTER EIGHTEEN

Since I wasn't able to fall asleep, I made it to work early. I wanted to get everything done, so I'd have more time to spend with the group. Jane still hadn't returned the calls I had made to her, but I wasn't sure that was a bad thing. I wanted to have time to focus on Sonya's thoughts and the others and Jane had a way of taking things over. I hadn't told Jeanine about this special meeting because I didn't want to give her the chance to tell me we couldn't meet. I blocked out my schedule, so she would know I was busy and not available to do any spur of the moment favors.

Norma was the first to arrive. We sat together in the conference room and made small talk while we waited for the others. Maggie came in next, she appeared less nervous and I hoped our meeting today wouldn't set her back. I started a pot of coffee while we waited for Sonya. I was beginning to think she got second thoughts and wasn't going to show up for the meeting she requested. "Let's just wait a few more minutes for Sonya before we get started. I wasn't able to get in touch with Jane, so it'll just be the four of us." I walked down the hall to see if I could see Sonya, but there was no sign of her.

I poured a cup of coffee in hopes of giving me enough energy to get through the day on zero sleep. Norma came over and made a cup and brought one over to Maggie. Between the lack of sleep and the absence of Sonya, I wasn't thinking clearly. "Sorry, I should have offered you some..."

"Good morning, beauties." Sonya's bubbling voice boasted over me. "Sorry I'm late; I had to stop for these." She placed a box of muffins from the local bakery on the counter. "Figured we could use a treat today."

"Isn't that nice?" Norma smiled as she placed her hand on Sonya's shoulder. "It's so good to see you, dear."

"Maggie, come and get it." Sonya smiled as she placed a blueberry muffin on a paper plate.

"I was worried you weren't going to make it, glad you're here."

"Of course, I made it, we have work to do today." Sonya winked at me as she looked around the room at the other ladies.

"Why don't we get started then?" I walked over to shut the door and found a seat between Norma and Maggie. "Sonya asked if we could meet a little early because she has been having some trouble since our last meeting."

"Not really trouble. I just...it's just that I'm having a hard time with everything I heard."

Maggie's eyes went to her untied shoes. "I'm sorry, I shouldn't have shared so much."

"Knock it off, Maggie. That's not what I mean. Hearing what that piece of shit did to you and your girls just made me furious. All I can think about is causing him as much pain as he caused all of you. I just wanted to see how everyone else was dealing with all this."

Tears filled Maggie's eyes, her head now looking up at the group. "I don't know what to say." She took a tissue out of the box and blew her nose. "I've wanted to hurt him for years now, but seeing what he's done to my girls makes those thoughts endless now. I never told anyone about that before. But, hearing you are feeling the same way helps. I don't feel so crazy."

"Wanting to make him pay for what he did to you doesn't make you crazy, Maggie, it makes you a mom, but what does it make me? I don't even know him, or you, or your girls."

"I think it makes you compassionate.... well, thoughtful..." As I searched for the right word, Sonya erupted with laughter.

"Did you hear what you just said?" Her laughter continued. "Killing someone makes me compassionate?"

"Yeah, I know I didn't say the right thing, but you know what I mean. You don't want to see someone taken advantage of; you want to protect them. That's what makes you compassionate, not the act of harming someone."

"I haven't harmed anyone. I just want to." Sonya twirled a piece of hair around her finger.

"I've been thinking a lot about you, Maggie, and your sweet girls, too. I can't say I wanted to hurt anyone, but my heart surely hurts for you." Norma reached over and patted her hand on Maggie's knee.

"Maggie, how have you felt since you shared with us?" I leaned in to try to get closer to the group.

"I don't know. I hadn't thought much about it, about the sharing part. I always think about what he did. I'm still afraid, but what you all said helped me feel a little safer. I didn't know they'd tell me when they let him out, so that has helped me ease some of the fear."

"I haven't been able to stop the anger. I can't even find the words to express the rage I feel."

"I hear you, Sonya. But what can we do to help you?" I turned to make eye contact with her.

"Help me? I don't need any help. I just want to let my rage do some good. You know?"

"Oh, honey, if you use your rage for bad, you'll suffer more. We don't want that, do we?" Norma picked up Sonya's hand and held it between hers.

"You mean, you don't want to cut his dick off?"

Laughter escaped from Maggie as she covered her mouth with her tissue.

"See, even Maggie thinks that's a good idea." Sonya slapped her hand against her leg.

"Honey, I don't want to think about his dick." Norma wrinkled up her nose.

The room erupted with laughter. The seriousness of the conversation took a back seat while we wiped away our tears. "So, there you have it, let's stop thinking about his dick."

"Why do you think this upsets you so much? Did something happen to you, honey?" Norma's question changed the mood in the room.

"Well, yeah, why else would I be here?"

"No, no, I know that, but did something happen to you when you were a little girl? Did someone touch you?"

Norma's question made my throat close. My heartbeat against my chest as I scanned the room. Memories flooded me, the images from Facebook from the night before filled the room. "Yes." It was too late to take back the words and deflect what I had just said.

All eyes focused on me. "Sonya, did someone touch you, as a little girl?"

"Wait a minute, you just said 'yes.' Do you have something you want to share with us?"

"No, I wasn't answering, I was agreeing with Norma." This was not going to turn into a therapy session for me. I was the counselor, not the counseled. These women had enough of their own problems, they didn't need to hear about mine.

"Hmmm, well, it sure didn't sound like that. No, no one touched me as a little girl. That's gross. I don't want to think about that."

"And you think I do? I can't get the image of that bastard violating my beautiful little girls."

"Awe, geez, I'm sorry, Maggie, I didn't mean that. I guess the truth is, I *was* molested by a neighbor when I was about eleven." Sonya paused. "I've never told anyone before." Sonya rocked back in forth in her chair as she looked around the room. "I didn't mean to say that."

"I'm glad you told us. It makes sense why Maggie's story upset you so much. Have you ever thought about harming the person who did it to you?" I waited for her response.

"No, I mean, not lately. I think he's dead. I don't know, it's been years."

"Do you want to tell us more about what happened to you? Do you think that would be helpful?"

Maggie spoke up, "I think it would help me. To hear about someone who understands what my girls went through."

"Well, I haven't thought about it for years. I almost forgot it even happened until I heard Maggie talk about her girls." Sonya took a drink of her coffee and a deep breath. "There was an old man who lived next door to us. He wasn't creepy or anything, well, he didn't appear to be. He brought groceries for my mom every once in a while. He got on her good side and then he offered to babysit my little brother and me. We didn't have family close, so my mom was relieved to have someone she could trust to help her out. The first few times we stayed with him everything went fine. It didn't start happening until we started spending the night there. My mom picked up some more shifts to get Christmas money, and my brother and I would spend the night at his house.

"One of the nights, I woke up and found him in my bed. He was naked. When he saw I was awake, he started kissing me. I didn't know what to do. I tried to scream, but he put his hand over my mouth. He told me if I wasn't quiet, he'd tell my mom I wasn't listening to him. He told me she knew what he was doing, and it was how she was repaying him for all of his help. I didn't want to let my mom down, so I stayed still and let him continue. He pulled off my undies and pushed up my nightgown. It made me sick. He got mad when I didn't do what he wanted. He said I was selfish because I wasn't making him feel good. I started to cry harder, but it didn't stop him. He stayed in my bed the rest of the night and wouldn't let me get up to go to the bathroom." Sonya closed her eyes and bit her bottom lip.

"Oh, Sonya. I'm so sorry." I handed her a box of tissues.

"In the morning, when I woke up, he was making us pancakes, like nothing happened. He had a bath running for me and told me I needed to go get cleaned up. My little brother happily ate his breakfast while I washed away the evidence. Before my mom came over to get us, he told me if I told anyone, he wouldn't be able to help my mom anymore, and if he couldn't help her, she would lose her job. I didn't want to make life harder for her, so I didn't say anything. For the next three years, he kept this up, and I kept it quiet. When he found out I got my period, he started using condoms, but he made me feel dirty about it like I was no good because he had to wear one. Thankfully, I didn't get pregnant, but the thought that I could have scared me. I mean, what would I have said? My mom had no idea what was happening. She would have been so angry. The only thing that made it stop was when I was old enough to stay home and watch my little brother. I was fourteen when my mom agreed it would be safe enough for us to stay home without her. Little did she know being home alone was way safer than going to that sicko's house."

The room stayed quiet as Sonya disclosed the horror she went through. Something in me wanted to tell her I understood what she had gone through, but I wasn't ready to share yet. I needed to be strong for her and the others. The idea that there were so many people silently suffering was becoming more of a reality. The need for revenge burned stronger, and I could relate even more to Sonya than before.

"Sonya, I am so sorry that happened to you. I can understand your anger now, and it makes total sense. Thank you so much for trusting us enough to share that with us."

Tears streamed down Maggie's face. She blew her nose in her recycled tissue and nodded her head to Sonya. "Thank you...for sharing that with us. It helps...to...to understand what my girls went through. I'm so sorry you couldn't tell your mom."

"I think I could have, but I believed him. And, after a while, I was ashamed. You know, after a while, I felt like I was just as guilty. After a while, I tried to pretend he was someone else, and, you know, enjoy it. It sounds disgusting, but, if I didn't fight it, it didn't hurt so bad. Don't get me wrong, I hated it, but I needed a way to get through it."

"That makes perfect sense, Sonya. I think that's a normal response. Sex can feel good, that doesn't make you responsible. It still makes him a sick son of a bitch."

"You think? That's kind of a relief. I always thought when I went along with it, it made me guilty, too. I seriously never told any of this to anyone before today. Not sure how I feel about that yet."

"That was very brave of you to release all that. Now, you can start working on healing." I realized the hypocrisy in my words, but I meant them.

"I didn't realize I wasn't healed. I figured I could forget about it and move on with my life. I never expected to react the way I did after hearing about someone else. I knew people sucked; I just didn't want to believe anyone else would have to deal with what I did. I guess the amount of anger I've experienced the last few days isn't healthy, but I'm not sure I want to give it up, you know?"

"Give what up?"

"The anger. I kinda like how it feels. I like how fired up it gets me." She took another drink of her coffee and tapped her fingers against the cup.

"Oh, honey, you don't want to live a life like that. You want to forgive, release the power that anger has on you."

"Oh, sweet, old Norma, that is not at all what I want. I don't want to forgive anyone. Not now. Not ever. You wouldn't understand."

"I just might. I have my own story, dear. Don't dismiss this old lady."

"Norma is right, Sonya, we each have our own way of dealing with the life we have been handed. Forgiveness might work for Norma, while anger might work for you. You both might be right."

"I'm with Sonya on this one, I'm not sure I could ever forgive Hank for what he did to Lexi and Sammy. If Lexi hadn't been pregnant, he would still be raping my babies. I think about that all the time. I can't forgive him, and I'll never be able to forgive myself."

"Maggie, you are not to blame for what happened to your girls. You did the right thing as soon as you knew. Not all moms do that, they are the ones that should never forgive themselves, but not you." I wish there was something I could say to make her believe me, but I know she's not ready to hear it yet.

"She's right, dear, you are a good mom, and your girls are lucky to have you on their side. Give it time, you'll see the good work you've done."

"I wonder what my mom would have done if I ever told

her what that sick fuck did to me. I can't tell her now, I mean, what would be the point?"

"Are you and your mom close?" Maggie waited for her reply.

"Yeah, I guess. Well, I don't know, not really, I guess. We get along, but we're not really close. I don't go to her to talk or anything."

"Do you have anyone in your life that you trust, that you can talk to?" I asked the question, knowing the answer.

"Yeah, sure, you guys."

"Okay, that's great that we have each other now, but do you have anyone else? I mean, we are all pretty new friends."

"No, I really don't. I have a few friends at work, but no one I trust." She paused for a moment as she looked around the room at us. "That's bad, isn't it? I'm pathetic, right?"

"No, not at all. It's quite normal, considering what you've been through. A lot of people who have been hurt by others in the past have a hard time trusting others. It can be easier to figure things out on your own when you've been hurt so badly by others in the past."

"Sounds like you're speaking from experience?" Sonya gave me the perfect segue to disclose my past, but it wasn't time yet. Tim was the only person who knew about my past, and he only knew a fraction of it.

"Fair enough. I think we all have been hurt in one way or another."

"That's true, dear. I think it's right on the money. I never had too many people I could trust, now that you mention it. I've had plenty of friends, but none I could share like this with. Thank you, Val, for getting us together. It feels so nice to be with others who understand."

"How about you, Maggie? Do you have anyone you talk with?"

"Hank made it so I couldn't have contact with my friends or family. I haven't tried to reconnect with any of them yet. I do have my therapist, and she has been helpful, but no one else outside of this room."

"How often would you all like to meet? We were scheduled for once a week, but do you feel like that will be enough?"

"I think twice a week would be better," Sonya answered for everyone. "Maybe Tuesdays and Fridays?"

"I'm not sure I can get this room consistently twice a week. It's scheduled for Tuesdays, but Fridays might be problematic. Maybe we could meet somewhere else on Fridays? Go get lunch or something?"

"I don't think that's a good idea," Maggie spoke up. "We wouldn't be able to be honest in a restaurant, people could hear us."

"She's right, dear. We could meet at my place. I live just down the road."

"Sounds good to me." Sonya stood up and brushed the crumbs off the front of her pants. "See you all on Tuesday."

"Do you have a few minutes to stick around today, Sonya?" Maggie and Norma stood up to walk to the door. "See you next week, ladies, thank you for coming in this morning. I think it's been helpful."

"I think so, too." Norma took my hand, patted the top of it and left the room with a smile. "Maggie, do you want to stop over for tea?" I heard the conversation continue down the hall as they left the hospital together.

"Thanks for sticking around." I pulled out my notepad and pulled the pen cap off. "Have you ever checked to see if your neighbor actually died?"

"No. I just assumed he's dead. I mean, he was old back then and it's been about ten years. Why are you asking?"

"I don't really know. I guess I just wanted to make sure you are safe."

"Well, he hasn't bothered me since I was old enough to tell him to leave me the fuck alone."

"If you don't mind my asking, what's his name? I just want to see if I can get any information dug up on him."

"Donald Brice. I still don't get why this matters to you."

"The same reason Maggie's story bothered you so much." I half hoped she would pick up on the clue I dropped, but not sure I was ready to discuss it any further.

Her eyes met mine, and for the first time since meeting her, a calm came over her. "I thought so. You know, sometimes, you can just tell."

"Yeah, I know. The curse of the damaged. All that self-doubt makes us second guess our gut feeling. I think that's the worst part for me."

"Hmmm, so I'm not the only one that second guesses everything?"

"I'm afraid not. Are you going to be OK this weekend?"

"Yeah, I don't have any other choice." She smiled as she started walking out the door.

"Thanks for sharing today, Sonya."

"Back at you."

CHAPTER NINETEEN

When I got to my office, I pulled out my phone and typed Donald Brice's name into the search bar. His name didn't come up. Like I tried with my gram, I added the word obituary in the search. Still, no results. He may be alive.

The story Sonya told was graphic and gruesome. As I replayed it in my mind, the anger inside me boiled over. I wondered if her mom would have believed her and if Donald would have been held accountable for his actions. I imagined Sonya as the innocent eleven-year-old girl and the fear she must have felt as he tortured her for his pleasure. I didn't understand how the people you thought you could trust were the ones that could be the most dangerous. All of the thoughts swirled through my head as I stared at the blank computer screen.

As the computer started up, an idea hit me. I could search for his name in our database. I knew how much trouble I could get in if anyone ever found out, but why would they look? I'd never even been written up for anything before. As I struggled with my inner voice, I knew I had to know. I had to know more about this man, and I doubted I could find anything about him on Facebook. What was the worst that could happen?

I couldn't fight the need to know. I entered his name in the patient portal and waited for it to populate. Donald Brice wasn't a common name, so the one hit that came up had to be him. I clicked on his name, and in seconds I had access to all of his information. He was seventy-five, so he wasn't as old as I had imagined. He lived in the next town over and his next of kin was listed as a woman with the same last name as Sonya. That must be her mother. How could that be? I wondered if Sonya knew...but what good would it do for me to tell her?

Before I could even think I picked up the phone and dialed his number. "Hi, this is Stephanie Mills from Lawrenceville Regional Hospital, is this Mr. Brice?"

"Yes, what can I help you with?"

"I'm calling about a new program we are starting here at the hospital. We are offering home visits for diabetes educa-tion. Would you be interested in a visit?"

"Well, that depends. Would you be the one coming out?"

"Yes, sir."

"Great. I'd love that. When should I expect you?"

"Hmmm, let me see...I could be there this evening, around 5?"

"Works for me. Do you need my address? Directions?"

"No, I have your address. What color house should I look for?"

"It's a white house with black shutters. The mailbox out front has my name on it."

"Sounds easy enough. I'll see you this evening."

I didn't know why I had such an urge to meet him. The idea of being in the same room with him fueled something in me I'd never experienced before. What would I even do? The phone rang and took me out of the trance I was in. It was Jeanine. She said Jane was on the way in to meet with her, but she didn't have time and asked if I could see her. This was the last thing I wanted to deal with today. Jeanine wasn't asking me; she was more telling me. She didn't have time for Jane, but it didn't matter that I didn't.

I listened to my messages and checked my email while I waited for Jane to arrive. My cell phone buzzed in my pocket, reminding me that I hadn't texted Tim yet. "Hello?"

"Hey, Val, are you okay?"

"Yeah, I'm fine, it's just been busy here. I have to work late tonight and Jane is on her way in."

"How late? I wanted to see if you wanted to get some dinner and watch some TV? I hear there's a *Snapped* marathon on tonight."

"That sounds nice. Come by around 7?"

"Sounds good, I'll bring dinner with me. Don't worry about anything else."

"How'd I get so lucky?"

"I was going to ask you the same thing." His laugh gave me the comfort I needed.

"See you later. Thanks for checking on me."

"My pleasure. And, thanks for helping Jane. I'm sure you're just what she needs."

A knock on the door startled me. "Oh, gotta go, I think she's here."

The only people that ever came down to my office were Tim, Jeanine, and some of the nurses. Typically, people didn't feel comfortable down here, and I didn't feel comfortable being down here alone with people. Some were fine, but the idea of having Jane down here made me feel unsafe. She was unpredictable, and it wouldn't be too far-fetched to think she would pull something.

When I opened the door, it wasn't Jane. "What are you doing here?"

Tim pulled me into a hug. I felt my body melt into his. I didn't know how much I needed this surprise visit. "Well, I hadn't heard from you all day, and you sounded a little stressed last night. I wanted to make sure you were telling me the truth, you know, that you really were fine."

"You goofball, you're incredibly sweet, and this surprise was just what I needed."

"I know." He handed me a coffee and kissed my cheek. "Better than who you expected to see on the other side of the door?"

"Absolutely. No comparison." I shut the door behind me and took his hand. "Want to walk me upstairs?"

"Oh, you think I can be trusted?"

"I'm willing to find out."

His hand in mine filled me with warmth. Feeling safe and protected was something new, but I was beginning to depend on it. That was something I swore I would never do. "Can't wait to see you later. Will you bring your backpack?"

"It's already packed." He bent down and gave me a quick kiss on the lips.

His lips against mine had my heart fluttering. I pulled my hand out of his when we reached the door. "I just want to keep the gossip to a minimum, at least for now."

"I get it. We wouldn't want anyone to think you might be happy."

"Yeah, I know, that would be brutal. I'd never be able to live that down. Thanks for stopping by, and for the coffee. It's the best surprise ever." He tipped his hat to me as he walked away. I hoped the awkwardness of our encounters would lessen over time, but I knew the real issue was with me. Living alone for the last sixteen years took a toll on my social skills. Tim was worth the slight uncomfortableness.

I pulled out my phone, turned on the lights in the conference room and waited for Jane to arrive. I wasn't sure how long it would be before she arrived, but I didn't want to risk her coming down to my office. It wasn't even something I had considered until the scare earlier. On my phone, I opened up the web browser and logged onto my fake Facebook account. I typed in Jane's name and scrolled through the results. I didn't see anyone that looked like her and wasn't sure how to find her. I typed in Carmen's name and clicked on the first smiling face that popped up. It was her. She was so different from Jane, she was beautiful, with a classy vibe to her. She looked like she was going to go places. I didn't see any pictures of Seth or even her mom on her profile. Pictures of her with her friends, hanging out at the beach, the typical teenager stuff. The more I looked, the less I could understand why she would want to take her life. It didn't add up. If she loved Seth as much as her mom said she did, why wasn't he in the pictures? And, where was Jane in these pictures?

I clicked on her friends list. Seth was not a friend, but Jane was. I clicked on Jane's profile and scrolled through the pictures. It didn't take long to come across one with her and Seth. That didn't add up. Seth didn't look happy, so I guessed it didn't mean anything. But where were the photos of him and his girlfriend? I looked at the date on the photo...it was posted three years ago. Carmen would have been sixteen. That seems strange that Jane would be hanging out with the older man dating her daughter.

Jane's page had so many selfies and drinking photos. It looked more like what I'd expect from a teenager, not a grown woman. She was hard to understand, and these photos made me lose more respect for her than I already had. None of it made sense, but neither did she. I scrolled through Jane's friends list and Seth wasn't a friend either. Maybe he just didn't have a Facebook account. Can't blame him.

Lost in Jane's photos and unstable posts, she startled me when she walked through the door. "You don't look like Jeanine. Guess if I wanted to talk to you, I would have returned your calls."

I hit the button to turn off my phone and turned it over before she could see I had been researching her. "I did leave you several messages, Jane. Is everything alright?"

"Well, I'm pissed off that you're calling me a liar." She plopped down in the chair next to me.

"How am I doing that, Jane?"

"You told Jeanine you returned my call, but I know you never did. I know you just don't like me."

"Oh, Jane, that's not true. I'm sorry you didn't get the calls I placed. Maybe I have the wrong number."

"Huh? How would you have the wrong number? How hard is it to dial the right one?"

I pulled out the folder of the intake forms from the group members and handed her a copy of hers. "Is that the right number?"

Jane threw her head back with laughter. "No. That's the made-up number I give to people I don't want to deal with."

"Oh, I see. So, it was you who didn't want to talk to me."

Frustration filled her when the truth filled the air. "Well, it's your job to find the right number. If I want to talk to you, you should do everything in your power to reach me."

She was impossible. I didn't want to waste my time with her, but I needed to try to make the best of this situation. It didn't appear she was going to go anywhere anytime soon. "Well, now's a good time for you to give me the number you can be reached at. That is if you want to talk with me."

She picked the pen up off the table and took the notepad away from me and wrote her number big enough to fill the whole page. "There." She pushed the notebook back at me.

I took a long, deep breath as I held my necklace between my thumb and index finger, rubbing it, reminding me how much she is probably hurting. "Thank you. I will use this number from now on." I glanced up at the clock in the room; she'd only been here a few minutes, but her presence was exhausting; it always felt like so much longer. "What can I do for you, Jane?"

"I just wanted to tell you that I think Carmen did kill

herself. You know, the more I think about it, the more it just makes sense."

"Really? Because I was going to tell you I believed what you were telling me before."

"No, none of what I said means anything. I just forgot to take my pills, and you know how that goes."

"No, Jane, I don't know how that goes. Why did you change your mind? Are you protecting someone?"

"The only person I am protecting is Carmen. I went to one of those psychic people, and she told me Carmen wants me to move on and accept that she did this to herself. I just need to respect her wishes."

"So, Carmen told you to drop the whole thing? No one else?"

"Yes. So, I just wanted you to know Carmen doesn't want anyone snooping around. I wanted to talk with Jeanine, to let her know you were knocking boots with that detective, so..."

"Hold on, you came in here to tell my boss you saw Detective Phillips at my place when you stalked me to find out where I live? Are you serious? What does it even matter that he was at my place?"

"I liked you before I knew about him, but now I don't trust you. Maybe you're an informant. Maybe you are after me. How do I know?"

"That's disappointing to hear. I wanted to help you, Jane, and I'm sorry you feel that way. I can tell you the one thing I am good at is keeping boundaries clean. I don't mix business with pleasure. I don't share information with people who don't need it, and I'm hurt you think that about me." I could feel the skin on my neck start to break out in hives. My body never did tolerate stress very well.

"Police are all the same. They can't be trusted. I'm worried he'll take you down the wrong path."

"Thank you for your concern." I cleared my throat. "Just seconds ago, you told me you came here to get me in trouble with my boss, and now you're worried about me?" I tried to shake the disgust away with a shake of my head.

"Yes." She reached over and put her hand on mine. "I miss being a mom so much, I guess I just wanted to mother you."

What the hell was happening? This woman clearly should not be left to her own devices. The judgment part of my brain was getting louder, and I knew it was only a matter of time before I said something I shouldn't. I used everything I had to inhale peace into my lungs. "Well, thank you, Jane. That's kind of you."

"So, is it OK with you if I come to the group meeting next week?"

"Sure, we'd love to have you." I forced a smile as I stood up. "I've got a lot of work to do, so I'll see you next week?"

"Wait, I'm not done." She reached into her large Coach purse and pulled out a piece of paper. As she unfolded it, I saw tears flood her eyes. "Here, just look at this. Please."

I took the paper and read the first few lines. I sat back down as I read the paper. My eyes met hers when I found what she wanted me to see.

"She was pregnant. I could have been a grandma. Not only did she kill my baby, but she killed hers, too."

"Oh, Jane, I didn't know. I'm so sorry."

"I can't help but be angry with her, even more now. But it makes sense. She never would have been able to take care of a baby."

"You think she knew?"

"Don't be stupid, a mother knows when they are pregnant. Didn't you?" Her eyes pierced my soul as she looked through me.

"I'm not a mom, Jane, so I couldn't answer that."

"Come on, you're what, forty? And, you're not a mom? Let me guess, you're a virgin, too."

"Let's not turn this into something about me, Jane, let's focus on Carmen."

"This just proves to me she did it. This was what I needed to believe the cops." She took that paper from me, folded it back up and returned it to her purse. "Case closed."

"How are you doing with this new information? Do you have anyone you can talk to about this? Do you have family?"

"I don't have anyone. Carmen was my family."

"What about Seth?"

"Oh, he can never know about this. He'd never be able to forgive her. She killed his baby."

"You think it was Seth's? You don't think she was seeing anyone else?"

"Are you just trying to piss me off? No, Carmen wasn't a little whore. She was dating Seth, and he was the only man she'd been with."

"No, I'm sorry, Jane. I didn't mean to upset you. I was just asking questions. We'd love to have you join us on Tuesday. Thank you for sharing this with me."

She stood up and walked to the door. "So, remember, case closed."

"It was already closed, Jane, that wasn't up to me."

"Just don't you forget it."

After I saw her exit the hospital, I went up to Jeanine's office. I couldn't keep this all to myself, especially if Jane didn't trust that I wasn't going to stick my nose into the case. The smell of grapefruit and cinnamon greeted me before I knocked on the door. She did not look as busy as she had said she was. "Hey, do you have a minute?"

Her eyes looked up at me, "Is everything alright?"

"I'm not sure." I closed the door behind me before she even invited me in. "Jane just left, and well, I'm not even sure where to start. Oh yeah, how about thank you for pawning her off on me." I crossed my right leg over my left as I leaned back in the armchair in front of her.

"Val, you know I'm busy, it's the end of the month, and there are so many reports that have to be done."

"Save it. I was more or less yanking your chain. But, seriously, that woman is unhinged. I didn't want to say anything before, because it isn't anyone's business, but when she came over to my place the other night, Detective Phillips was there."

"Wait...when she came to your place?"

"Oh, I thought I told you that?"

"No, I think I would have remembered that."

"Yeah, well, the other night, she showed up. I opened my door, thinking it was Detective Phillips, and she walked in. She said she wanted to talk. I was super uncomfortable...for obvious reasons, and I tried to get her to leave. I told her I had company coming, but she didn't care."

"Oh my god, Val. You need to tell me this when it happens. I wouldn't have had you meet with her if I had known."

"She's in the group, I can't just kick her out of it."

"True. But, I'm not comfortable with this."

"I knew you wouldn't be. I told her she couldn't come to my place and she agreed. But today she told me she was coming to tell you about Detective Phillips and me. I know I don't have to explain myself, but I just wanted you to hear it from me."

"Val, it's not really a surprise. It's easy to see the chemistry between you two. It would do you good to have a little fun." She winked at me as she folded her hands on her desk.

"Gross."

Her lack of laughter made it even more uncomfortable. "What's gross about two grown adults having a little fun? It might help you enjoy life a little."

"Anyway, I just wanted to let you know that I'll make sure it stays professional."

"I don't doubt that. Thanks for telling me, but it isn't my business. I trust you, Val. You have nothing to worry about. If it gets too much with Jane, please let me know. Don't try to handle her on your own. Okay?"

"Okay. Thanks for the awkward talk."

"Anytime. You're doing a great job here, Val. I enjoy working with you."

I nodded my head and headed back to my office. It was hard to hear the compliments from Jeannine. It was so much easier to not get connected to people. My visit planned with Donald Brice at the end of the day would not be something she would approve of. It was not something I would have ever done before, and I wasn't even sure why I was going. There was just something in me that needed to go and meet this monster.

CHAPTER TWENTY

I pulled into the driveway at Donald Brice's house and nausea crept up on me. I put my car in park and pulled out the handouts I had picked up in the nutritionist's office at work on diabetes. I wasn't an expert on nutrition but knew enough to slide by. I checked my shirt and cardigan to make sure I had taken my name tag off. It was always embarrassing having strangers greet me by name and having no idea how they knew me, then realizing later I had left my name tag on.

My heart raced as I played the visit out in my head. What was my purpose here? I really didn't know. All I wanted to do was put a face to the evil monster Sonya told us about. I pushed a pen into my pocket, opened the door of the car and started to walk toward the front door. The world went quiet as thoughts began racing through my head. *What if he knows my real name? What if someone else is here? What if he knows?* I took a deep breath that filled my lungs and pushed it through my pursed lips. *I'm not doing anything wrong. I'm just visiting an old man.* A calmness washed over me as I pushed the worry out of my mind. I raised my hand to pull the brass knocker back when the windowless door opened. "Stephanie?"

Startled by his eagerness to greet me left me speechless.

"Stephanie Mills? You're here to see me? Correct?"

There was a slight stutter in my response, "Y-yes, that's correct."

"Well come on in, I've been waiting for you."

He held the door open for me to enter and then closed it behind us, taking extra care to lock it before walking away. The click of the lock made me turn my head. "Oh, sorry, just habit." He said as he went back to unlock it.

He motioned for me to enter the living room where he asked me to have a seat. I scanned the room and noticed framed photos of young children lined the wall leading to the stairs. I sat in the seat furthest from the maroon recliner, hoping it would put a distance between us. I set the manila file folder next to me to keep him from sitting next to me.

He made his way to the recliner and turned off Family Feud that was playing on the flat-screen television perched on top of a stand. "So, how does an old man like me get lucky enough to have a pretty young lady stop by for a visit?"

The taste of bile climbed up my throat. "Um, there's a new program at Lawrenceville Regional Hospital that provides education to people with diabetes."

"This is a new program? I seem to remember meeting with someone at the hospital years ago and walking away with a bunch of pamphlets. I didn't learn anything. I threw that rubbish away once I got it home."

"Well, the new part of the program is that we, um, we, ahh, take the program to people's homes. We want to see if it helps to have the discussions in a comfortable place."

"I see. So, what information are you going to be teaching me?" He winked his droopy eyelid at me.

I swallowed hard to keep myself from materializing the vomit that danced in my throat. "Well, what is it that you would like to learn?"

"Oh, sweetheart, I thought you'd never ask." His laugh reached the parts of myself I hadn't seen in years. Rage filled my core. His words reminded me of the way Chad first talked to me. It was then I knew why I was there and what I had to teach him.

The plan was set into motion without much time to think. An episode of *Snapped* came to mind, and I knew what I had to do. I pushed up a seductive laugh and played along with him. "Oh, Mr. Brice, I know just what I want to show you." I unbuttoned the top button on my shirt and licked my lips. "But we need to take care of business before we play."

The sparkle in his eyes glistened in the light of the lamp. "I'll be a good student, as long as I can spank the teacher."

"I do like a good spanking." I winked at him as I took my hair down out of the messy bun and shook it free. "So, Mr. Brice, does your diabetes require you to take insulin?"

"Yes. I've been doing that for a few years now."

"Where do you keep it? I'll need to have a look at it."

He pointed to the kitchen. "It's in the fridge."

I walked into the kitchen; I was still in his line of sight as I opened the door to the refrigerator. I noticed a bag of syringes and two bottles of Lantus. "Did you just fill your prescription?"

"No, I get a three-month supply in the mail. I think I have a couple months left."

I shut the refrigerator door as my mind raced with thoughts. "Could I use your restroom?"

"Oh...do you want to get more comfortable before the exam?"

His words brought me back to my purpose for being there. There was no way I would be able to return, I had to do everything in one visit. I forced a smile as I bit my top lip. "Yes. I want to get to the good stuff."

"Down the hall, on the right."

I flipped on the light and shut the door behind me. In the mirror, I didn't recognize the person looking back at me. "Val, what are you doing?" The words left my lips without feeling connected. My heart flipped in my chest as I opened the medicine cabinet. A bottle of Tylenol PM sat on the top shelf. I removed the bottle and took three pills out and put them in the pocket of my cardigan. *What am I doing?* The question kept coming, but I didn't really know.

I flushed the toilet, washed my hands, and returned to the couch. "Do you have any family, Mr. Brice?" I picked up the file and pulled out the notebook, looking down to take my focus off of him.

"Not exactly. I have friends."

"Oh? Those aren't your grandkids?" I pointed to the photos on the wall.

"Them? No. Those are...friends."

I took a closer look at the photos on the wall. They were

all young girls, they looked to be around twelve years old. Trophies. These were his keepsakes to remember the girls he damaged. The thought of their pain fueled my fury. "How often do you have visitors?"

"Not very often. I could be dead and no one would find me for days."

It was like he read my mind. "So, no one checks up on you? Not even a phone call?"

"If you're asking if anyone will walk in on us, the answer is no. I'm just a lonely old man. A very, lonely old man."

I pulled the blue pills out of my pocket and handed them to him. "Take these for me? I like my men hard and stiff."

His excitement didn't leave room for questions. He popped the pills in his mouth and washed them down with the can of diet Coke sitting on the coffee table in front of him. "Oh, sweetheart, I'll deliver all of your desires. These pills will only intensify my manhood."

"Do you have anything to drink? I need a little something to loosen up."

"There's some beer in the fridge or some scotch on the table."

"Want a glass of scotch with me?"

"I'll never pass up a drink with a beautiful woman."

I got the bottle of scotch and brought it into the kitchen, where I poured a little in one glass, and more in the other. I handed him the glass with more, while I took a small sip from my glass. "Drink up." I smiled as I held my glass up. He took a large sip, and as I held the glass to my lips, he matched my drink with another. His glass was empty before I sat down. The excitement from this old pervert was almost too predictable. I unbuttoned my shirt another button and placed my hand on my breast as my eyes met his. "Do you want to feel?"

I walked over to him and got on my knees between his legs. He eagerly placed his hand on my breast, and I put my hand on the top of his pants. I felt the blood rushing to his penis, and I felt more in control than I had ever before. "Let's go to the bedroom and get more comfortable." I held his hand against my breast as our eyes met.

"I'm going to give you a ride you'll never forget." He stood up and took my hand and led me to the bedroom. He took off his pants and white underwear and laid on the bed, his erect penis in his hand, stroking it as he watched me take off my cardigan and top. I crawled on top of him, my pants still on, and rubbed myself against his penis. He reached up and grabbed my breasts, fumbling, trying to expose them. I backed up, out of his reach.

"Stroke it for me. I want to see how you like it."

"No, put your mouth on it." His words brought me back to Sonya's story. I imagined her little body quivering under his.

"I've got a better idea." I opened his closet and found some neckties hanging on a hanger. I pulled one out and wrapped it around his wrists. "I like it kinky. Wanna get dirty with me, old man?" I took the end of the tie and wrapped it around the spindle on the headboard, pulling tight to make sure he could not get loose.

"Oh, I've always wanted to try this."

Once his hands were tied above his head, I got back on top of him and rode him with my pants still on, getting him to the brink of ejaculation, and stopped. I got up and put my shirt back on, and then my cardigan.

"Hey, where are you going?" He wiggled his hands to try to get free. "Get your tits back here and finish what you started."

"Oh, I fully intend to." I walked out of the bedroom and back into the kitchen, opened the refrigerator, and removed the bottle of insulin and two syringes. I took the orange cap off the first needle and put it into the Lantus and drew out 100 units. I repeated the steps with the second syringe and put the covers back on. I returned the bottle of insulin and returned to the bedroom.

Still fighting to get untied, his penis was no longer erect, laying limp against his leg. "Ah, look at your little limp dick. Not such a stud now, are you?" I walked closer to him and took his penis in my hand, and squeezed it until he screamed.

"What are you doing, you crazy bitch?" The fear in his voice satisfied my desire to continue. I pulled the first syringe out of my pocket and removed the cap. As I held it up, I flicked the side to remove the air bubbles. I lifted up his shirt and stuck the needle into his stomach. I carefully replaced the cover and removed the second syringe from my pocket.

"Where should I put this one?" I held the needle up for him to see. "How about in your penis? Or your balls?" I flicked the side of the syringe and brought it down near his legs. He kicked his legs at me.

"Get the fuck away from me, you psycho bitch."

"I haven't heard that one before." I climbed on top of him to keep his legs still, the syringe in my hand. I shoved the needle into another spot on his stomach and pushed the insulin into him. "That should do it." I looked down at him and saw the terror in his eyes.

"What the fuck are you doing? Why are you doing this?"

"Do you remember Sonya?"

His eyes went wide. "Sonya?"

"No, you sick fuck. I'm not the little girl you raped. I'm her friend." A laugh I didn't recognize climbed up my throat. "What's that saying? Karma's a what? Oh, that's right, a bitch." I got off of him, put the caps back on the needles, put them into my pocket, and went to clean up the kitchen. I put the glasses of scotch in the sink and ran the water over them. Under the sink, I found a pair of rubber gloves and put them on my hands. I found a jar of Clorox wipes and pulled one out. I ran the wipe over the handle of the refrigerator and then went to the bathroom to try to erase my fingerprints.

The vision of a crime scene flashed in my mind. I looked around and saw all of the potential evidence I might leave behind. There was no time to get rid of everything, and I couldn't remember everything I touched. I knew the bottles of insulin and Tylenol PM were the most essential things to wipe clean. I wet a paper towel and washed both bottles, drying them, and returned them to where I found them. I remembered the bottle of scotch. I wiped down the bottle with the same damp paper towel and tossed it in the trash in the kitchen. I finished washing the glasses in the sink and dried them with a dish towel, returning them to the cupboard where I found them.

I picked my folder and pen off the couch and went back to the bedroom. I removed the glove to check Donald Brice's pulse. He was still alive, but not responsive. From the episode of *Snapped* I'd watched about murder by insulin, I knew it could take a while to kill him. I was confident he would die before he was found. I untied his hands and placed them in a more natural position. His wrists didn't show signs of being disturbed, no cuts or marks. I lifted his shirt to check the injection sites, they blended in with the others. I put a blanket over him, to make it look like he was sleeping, and turned off the light.

I looked around the house one last time and didn't see anything out of the ordinary. When I closed the door behind me, I removed the gloves and looked around to see if my car had been visible to neighbors. The giant oak tree appeared to shield the house from the road, and no other homes could be seen from where my car was parked. "Good work, Stephanie Mills." I looked down at the clock on my dash to see I had fifteen minutes before I was supposed to meet Tim. There was no time to take a shower or get the filth from Mr. Brice off me.

I pulled into a gas station to fill up and remembered I needed to get rid of the syringes in my pocket. I reached down on the floor of my car and picked up a bag from McDonald's and carefully placed the syringes and rubber gloves in the bag. I crumpled it up before placing it in the trash can by the gas pumps. After filling up my car, I continued on my way home.

When I pulled into my driveway, Tim was already there. He was still in his car on his cell phone. The smile on his face when he saw me was enough to wipe away the doubt that started to creep into my mind. I walked over to him and wrapped my arms around him, kissing him longer than I expected. "I'm so glad to see you. It's been a long day."

"Well, I'm happy to see you, too. I'm even happier at how happy you are." A nervous laugh filled the cold night's air. "That's a lot of happy."

"It's going to get happier." I reached up to kiss him again.

"Oh, really?" He opened the back door and got a bag off the backseat.

"If all goes well." The adrenaline that had been pumping through my veins left me feeling surprisingly calm.

Gabriel was at the door again, yowling when he heard my key enter the lock. "We're home, buddy." I turned to see a smile on Tim's face.

"Yeah, buddy, we're home. And Daddy brought you a surprise."

"Daddy?" I laughed at his attempt at humor. "Hmm, that kinda sounds good."

"Sorry, too much?" He set the bag on the table and pulled out a can of Fancy Feast. "I got my favorite boy the good stuff."

"He does love that stuff." I got a saucer out of the cupboard and emptied the can out. "I need a shower before dinner. Want to join me?"

"Sure." As he set the sandwiches on the table, what I said registered. "Wait...did you just ask me to join you?"

I nodded my head as I kicked off my shoes and took off my cardigan. It dropped on the floor by his feet. "So, do you?"

"Um...yeah...what's gotten into you?"

"I hope...you."

"Holy shit." He followed me into the bathroom, removing

his clothes as he walked. I slid off my pants and panties and unbuttoned my shirt and let it drop to the floor. When I unhooked my bra, Tim helped take it off. I finished pulling his pants and boxers off and stood up to kiss him. He pulled my body into his and kissed me, his penis pushing into me.

"Are you sure you're ready for this, Val?" He whispered between kisses.

"Yes. I want to make love to you." We stepped into the shower, and I turned the hot water on. As it cascaded over us, we kissed as he guided his penis inside of me, and carefully thrust inside me as he held me against the wall. "Oh my god. Oh, Tim, it feels so fucking good, don't stop." He increased the rate and pulled out.

"Fuck, Val, I don't think I have a condom."

"It's okay, just don't stop." My hands grabbed his butt to pull him closer. "Mmm, don't stop." The water hit my face as he thrust deeper inside of me, staying there as he kissed me.

"Val, I don't think I can last much longer." He pulled out and thrust back in, pulling out one last time. He pulled me into him as he kissed me and moved the wet hair out of my face. "Wow. I wasn't expecting that."

"Yeah, me either." I kissed him with the hot water beating down on his strong back. "That was amazing. Can we do that again?"

"Absolutely. I'll come prepared next time."

"Oh, I was talking about later." My nipples hardened when the cold air hit them. Shivering, I stood under the water to wash my hair.

"You're so beautiful, Val." He ran his hands over the outline of my body.

I poured the Ivory body wash into my hand and lathered it up to rub over his muscular body. He took the bottle and did the same to me. We took turns under the water until we both finished our shower. When I turned the water off, I gave him a towel and put my hair into one and took another one to dry my body off.

"That was the best stress reliever I've ever tried. I can't believe I waited so long to try it."

"At your service." He winked as he opened up his back-pack to pull out his sweatpants.

"I'm starving. What did you make us tonight?"

He laughed as he pulled his shirt over his head. "I forgot about dinner. Your beautiful, naked body could make me forget about anything." He walked over to the counter and held up the sandwiches. "This seems like a pathetic dinner after the gift you just gave me."

"Oh, stop." I kissed him as I took a turkey sandwich out of his hand. He pulled out a bag of sour cream and onion chips and a bag of pretzels and held them up for me to pick. "Bring them both." I went to the refrigerator and took out two Sam Adams and brought them into the living room. We sat together on the couch as we savored our dinner in silence.

CHAPTER TWENTY-ONE

I rolled over and hugged Tim's naked body as he slept. We hadn't talked much last night, just enjoyed each other's company. There was so much I wanted to tell him and equally as much that I couldn't. I never felt the need to share my life with anyone before, and now the thought of having to keep secrets tainted me with guilt. There was no way I could tell him what I did. I couldn't tell anyone.

Panic settled into my chest as I replayed the day before. I wasn't even sure who that was, surely it wasn't me. But it was. How could hurting someone else feel so good in the moment, and now plague me with fear? I sat up and put on an oversized t-shirt and made my way to the bathroom. I closed and locked the door behind me, I didn't want to risk Tim walking in on me. I turned the shower on and sat in the corner by the door and cried.

Unable to catch my breath, my sobs turned to hyperventilating. Images of Donald's dead body, rotting in his bed, appeared every time I closed my eyes. What if no one ever found him? What if Sonya's mom was the one who did? What if they did find him and knew it was me? What if he wasn't dead? What if I lost my job? Or they sent me to jail? What about Gabriel? Who would take care of him? What if my Gabriel comes looking for me, and he found out his mom was in jail?

The endless thoughts swirled around my head. Each possible scenario played and replayed. There was no way Tim would love me if he found out. No way anyone could. I stood up and made my way to the toilet in time to raise the lid and throw up the contents of my stomach.

Breathe Val. I took a deep breath to try and gain control over the emotions that were drowning me. *He was a monster. You did what you had to. Think about the children you saved. You did the right thing.* As the thoughts changed, the power returned. This was for Sonya, and for all the other young girls he violated. Monster didn't even begin to describe him. I took one last deep breath and turned off the shower. I picked up the mouthwash and swished the taste of vomit out of my mouth. The actions from the day before were released, and the feeling of guilt left with them. Some secrets were necessary.

When I returned to the bedroom, Tim was still asleep. I took the t-shirt off and snuggled up next to him and placed my head on his chest. Feeling his breathing under me brought the calmness I needed to focus on. I wouldn't let any more time pass without living the life I deserved. If I learned anything yesterday, it was that I had the power to take a situation I didn't like and change it to be what I wanted. From ending the life of a predator to finding the life I was missing.

No more time spent being cautious. No more time spent being a victim.

Tim's breathing must have lulled me back to sleep because the familiarity of the stark white hospital wall and the sound of a crying baby came back to me. This time, I found him. I found my beautiful little boy and hugged him in my arms. The love I felt between us righted every wrong I ever experienced in my life. I held him close to my heart and rocked him in my arms. The color returned to the walls, and we were no longer alone. When I woke up, I didn't feel empty like the dream always left me before. That was the sign I needed. I knew now, without a doubt my actions yesterday, all of them, were the right ones.

Tim was awake when I opened my eyes. "Hey, sleepyhead." He kissed the top of my head. "Last night was...amazing." He stretched his arms above his head and placed me in another hug. "I'm not just saying that. It sounds kind of lame, but I mean it."

I hugged him tighter and kissed his chest. "No, I agree. It was amazing."

"What are your plans for today?"

"I don't have any. How about you?"

"Nothing. Too cold to do anything outside. Do you want to do something, or are you sick of me yet?"

"I'd love to spend the day with you. I have an idea." I sat up and pulled the sheet up to cover my bare chest. "I want to see if I can find out if my grandma is still alive." I paused as I realized how crass that probably sounded. "When I left home, I never looked back. I stopped all contact with everyone. I didn't want my mom or stepfather to find me, and I knew my grandma wouldn't have been able to keep my secret."

"That's incredibly sad. I'm sorry your life has been so hard, Val." He sat up, his feet on the floor. "I'd love to help you. If you tell me her name, we can try to look her up on the computer system at the barracks."

"Won't you get in trouble for that?"

"It's Lawrenceville, Val, do you even think they'll notice?" As he stood, he arched his back as he stretched and pulled on his boxers. "Besides, my uncle is the Chief, no one cares what I do, or at least they don't say anything."

"Thank you. That would be helpful. I tried my hand at Facebook stalking, but she's old." I laughed at the thought of my gram scrolling through the X-rated memes and teenage drama. I got dressed while Tim was in the bathroom and started a pot of coffee. Gabriel met me in the kitchen, meowing for his breakfast. I bent down to scratch under his chin and scooped him up. I hugged him against my chest and kissed his head. "You're such a good boy, Gabriel. I know, I know, breakfast is late this morning." I placed him back on the floor and poured his food into his dish.

I opened the refrigerator to look for something to make for breakfast, but the shelves were empty. I took out the creamer and set it on the counter. "Looks like I need to go shopping, buddy."

"I'm not a big breakfast guy, coffee is all I need." Tim's voice surprised me. "Whoa, sorry to scare you."

"Oh, it's not you, just that pesky startle reflex years of trauma leaves behind."

"I hate that you've had such a shitty life. It gives me all

the more reason to make sure you have the best rest of your life."

"Corny. I didn't know you work for Hallmark." I laughed as I handed him a yellow smiley face mug.

"Says the lady that owns this mug?" He shook the empty cup in the air.

"Fair enough." I smiled as I took out my favorite blue ceramic mug. "I really do love that you want to protect me. It's hard to believe you mean what you say, but I'll try my best."

We took our coffee into the living room and sat together on the couch, Gabriel between us.

"What's your gram's name?"

"Marianne Cooper. I think she's eighty-seven now. She's what I've missed the most since I left my old life behind." I rubbed my blue mug between my hands. "She actually gave me this the last Christmas I was home. This and an assortment of tea." I took a sip of coffee as memories came back. "She had no idea what happened to me. My mom told me we couldn't tell her because she would have been disappointed in me. She said I was an embarrassment to the family."

"Jesus, Val, your mom sounds like a real bitch."

"Yeah, she's worse than that. She's evil. You only know part of the story." I looked up at him to see if he was ready to hear my truth. "There's so much more I've never told anyone. My mom is the only one who knows, but she wouldn't believe me."

"You can tell me if you want, Val. I'll believe you." He put his coffee down and put his hand on my knee.

"Are you sure? I mean, it's early and this is...disturbing."

"I'm sure. Wouldn't it be nice to get it out? I know when I talk about something, I feel better about it. One of my counselors once told me that once you let it out, either write it or speak it, you're free from its power. I think that is some of the best advice I was ever given."

"You've been to counselors? As in plural?"

"Yeah, after my mom and dad got divorced, I had a tough time. They fought so much, I felt guilty for pretty much everything. Do you see one?"

"No. I haven't been to a counselor since my time at the group home before they took my baby. That's actually part of the story you don't know."

"So, when you say you haven't told anyone, you mean you haven't told anyone?"

"Yeah, Gabriel knows, but who is he going to tell?" I scratched behind his ear as I focused on his shiny black fur. "When I was about thirteen, my mom brought me to see a counselor, psychologist, actually. She said I needed to work through my anger. I didn't think I had a problem; I mean, I was thirteen and my hormones were going crazy. Looking back, I think I was just a normal teenage girl. That ended shortly after I started seeing Dr. Ross.

"My mom didn't like it when I talked back to her or rolled my eyes. My dad hadn't been in the picture for years, but she started threatening to send me to go live with him. After a while, I told her that it didn't sound so bad. When I wanted to go, she told me he didn't want anything to do with me and I was stuck with her. She said I was lucky, at least she wanted me. I told her I didn't think that made me lucky, just cursed. She didn't like it when I started to fight back. That was when she said my anger was out of control and I needed to talk to someone. She made a point of finding someone with a Ph.D., because that made them professional and they'd be able to see through my bullshit."

"She does sound evil."

"Yeah, well, it gets better." I took a drink from my now cold coffee. "I didn't like him the moment I met him. I told Mom I didn't want to go, but she wouldn't listen to me. She started going to see him when I was in school for parental meetings. The more time she spent with him, the worse my visits with him became."

"He told me he had a treatment that could fix me. He went on to tell me if I told anyone about this treatment, they wouldn't believe me, and I would be put in a mental institution. This was after several visits where we talked about how awful mental institutions are, and how unsafe they are. So, I have this in the back of my head. This fear that left me open to anything."

His sigh filled the silence while I took another drink. "Things started slowly. First, he put his hand on my knee, then he moved it to my back, then to my chest. He told me he had to see my breasts to make sure I was developing correctly. When I questioned him, he reminded me he was the professional. When I took my shirt off, he removed my bra. The looking turned to touching. Each visit, we would start with him feeling my breasts, telling me if they had grown."

"Jesus."

I cut him off before he could say anything else. "Things escalated to him showing me his penis. He sat on the couch next to me, his pants off, with it in his hand. He proceeded to masturbate and then put my hand on it, telling me to do what he had been doing. He said he would show me more next time."

Another heavy sigh escaped from Tim as I continued, holding the empty mug between my hands, trying not to make eye contact. "I begged my mom not to bring me back. I couldn't tell her why. She told me to stop being difficult and basically told me to shut up. The next visit, he told me to get naked. He skipped the small talk and took his clothes off, too. This time he finished the lesson by raping me. I didn't know what it was called then, I was just scared. I hadn't even had a boyfriend yet, hadn't even kissed a boy. And this grown man was shoving his dick in me. I had never experienced pain like that before. I cried the whole time he was on top of me. I closed my eyes as tight as I could and tried to imagine myself anywhere else but under him. When he was done, he said if I ever wanted to be anything, I had to know how to please a man. When he collapsed on top of me, he told me I had a lot of work to do, but not to worry, he would teach me."

"Oh my God, Val. I am so sorry."

"This went on for the next couple of years. Not every visit, but every visit involved something gross."

"Oh, Val."

"No, wait, there's more." I took a deep breath, set my mug down, pushed my back against the couch, pulled my legs up to sit like a pretzel and continued. "All those parental visits must have turned into the same as mine, because before long we had a joint meeting at our house where they announced Mom was going to become Mrs. Dr. Chad Ross and we were going to move into his house." Years of pent up anger came crashing down on my shoulders. I sat up straight to hold the newfound weight. "Once we moved in with Chad, I had to change schools and get rid of most of our stuff. We moved away from my grandma and all of my friends, and then...the 'treatments' intensified. I never knew when he'd be in my bed, or if he would walk in on me when I was in the shower."

Tim moved closer to me and placed his hand on my back, his head hung low. "I'm so sorry."

"Still more. But can you please stop saying you're sorry? I'm okay now, and I'm not telling you this for pity."

"I'm sorry...I mean...it's just hard to hear about someone I love being hurt. I'll just listen now."

Someone he loves. His words pushed out some of the shame. "I started getting sick. I couldn't keep anything down. My boobs started hurting. Funny thing is, I didn't even notice when my period stopped coming. At fifteen, they hadn't started being regular yet. My mom finally took me to the doctor's after months of my complaining. They ran so many tests; everything came back negative...until the pregnancy test. When the doctor walked into the room and told my mom I was pregnant, the look she gave me probably hurt more than the years of being raped by her husband.

"On the way home, she lectured me about being a tramp, a whore...you name it, she called me it. Without thinking, I yelled at her to shut the hell up and told her if she could have kept her husband off of me, it never would have happened. She slapped me across the face and told me I was lying. When we got home, she ran straight to him and told him. He told my mom it would be best for me to go away, and before the weekend, they delivered me to Sawyer's Home for Unwed Girls.

"I didn't know the social worker was working with my mom behind my back, and no one told me they were stealing my baby from me until it was too late. The whole time I was pregnant, I thought about the kind of mom I wanted to be, and I promised my baby I would take care of it, no matter what, and they made me break my promise. They knew all along, but Chad must have told them to lie to me, play along because they all pretended I was going to be leaving with my baby.

"After I had Gabriel, my mom was waiting for me. She was there when they took him from me, and she signed all the papers to terminate my rights. She drove me home from the hospital. I didn't even have a chance to pack up my stuff. Some of the girls packed it for her and loaded it all into the car. The whole ride home she told me how lucky that little baby was that he didn't have to grow up with a whore of a mother. Chad was waiting for me at the house when we got there and gave me a list of rules. Mom took his side and assumed I was lying. He had a list of prescriptions waiting for me that one of his friends prescribed me. He told them I was psychotic and the drugs would help me with my hallucinations. I refused to take them, so they tried to sneak them into my food.

"Eventually, I just stopped eating, unless it was something I cooked myself. Chad never got in trouble for what he did to me. My mom never left him."

"That's a lot of shit to have to go through. I totally get why you don't trust people and why you keep to yourself. I know you don't want me to say I'm sorry, but I want to tell you how brave you are and... thank you for trusting me." He picked up my hand a kissed the top of it.

"Not only do I trust you...but I lost my virginity to you last night." My stab at sarcasm came a little too soon.

"Well, thank you for the beautiful gift."

I couldn't hold the laughter in. "I should have saved it for Christmas. Now I won't know what to get you."

"Jesus, Val, I was being heartfelt. You know how to kick a guy when he's feeling vulnerable...but I wouldn't mind a repeat of last night for Christmas...it just feels a little wrong to joke about it after hearing all that."

"You're a detective...you must hear horrific things all the time."

"Yeah, but it's never about the woman I love."

And there it was again. "Love?"

"Yes, Val, I love you. I can't pretend any longer. I've loved you for a long time, but last night just sealed the deal." His dimples pushed through his day-old scruff. "You're so hard to read, but I love that about you. You're mysterious."

"You have no idea how mysterious I can be." I winked at him as I stood up to stretch.

"And..."

"And what? Oh, yeah, and I love you, too. Are you happy?"

"Incredibly so."

CHAPTER TWENTY-TWO

When we pulled into the parking lot at Tim's office, it was empty. There was no excuse for not doing what we came for. Tim pulled a chair up to his desk and pushed the button to turn his computer on. "Marianne Cooper, right?"

"You remembered, I'm impressed."

"This is important to you. Of course, I remembered." He typed her name into the search bar and waited for the results to populate. "How old did you say she is? Eighty-seven?"

"Yeah, I think so. Did you find her?" I scooted my chair closer to try to see the screen.

"There is one that looks like it might be her in Windsor. Is that close to where she was living before?"

"Yeah, pretty close. Does it give an address?"

"Um...445 Bluebird Lane. Let me try to pull that up... something called The Nest; it looks like it may be a senior housing complex. That would make sense."

"I'm not surprised Mom would dump her there. Can you tell how long she's lived there?"

"Well, at least a year, but I can't tell. Sometimes they don't update this system as often as they should, especially the non-criminal side of things."

"Can you look up Chad Ross? And see if there is anything on him?"

"Yeah, sure...hold on...um...it looks like he's clean."

"Hmmm...so either he's never done it again, or some other girl has been bullied into staying quiet." I pushed my chair back and stood up. "That really pisses me off...he never got in trouble...and he probably never will. It's too late for me to do anything to him now."

"Val, it's not too late to charge him with the sexual assault. You were a minor...that means you don't have a time limit to report."

"I don't know...I mean, they probably wouldn't believe me anyway." Memories of that time came rushing back. My mom's red face took over the room. I could feel her hot breath in my face as she called me a whore. She wouldn't even listen to what I had to say. She was under Chad's spell. I stopped trying to explain what happened because it didn't matter.

Tim's hand on my shoulder broke me out of the memories. "Val, I believe you."

"I hadn't even considered you didn't. Huh...that's strange, isn't it? I held all of it in for all these years, because I didn't trust anyone, and just like that, I pour it all out for you. I didn't even feel like I had to prove anything to you." Our eyes made contact. "I do trust you. Thank you...for believing me... and for loving me."

"I do love you, Val. I'm so glad you trust me. I really want to help you make the bastard pay for what he did to you."

"I'm not sure I'm ready for that yet. I don't think I'm in a good enough place to face him or my mom yet...I'm not sure I ever will be."

"I get it. That's a lot to think about. I'll be here whenever you are ready, even if you never are."

"It's kind of a joke that Jeanine asked me to start that trauma support group. I mean, me? What the hell do I know about trauma?"

"Um...probably more than most people do. You lived through some horrific shit; I think that's what makes you so easy to talk to. You get it. Not many people have that gift."

"Gift? I always thought of it as a curse." I picked up the broken heart pendant around my neck and rubbed it. "But maybe you're right. I do understand the pain of losing people I love. That's what landed me the awesome title of deceased patient coordinator. Most people want to run away from sadness, but I want to wrap myself up in it. When other people are in pain, it helps me feel normal. That's kind of twisted, isn't it?"

"Not at all. I'm a detective for the same kind of reason. When my dad left, he would disappear for weeks at a time. I never knew when he would show back up, or if he ever would. When I meet with families in crisis, I know what they are going through. It's not just a job to me."

"You're pretty amazing, Detective Phillips. I never knew this soft side of you."

"Same." He laughed as he pulled me into a hug. "All that sarcasm had me fooled."

"Ha-ha, you're so funny."

"And there it is." He pulled me in tighter before he kissed the top of my head. "Do you want to go see if we can find The Nest today?"

My heart dropped to the bottom of my stomach. "I don't know. I don't know if I'm ready to visit my old life yet."

"We don't have to visit anyone; we can just take a drive and have a look around."

"I guess it's a nice day for a drive."

We stopped to get coffee and filled the car up with gas. Tim entered the address into his GPS and we hit the road. Windsor was about two hours away from Lawrenceville and about an hour from Benton, where my mom and Chad lived. The trees had lost most of their leaves, leaving the countryside brown and dreary. The clouds filled the sky, leaving no room for the sun to peek through. The day matched my feelings about the trip; melancholy. I always loved that word because, like me, it had more depth to it than just letters on the paper. On the surface, it appeared to be more than it was, but under the layers of it, the truth was revealed.

Since moving to Lawrenceville, Vermont, I never left the area. It seemed safer to stay in the little cocoon I created. Work took up most of my time, the rest of it was spent at home with Gabriel. Everything I needed could be found in the grocery store in town and if not, I had become an expert at online shopping. So much of my life had been spent hiding away. The last sixteen years had slipped by so quickly and yet so slowly. Stuck in time and yet floating through space. Life was so hard to understand.

"This is such a pretty drive. I've never been to Windsor before."

"Yeah, it is beautiful, probably more so a few weeks ago, before all the leaves fell off."

"I think the look of death is nice." Laughing, I put my hand on his thigh.

"That's right, I forget you're the queen of death."

"Hmm, I've never heard that before...I like it. I guess you must be my king of death."

"I don't think it has the same ring to it. I'm OK with being your king, though...but let's leave the death to you."

A sharp ping of anxiety rang through me. How did he know? He can't know...can he? "Is it alright if I turn some music on?"

"Of course." He turned the radio on and pointed to the button. "Go ahead and pick something you like."

I flipped through the channels, unable to find anything worth listening to. "Do you have any CDs?"

"What do you think this is? 1999?" His deep laugh filled the interior of the Volkswagen Touareg. He pushed a button to turn the Sirius radio on. "What kind of music do you like? I'm sure you'll find something here."

"Tom Petty is my favorite...I mean, who else is there?"

"No shit? I love Tom Petty." His finger went to one of the preset channels. "Ever heard of Tom Petty Radio?"

"Tom Petty Radio? What's that?"

"Just listen."

The end of *Free Fallin'* was playing. The sound of Tom's voice chased away all of my worries. I closed my eyes as I let his words fill my soul. I always forget how healing his music was. It melted away all of the pain, literally what saved my life so many times in the past.

Something Good Coming started to play. "Another one? This has to be the best station ever."

"It's Tom Petty Radio...that's all they play...well, sometimes they play some of the songs that he loves, which is pretty much the same thing."

"Careful...there is nothing that compares to his songs."

"Let me rephrase that...it's cool to hear what music helped shape him into the amazing musician he is. How was that? Did I redeem myself?" His eyes glanced over quick enough to light the spark in me.

"Good save. I love this song...I mean...the hope of something good coming has helped get me through some pretty shitty times."

"Yeah, this is one of my favorites from the *Mojo* album."

"Same, and *The Trip to Pirate's Cove*, and *No Reason to Cry*. Oh, and *I Should Have Known It*, I love to listen to that super loud when I'm having a bad day...so pretty often. Safe to say that's one of my favorite albums."

"No...I never could have guessed."

"You're lucky you're so cute. Seriously, though, I can't believe you love Tom Petty, too."

"Well, I do like him. I'm not so sure I love him as much as you do, but I totally get it."

As the trees sped by the window, the sun started to peek out from behind the clouds. The longer we were in the car, the closer we were to my mom and Chad. What if they were visiting with Gram when we drove by? What if she notices me? I hadn't thought about any of these possibilities when

Tim asked if I wanted to go. I never let the distance between us shrink enough to put myself in this predicament before, and now I knew why.

My mouth went dry and my heart raced. My mother stole so much from me and I always let her get away with it. Years of distress morphed into resentment. I thought I left to escape them, so they couldn't hurt me any longer, but now I know it was so I wouldn't hurt them. The fear held me hostage and now I was no longer its prisoner.

Out my window, the sight of a hanging deer carcass caught my attention. As a kid, I always hated hunting season. Dead deer tied to the hoods of little sedans or thrown without regard in the back of ratty old pickup trucks. I never understood why people got a thrill out of taking a life. My teacher told me people depend on the meat they get from the deer; for some people, it was all they had to eat. I still didn't understand how it gave someone the right to end a life. Murder was justified when it was done for good, with purpose. That was a lesson I understood now.

"We'll be there in about twenty minutes. You doing okay?"

"Yeah, sorry. Just lost in my head."

"I figured you might be. Do you want to talk it out?"

"Not really." I hoped my smile showed him what I couldn't say.

"That's OK, Val."

The rest of the ride there, my body tightened and there was a catch in my breath. It was hard to tell if it was anxiety or rage that was taking over. I missed my gram so much, and I would be able to see where she lived, but I wouldn't be able to see her, or talk to her, or hug her. All because of them and what they did. "I think it's bullshit that my mom has been able to see my grandma whenever she wanted, and it's been over sixteen years since I saw her."

"Who was stopping you?"

"She was. I didn't go because I didn't want her to know anything about me. I wanted her to think I disappeared or died, or whatever."

"So, you were trying to punish her, and you were the one who suffered?"

His words hit hard as they sank in. "Yeah, I guess you're right. I bet she didn't even think about me, but I know Gram missed me. We were so close. I know it must be killing her."

He parked the car on the street, under a giant oak tree. "Do you want to change that? Take your power back?"

"We're here?"

He nodded his head and pointed to the blue building across the road. "Do you want to go see your grandma?"

Butterflies multiplied in my stomach. "Will you come with me?"

"Already meeting the family? I think that's good news for me." His smile alleviated his poor timing of sarcasm.

My raised eyebrows spoke louder than I could have.

"Bad timing? I suck at this quick wit crap. Let me try again...I'd love to go with you."

"Much better." As I opened my door, I tried to slow my breathing down. The Christmas lights were already on the pine trees in the courtyard. The twinkle of the white lights took me back to my childhood when my gram would drive me around town to look at lights on Christmas Eve. I missed her more than I knew. Tim reached over to take my hand and gave it a little squeeze. "Thank you." It was too late to hide the tears in my eyes. "You go first?"

"Sure." He led me down a winding paved path past identical doors adorned with simple green wreaths. "You want me to knock for you?"

I nodded my head and took a step behind him.

His knuckles tapped against the white door and we waited. He knocked again, louder this time. No answer. He put his head to the door to listen. "The TV is on in there, so she must be here." He tried the doorknob and as it turned open, he looked back at me with slight hesitation. "Mrs. Cooper? Mrs. Cooper, are you home?"

"Come in."

He squeezed my hand tighter and pulled me through the door. "Good evening, Mrs. Cooper."

We entered through the kitchen, guided by the sound of The Wheel of Fortune, she was sitting in a navy-blue recliner. When I saw her, it was like no time had passed. She had aged, but she was still my gram. Her silver hair was still cut short with messy curls; she used to have her hair done every week to keep the curls in tight. She had a pink sweatsuit with a small patch of purple flowers embroidered on the chest. She dressed much more sophisticated when I knew her, but her eyes remained the same, sweet baby blue.

"Hi." The only word I could muster.

"Hi. I wasn't expecting any visitors. Or was I? Do I know you? Did Elaine send you?" The confusion that followed her words made her feel like more of a stranger. She didn't recognize me. I squeezed Tim's hand as I changed the plan.

"No, Mrs. Cooper, my name is Stephanie, and this is my partner, Tim. We are with the US Census Bureau. We did check with Elaine, and she said it would be fine to stop by and ask you a few questions."

"You talked to Elaine?"

"Yes, ma'am."

"Well, as long as you're sure she knows. She yells at me when I talk to strangers."

"It can be dangerous to talk with strangers. Your daughter is only looking out for you." The lie tasted like poison. My mother's venom was powerful enough to fill the room with tension without even being present. I knew my mother well enough to know what my gram needed to hear to trust me.

"I suppose so." She fumbled with the remote and turned the TV off. "What would you like to know?"

"How long have you lived here?"

"Oh, I don't know. I can't remember when I moved here. Elaine could tell you that."

"That's okay. How often do you see Elaine or other family?"

"That's a good question. I'm not sure. Elaine doesn't come very often. She's really the only family I have."

The honesty in her words stung. *What about me?* A thought I didn't dare put into words. "Do you have other visitors?"

"Yes. I have a nurse that checks up on me."

"Are you able to cook your meals?"

"I can, probably, but the nurse does the cooking." She paused. "I guess I don't really do anything for myself anymore."

"That's alright, sometimes it gets hard. Don't feel bad about that." I wanted to tell her who I was, but I wasn't even sure what stories my mother had told her. Had she wiped me entirely out of her memory?

"You're a sweet girl. It's hard getting old. Simple things become too much, and time passes by so slowly...or quickly. I'm never quite sure how that one goes."

"I understand that." I ached for her to see me, to go back to how we were so many years ago. I missed her so much, even with her sitting right across from me.

Tim saw my emotions had taken over my thoughts and stepped in. "Do you like the people who help you, Mrs. Cooper?"

"Yes, I do. She's a nice girl. She reminds me of my granddaughter. I haven't seen her in ages, but I remember the fun times we had together." The smile on her face was almost too much to bear. It wasn't time yet...not now.

"She sounds like a nice girl." Tim's eyes met mine as he tapped my knee.

I shook my head and fought back the tears. "We have to get going now, thank you so much for your time tonight. We will be back with some more questions if that's OK."

"That would be fine. It's always nice to have someone to talk to."

"Before we go, is there anything we can do for you? A cup of tea?"

"Oh, that would be lovely. I love..."

"Peppermint tea?" The words slipped off my lips before I could get them back.

"How did you know?"

"Well, that's my grandma's favorite tea...so, just a lucky guess." I went into the kitchen and put the kettle on. The matching blue ceramic mug she gave me so many years ago was resting in her dish drainer. I picked up the mug, held it in my hands and flashbacks to our last Christmas filled the room. She was so excited to show me the matching mugs she had bought at the local Christmas Bazaar. We sat by the light of the Christmas tree and sipped on peppermint tea and shared a plate of Pecan Sandies while we laughed and talked about everything.

The whistle of the tea kettle brought me back to reality. So much time had been wasted. I didn't know how much I had missed her. I kind of pushed all of my memories out of my head so I could manage my stone-cold exterior. Tim continued talking with Gram. They seemed to be having a good time together. Just one more reason he was a great guy. I just hoped I didn't screw it up.

The hot water hit the tea bag and as the smell drifted up to my nose, I knew I wouldn't be able to pretend for much longer. Just not today. Too much had happened over the last twenty-four hours to add that to the mix. A lifetime took place in those few hours. My life was changed and there was no way back to the way it was any longer. That door was closed tight, locked and the key disposed of.

"Here you go, Gram...I mean Mrs. Cooper."

"It's been years since anyone has called me that." She put her hand to her heart and smiled. She took the mug of hot tea and held it between her hands, letting the heat warm her hands, just like I do.

"This might sound strange, but would it be alright if I gave you a hug?"

"That would be lovely." She placed both hands on the arms of her chair and pushed herself up out of the chair.

I walked over to her and bent down to wrap my arms around her. My head rested on hers, I took a long, deep breath in. The familiar smell encased me in love. I didn't realize how empty I had been all those years. There was nothing that was going to keep me from her, not even my mother.

CHAPTER TWENTY-THREE

Tim's phone rang, waking us. I rubbed the sleep from my eyes to look at the clock. Who would be calling at eleven o'clock at night? I sat up to try to hear the other side of the conversation.

"Yeah, OK, I'll be right there. Text me the address."

"What's that all about?"

With one leg in his jeans, he fell on to the bed. "I forgot I was on call this weekend. You're such a great distraction."

"Oh no, that's a good way to get in trouble. Good thing you didn't get a call when we were in Windsor."

"You're not kidding. But, it's Lawrenceville, and no one really cares about anything in this town."

"So, what's up? Where are you off to?"

"Oh, probably nothing, one of the other guys was called to do a welfare check on some old guy and they found him dead in bed, without his pants."

Pressure filled my head, a weight settled onto my chest

and my right eye started to twitch. My tongue felt like it tripled in size and I lost my ability to swallow.

"Do you want to tag along?"

"No." The word came out harsher than I intended.

"What, the queen of death doesn't work overtime?"

"I'm just exhausted." I pulled the blanket up to my chin and laid back down.

"Relax, Val. I was only kidding." He bent down and kissed my head. Unable to meet his lips, I laid still. "Are you mad at me?"

"No...I just have a migraine coming on."

"You sure? You know I'm just messing around, right?"

"Yeah...yeah, I'm sorry. I just need to sleep and I should be fine."

When the door shut behind him, I called for Gabriel to join me. His meow entered the room before he did. "I'm sorry to wake you up." He jumped up on the bed next to me and curled up on my chest. "It's been a crazy couple of days, buddy. I don't know what I'm going to do. I mean, what if Tim thinks things look suspicious at that house? It's got to be him...how many other old guys could be half-naked and dead?"

As I thought about what had happened, I thought about Sonya. I thought about all of the young girls he hurt and anger replaced my fear. "No. I'm not going to let him hold me prisoner like he did to all those others. I cleaned up after myself and no one even knows I went to his house. There is no way this can get pinned on me. I didn't even really kill him...he was alive when I left." Gabriel was fast asleep, his chest rising and falling on top of me. "You always know how to make everything better."

Tim woke me up when he returned to bed. He tried to be quiet, but I felt the bed move when he laid down. I rolled over to greet him. He kissed me and pulled me close. "How did everything go?"

"Oh, it was nothing. Just a dirty old man that died in his sleep. No crime scene. It was a pointless call...but it's protocol."

"So just like that, case closed?"

"Well, sort of, although the case was never opened for it to be closed."

Relief pushed any remaining apprehension out of my body. "I love you." I lifted my head to kiss him. "Thank you for everything."

"I love you, too, Val. But you don't need to thank me."

He had no idea how much I owed him and he never could know the extent of my gratitude. I let the weight of all that took place over the last forty-eight hours fade away as I fell back asleep in his arms. The love I felt when I hugged my gram was close to this. For the first time in years, I felt whole. I didn't want these feelings to end.

When morning finally came, Gabriel pounced on the bed between us. His purring echoed in the quietness of the morning. "Good morning, Gabe. Are you hungry?" He jumped off the bed to follow me to the kitchen, where he devoured his breakfast. Watching how thankful he was for just having his basic needs met, I loved him a little bit more. I crouched down next to him and scratched the top of his head while he finished his food. "How did I get so lucky?"

"You get what you give, Val." Tim's voice behind me made me jump. "We're just as lucky."

"It's going to take some getting used to, remembering someone else is here."

"Is that an invitation to move in?"

"Whoa...slow down."

"We only have so much time on Earth. I don't want to slow down. I don't want to waste any more of my time without you."

"If you weren't so damn cute, I might be a little freaked out by your neediness...but it works on you."

"Neediness? Hey..."

"I said you're cute...that should cancel out anything else I said."

"Fair enough."

"I've got a lot to process...I'm still using my defense mechanisms. I don't mean it...I'm just not used to spending my time with anyone, except Gabriel."

"I get it, Val. I'm grateful you've opened your heart to me as much as you have. I'll back off a little and slow things down."

"You're pretty amazing. I love spending time with you. Let's not slow it down too much. Some of this new stuff is..."

"Dreamy? Spectacular? Orgasmic?" He laughed at his attempt at a joke that I had to laugh, too.

"Yeah...that's the word I was looking for."

"Which one?" He winked as he pulled me into a hug.

"I'll let you use your imagination."

"That's my girl."

"You mean, here comes my girl?"

"Yes, of course, that's what I meant."

"I've waited my whole life to hear those words. You get major bonus points for being a Tom Petty fan."

There wasn't anything left that would make him a better match for me. His humor and tenderness were perfectly proportioned. I wasn't sure why I pushed him away before. I guess I wasn't ready to be open to these feelings. I wasn't worthy of love from anyone. I wasn't sure if I still was, but I wouldn't spend any more time pushing it away. I deserved happiness. I had so many years to make up for.

CHAPTER TWENTY-FOUR

Donald Brice's death didn't even make the paper. His body was cremated and his funeral was planned. Sonya's mother was the only one listed in his mediocre obituary as a "friendly neighbor." There were no children or other family listed. Any guilt I held about stealing someone's father, brother, uncle or friend lifted. No one was going to miss him. His death had to happen. He did it to himself. If he hadn't been so eager to get into my pants, he might still be alive.

At the office, I opened up the trauma group folder and found Sonya's number. I picked up the phone and gave her a call. "Hey Sonya, how are you doing?"

"I'm fine...well, actually...nah...I'm okay."

"Are you sure? Sounds like you need to talk."

"No, I'm okay...really...I'm just at work."

"Alright. I just wanted to remind you about our meeting tomorrow and wanted to make sure you're OK."

"Thanks, Val. It means a lot to know you've got my back."

"See you tomorrow?"

"Absolutely. See you then."

Maybe she didn't know yet. Or, perhaps she just didn't care. I didn't need notoriety, but knowing that taking Donald Brice's life gave her some freedom and safety would be nice. What was the point of taking his life if it wasn't to make the world a better place? Even if she didn't know he was gone, it still helps...his death was the only way to make sure he'd never touch another child again. I only wished he would have suffered a little more. The years of pain his actions caused Sonya was worth more than the few hours he had to endure.

What could I have done differently? I didn't even know my intentions were to kill him. I just wanted to get some information. It all happened so fast and everything fell into place so smoothly...and now any of the evidence I may have left behind didn't matter. His body had been turned to ashes. His footprint on this Earth was now as insignificant as his time here was. I wasn't ever going to be sorry for that.

The anticipation for Tuesday's group made everything else fade into the background. I wanted to hear how these ladies were doing and how their week went. The only part I wasn't looking forward to was Jane. She was next to impossible to figure out. As much as I didn't want to have this group, I was so glad Jeanine asked me to do it. We were the perfect mix of people and having such a small group made it easier to share some of the most intimate parts of our lives.

I spent Monday night writing down parts of my story. I had always suggested it to clients, but I never tried it. After hours of writing, I took a break to read what I had written and the fury inside me grew. There was something about seeing it all on paper that gave it more power. I spent so much time trying to move forward in my life without acknowledging the past. I thought by ignoring it, the power it held over me would disappear. All it ended up doing was taking over my life, kept me guarded and alone. There were so many times I wished I had someone I could talk to, but I never trusted anyone enough to share.

Telling Tim my story was easier than I anticipated and it didn't scare him away. I was sure if he knew what had happened, the sight of me would disgust him and he'd never want to see me again. He surprised me and made me ready to share my story with others. I thought about what I would say to the group. How I would say it and what I would share. It would be unprofessional to share my story; the group was for them, not me. But what if sharing made them see I understood their pain? What if my story helped them see me as more than just some professional doing their job? Maybe I wasn't ready to share with them just yet. Or perhaps I was.

The incident with Donald Brice showed me what occurs when I just let things happen. If I had planned what transpired, I never would have done it. In the moment, I did what I needed to do. There was no fault for that. And the world had one less child molester out there preying on innocent lives.

I put my pen back to the paper and wrote as more flashbacks came. Memories of what Chad made me do filled the page. With each word I wrote, my hatred grew stronger. I closed my eyes and imagined Chad in place of Donald Brice. The rage inside of me beat louder with every pump of my heart. I wanted to see his lifeless body in bed, found days later, with his pants off. I wanted to give him as much shame as he gave me all those years.

The anger switched over to sadness as I thought about Gabriel. I loved my son, regardless of how he came to be. I loved him without knowing him, and I loved him without knowing if I ever would. The pages soon filled with tear-stained paper and smudged ink. What would he think if he knew why I had to give him away? How would it change his life if he knew how he was conceived? Would he understand I had no choice, or would he be angry at me for not fighting for him?

Page after page, question after question, I still had no answers. I closed the notebook and tucked it into the box in my closet. I wasn't sure why I felt I needed to hide it, although reading the words on those pages would not be beneficial to me, not yet anyway. After hours of this, I had come to the conclusion the group wasn't my place to share. My pain was too much to share with others who knew what pain was. My job was to help them find a way to heal their pain.

Morning had come quicker than usual, which made it twice as hard as normal to get out of bed on time. When I remembered group was only hours away, my dread for another day was replaced with excitement. I was looking forward to seeing the ladies and even more anxious to see if Sonya would be sharing. It wasn't like I could ask her, I would just have to wait and see.

When I pulled into the hospital parking lot, a rusty blue Dodge Caravan was parked in the employee lot. It was not a car I recognized, although that wasn't uncommon for patients to use our spaces when the rest of the lots were full, but this one had given me an uneasy feeling. I pulled out my cell phone to have it ready to call for help and put it to my ear and pretended to be having a conversation as I walked to the building. When I was about ten steps away from the van, I heard the door open and close. I didn't turn around to see who got out, but the hair on the back of my neck stood up.

I increased my stride but was unsuccessful at reaching the hospital before they caught up to me. "Val...hey, Miss Social Worker, I need to talk to you."

I recognized the voice right away. "You're early, Jane." Annoyance replaced the adrenaline that was festering inside of me.

"For what?" Her eyes looked wild and her hair a mess.

"For group. That's why you're here, isn't it?"

"I've been here all night. I didn't have anywhere else to go." She wrung her hands as she walked with me into the building. "Seth kicked me out..." Her sentence was left unfinished as she realized she said too much.

"Seth kicked you out? What are you talking about?"

"You heard me wrong. I said...uh...Ted kicked me out... we got into a fight last night. He said he'd kill me if I didn't leave."

I turned on the lights in the conference room and set my bag on the table. "Jane, what is going on? Who is Ted? I thought you lived alone...I thought you and Carmen lived alone."

"Why would you think that? I'm not capable of living alone. Besides, why does it matter?"

"Did you go to the police?"

"What the hell are they going to do?"

"Oh, I don't know, maybe protect you from a guy who said he is going to kill you."

"No...they wouldn't understand. I told you I don't like cops...well except for...what's his name?"

"I think you need to call them. Do you want me to help you? No one should treat you like that. Did Carmen know Ted?"

"Yeah, we lived with him. That's a dumb question."

"Was he the one who hurt her? Do you think he could have killed her?"

"I told you to drop that shit. I told you she killed herself and to stop putting your nose where it doesn't belong. Jesus fucken Christ."

"Jane, calm down. You came to me for help, that's what I'm trying to do."

She let out a heavy sigh and slammed her hand flat on the table. "I just wanted you to give me some money, not stick your damn nose in my business. I need some...food. I don't need your help with anything else." She turned her back to me and crossed her arms. I noticed a slight tremor as she tried to sit still.

"I'm sorry I upset you. Come with me, I can get you some breakfast."

"I don't want to eat here. I just need money. God damn it. Why are you such a bitch?"

My disgust for her grew with every name she called me. I took a deep breath to replace what I wanted to say with what I should say. "Jane. What's going on? What do you need money for? I can't help you if you don't talk to me."

"I told you, it's none of your goddamn business."

"I'm sorry, then I won't be able to help you. I can't just hand cash out to people without a reason. That's not how it works. But if you want to talk, maybe we can figure something out together."

My calm tone took some of her edge off. Her foot feverishly tapped under the table. "You know, I try hard not to like your smart ass, but I just can't help myself." She turned back around to face me. "If you were just a bitch back to me, I would just leave you alone, but you're so fucken sweet." Tears started falling onto the table. "You kinda remind me of Carmen. She was a sweet girl, too."

I placed my hand on hers. "Oh, Jane, this must be so hard for you. I'm sorry you're struggling so much."

Her tears turned to hysterical sobs. As I sat with her, I noticed some track marks on her left arm. When I looked closer to her, I saw the red marks all over her face. I had noticed them before but never put it together. When her sobs quieted, I put my finger on her arm. "Jane, what happened here?"

"What do you think? I donate blood a lot." She pushed my hand away and wiped her tears with her dirty hands, leaving smear marks on her face.

"Jane. Come on, please be honest with me. When did you start using?"

Her eyes averted mine. "When I was fifteen. But...I don't do it that often...only when I need to stop the pain, you know?"

"No, Jane, I don't know."

"Yeah, you wouldn't. What do you have to deal with

anyway? Your life is perfect. You probably never had to struggle a day in your whole life."

"That's not true. Not at all."

"I don't need an intervention; I just need some money...I just need to get high one last time."

"Jane, I can't give you money to do that. I can help you get some food or even a place to stay, but I can't buy your drugs."

"Come on, can't your boyfriend get me some? I just need a little."

"He's a cop, Jane...probably the last person you should be asking for drugs."

"Oh, come on, that's where the best stuff comes from."

"Jane, are you hungry?"

"I don't give a shit about food. I just need some cash."

"Come on, let's just get something to eat, please? Then we can go to group together and talk with the others. Maybe they'll be able to offer some ideas."

She wouldn't stand up and her body went limp in her chair.

"Oh, come on, where else do you have to go?"

"Yeah, fine, you win." She stood up and followed me to the cafeteria.

After we got our trays of breakfast, we found a table in the back and sat together. Jane picked at her bacon and scrambled eggs, moving it around the plate more than she ate. She didn't even want coffee; instead, she opted for a bottle of orange juice.

"How do you manage without caffeine? I don't think I'd make it through the day without coffee."

"Oh, so now the truth comes out." She smiled before she continued. "You're a druggie, too." She reached out to give me a high five.

Leaving her hand in the air, I said, "Ahh, I think I understand what you were saying now. You know, I never thought about that before, but if I wasn't able to have coffee, I'd probably go insane."

She nodded her head as she lowered her hand. With my acknowledgment of understanding, she started eating her breakfast. Her food disappeared quickly and she placed her fork down on her empty plate. "Do you want to go back up for anything else?"

She looked down at her plate and back up at me. "I don't know the last time I've eaten a full meal. I usually don't have time...or money...and God knows I don't cook."

"There's still time if you'd like more."

"No, I'm good."

There was still some time before the others arrived, and I still needed to go to my office to check my messages and emails, but the thought of having Jane downstairs in my office with me still made me uncomfortable. "Jane, when is the last time you saw a doctor?"

"I don't know. It's been a while I guess."

"We have some time before group starts. Would you like to go have an examination? If nothing else, maybe they could help you with something for sleep. And, no need to worry about the cost, I can take care of that."

"Really? You'd want to do that?"

"Yeah, of course. It would be good to see if there is anything they can help you with and you're already here."

Jane followed me to the urgent care unit of the hospital, where I asked her to wait for me while I updated the nurse on duty. As I left the waiting room, they called Jane's name for her appointment. She was exhausting. I never knew what mood she would be in or how I needed to react to her. I made sure to tell the nurse about the marks I saw on Jane's arms and face and warned them not to prescribe anything with a street value. The patient care fund would pay for her bills, but I wouldn't let that fund pay for something that could potentially kill her...or someone else if she decided to sell them.

In my office, the red light on my phone illuminated my dark office as I opened the door. That blinking red light was the one part of my job that never changed; it was the only consistency in my day. Emails were equally predictable; there was always something that needed my attention or a new policy to learn.

The group was only an hour away, giving me just enough time to return the calls waiting for me. After listening to the messages, the only calls I needed to return resulted in an annoying game of phone tag. With the extra time, I logged on to my fake Facebook account and pulled up Jane's page. I wanted to see who Ted was, but there was no Ted listed on her friends list. Scrolling through her page, I didn't see any mention of him or any photos with him, still just the pictures of Seth.

I clicked on Carmen's Facebook page again to see if she had any friends named Ted, but that came back empty as well. Carmen's sweet eyes looked back at me as I scrolled through her profile. My heart told me she didn't take her own life, but there was no evidence...no proof I wasn't just trusting my gut when I shouldn't.

In the few minutes I had left, I called Tim. We hadn't talked yet this morning and I wanted to see if he would answer some new questions that came from my morning with Jane. My call went straight to voicemail. I didn't bother leaving him a message. Instead, I sent him a quick text message with a few sickly sweet emojis. What was I becoming? I always hated those things before, but Tim was changing me, helping me find the pieces of myself I didn't even know I was missing.

I went back to urgent care to retrieve Jane, but she wasn't done with her appointment yet. I went back to see if I could find a nurse to let me know how much longer they needed her. The nurse told me they were going to be admitting her to give her IV antibiotics for a bacterial infection they discovered during her exam. If left untreated, she could die.

I walked into the exam room where Jane was waiting to be transferred to a room and found her crying on the cot. "Hey, Jane, what's wrong?"

"I don't know if I want to stay...but they said I don't have a choice."

"You're extremely sick, Jane. Did they tell you how sick you are?"

"Yeah...the doctor said I have an infection...and I'll die if I leave...is that true, or is he being dramatic?"

"He's a great doctor, I'd trust what he says. Besides, you don't have a safe place to stay right now. This will be good for you. Will you stay, at least for a few days?"

She rolled over onto her side in the cot, pulling her legs

up to her chest. "Hmmm...I guess you have a point. It couldn't hurt to stay...at least until Seth calms down."

"Seth? I thought you said, Ted?"

She closed her eyes. "Yeah, yeah, whatever, I'm tired. Can you go so I can get some rest?"

I thought it was strange Jane hadn't mentioned Ted before, and now I knew why...because he didn't exist. Was Seth the violent one? Or was she lying about that, too? She's so hard to read. Hot one minute, cold the next. All I wanted was answers. I wasn't sure I'd ever get them. Not from Jane, anyway.

CHAPTER TWENTY-FIVE

Sonya, Norma, and Maggie were already in the conference room, waiting for me to arrive. They were in the middle of a conversation that went silent when I entered the room. "Sorry I'm late, ladies. I was just with Jane over in Urgent Care."

"Oh, dear. Is everything okay with her?" Concern washed over Norma's face.

"Well, she will be if she stays for treatment. But that's all I can say without her permission. What were you ladies talking about when I walked in?"

"Go ahead, Sonya, tell her the great news." Maggie's excitement made me anxious to hear what Sonya had to say.

"So, you know that old pervert I told you about last week?" She laughed before continuing. "The old sicko really was a perv. They found him dead over the weekend...but get this...the best part, ...he was jacking off when they found him."

Norma let out a gasp. "Oh my."

"What, you never heard of someone jerking off? Masturbating?" Her words were swallowed by laughter. "They found him with his pants off...and a stiffy."

"A stiffy?" Norma's eyes questioned the meaning.

"An erection," Maggie explained while Sonya continued laughing.

"Oh, wow, Sonya. How did you find out about it?" I sat on the edge of my chair as she caught her breath.

"My mom told me. He had her listed as his emergency contact. The cops went to her house to tell her the news...and the cop told her how they found him."

"How did your mom take it?"

"She didn't say. She thought it was pretty funny. But...the best part is he left her his whole estate. He didn't have any family, so he gave her everything."

"Wow. That's great news, Sonya. How are you doing with the news? Did it bring anything up for you?"

"I think it's fantastic. And, my mom gets some money out of the deal, which makes it even better."

"Well, then, that's great news. I think we should celebrate."

"I'm glad your monster is dead, Sonya. It makes me wish Hank was dead, too." Maggie paused for a moment. "Don't get me wrong though, I am happy for you and your mom. I guess I'm just a little jealous."

"It's okay, Maggie, I get it. Maybe someone will take him out while he's in the slammer."

"I wish they would. He's got a life insurance policy, over $250,000, not to mention the monthly social security

survivors benefits for the kids. That would really help us out."
Maggie's eyes stared straight ahead, as though she was
imaging the life waiting for her and her girls. I wanted to
help. I wanted to grant her wish and solve all of her problems,
but there was no way I could get to him while he was in jail.

The desire grew with every thought. Festering inside
like gasoline on a fire. The heat radiated throughout my
core as I tried to develop a plan. Norma's hand on my
shoulder took me out of my trance. The thoughts took me
out of the room longer than I realized. "Are you alright,
dear?"

"Oh, yes, I'm sorry...I guess I...I was just thinking."

"Is there anything you want to share with us, dear? We'll
listen...we're in this together." Norma said what I had been
feeling since our first meeting. These were ladies I could
count on, just as much as they could count on me.

"Thank you, Norma. I think I'm okay, but I will keep that
offer for next time." She took my hand and sandwiched it
between hers.

"Alright, I'll let you get away with it this time." Her smile
took me back to the hug I shared with my gram over the
weekend. That love word was something I just could not
escape any longer.

"Norma, how are you doing? Do you have anything you
want to share with us?"

"Oh, no, not today, dear. I don't have anything important
to talk about."

"Of course you do, or you wouldn't be here." Sonya
leaned in closer to the group. "Come on, Norma, you've got
to spill the beans sometime."

"Sonya, no one has to share until they are ready. We need to respect people's choices, okay?"

"Yeah, I know. I know. I just know how good it felt talking about some of my shit, I wanted her to have the chance, too. That's all."

"That's kind of you, dear. I guess I'm just not ready for that yet. I just don't want to open up something I can't turn off, and with the holidays coming up, it's not good timing."

"Norma brings up a good point...how does everyone feel about the holidays? What are your plans?"

Maggie began to cry. "I hadn't been thinking too much about it. I won't have any money to get the girls any gifts, and we don't have any family around here. We..."

"How old are your girls again?" Sonya pulled her chair in closer to Maggie.

"They're fourteen and sixteen."

"So, the Santa ship has sailed? OK, tell me what they like. I love to shop...let me help with some gifts. We can have a girl's day, go to the mall, have lunch, maybe a drink. How's that sound?"

"Oh, you don't have to do that. I didn't mean for you to..."

"Nonsense. I want to. I don't have any kids of my own yet, and I remember how hard my mom worked to make everything perfect for us. Let me? Please? Besides, I love a good excuse to get to the mall."

Norma chimed in, "I might just be an old lady, but I'd love to come, too, if that's okay. I'd love to help out with some gifts for the girls. And, you know, I've been meaning to host a Thanksgiving meal at my house for a long time, but I just never had anyone to invite. I'd love to have you and the girls. And, there's plenty of room if you'd like to come, too." Her kind eyes met Sonya's and then mine.

"Wow, that's sweet of you, Norma. I'm not sure what my plans are right now, but that's the nicest invitation I've received in a long time. And I'd love to join you on that shopping trip...I mean, if that's alright."

"Sure, it's fine. That sounds like fun. What do you think, Maggie?"

Her tears continued, but the look on her face had changed from desperation to hope. "You're all so kind. I haven't had a girl's day in years...well...I don't think I've ever had one. What can I do to repay you all for your kindness?"

"Just let us help you. It will help me to have something to be a part of. I could use a little fun."

"And it will be so nice to have some life in my house. It gets so lonely...especially this time of the year." Norma reached over to hold Maggie's hand. "This will be so much fun."

"So, it sounds like the holidays just got a whole lot better. This will be the best year in a long time for me, too. Thank you for including me." The offer made me realize how much these ladies mean to me.

"Why wouldn't you be included? You're part of this group, too...you don't get off the hook just because it's your job." Sonya placed her hands on her knees before she stood up. "Now, if we could just solve Maggie's other problem."

The room filled with laughter. This really was going to be one of the best holidays in a long time. There was so much going right in my life. Tim, seeing my gram, and now these ladies. The only thing that would complete my wish list would be finding my son. That was something I never let myself think too much about because I didn't want to keep feeling the repeated disappointment. But now, I was starting to believe anything was possible.

CHAPTER TWENTY-SIX

Enjoying a hot cup of tea, I sat at the kitchen table, researching Jane's Facebook page. Not sure what I was looking for, I kept scrolling. There were years of posts, some about Facebook games, some of memes, and some of the usual drama you find on social media. A knock on the door startled me so much I shut the laptop closed. My heart raced in my chest as I imagined who might be on the other side.

"Just a minute."

"Come on, Val, it's your knight in shining armor." His smile broadcasted through his voice.

As I opened the door, I noticed the pizza and flowers in his hands. "What did I do to deserve this?" I reached up to kiss his lips as I took the flowers from him.

"I figured you could use a visit." He set the pizza on the counter. "Well, actually, I could use your company. Today was a day from hell."

"You're welcome here anytime. I love spending time with you."

"Did I interrupt something? You sounded busy."

"Oh...no....I was just doing some research." I cut the stems of the pink carnations and placed them into a vase with water.

"What kind of research? Is it something I can help you with? Don't forget, I'm a wealth of knowledge." He chuckled as he pulled out a slice of pepperoni pizza.

"My human encyclopedia, how cute." I reached into the cupboard to take out some plates. "No, it's nothing, really." I took out two Sam Adams and held them up.

"You read my mind." He carried the pizza and his plate to the living room.

I followed behind with the beer and my plate. I sat down on the couch, my feet under my butt. "So, tell me about your day."

He let a massive sigh escape and took a swig from his beer. "It was a rough one." He balanced the bottle on his knee as he slowly spun it around. "Days like today make me want to find a new career. It might have been one of the top ten worst days of my life."

"Oh, my goodness, that sounds awful. Do you want to talk about it?"

He closed his eyes and took a deep breath. "I really hate it when I have to tell a family that their..." Tears ran down his cheeks, he let them sit there as he went on. "their kid is dead."

My heart dropped into my stomach. "Oh, Tim, I'm so sorry."

"You know, I've done this job forever, and it never gets

easier...but this time...I was the first one on the scene. I don't think I can unsee what I saw today. The car was mangled. And the blood...it was like a horror movie. It...it was the worst accident I've ever seen."

"Oh, Tim."

"When I saw the car, I knew there was nothing I could do. He was already gone when I got there. Do you know what a hopeless feeling that is? This poor kid hadn't even started his life yet. He was only sixteen...on his way to school. His mom told me it was his first day on his own. He promised her he'd be careful. And I had to be the asshole to tell her he'd never be coming home."

"I can't even imagine the pain she must be in...and you...I don't know how to take this away from you." I put my plate down on the coffee table and got on my knees to hug him. "I'm so sorry." He leaned into me and sobbed. "You're a good man. I love you."

"I love you, too, Val. I don't want to waste any more of my life. I don't want to live another day without you in it."

The words hit my core. I had never thought about forever before, and here it was in my face. Could I imagine my life without him? I wasn't sure anymore. He'd become such an important part of my day in such a small amount of time. Was I ready to let my guard down and trust he meant what he said? But, he was right, life was short...and I'd wasted so much of it already.

"Val, what do you think? Do you want to spend the rest of your life with me? Do you want to get married?"

My throat went dry, and I pulled out of his arms. "I... I guess I never thought I'd ever be married. This is a lot, Tim...

I don't know what to say. Your emotions are going crazy today, you might change your mind when things calm down."

"No... you don't understand. I won't. I've wanted you for so long and I don't want to think about my life without you. I'm not saying this just because of what happened today. I mean it. Think about it, at least?"

"I can do that. I do love you...this is all just happening so fast."

"I know. Just don't give up on me, okay?"

"That shouldn't be too hard...you're pretty amazing."

"So, now that I've made this awkward, how was your day?"

"It was fine."

"Hmm...that sounds like you're not telling me something. Come on, I really want to get out of my head. Tell me about your day."

"Well, my day was...strange...it started with Jane."

"Wow, that lady is like a bad penny."

"Be nice." I tapped his knee and laughed. "She was sleeping in a minivan in the parking lot. When I walked into work, she called my name. She was trying to get some money from me and had this weird story about some guy named Ted. She said he kicked her out of the house, and she didn't have any place to go."

"You're lucky she didn't come here last night."

"Hmmm...you're right, I didn't even think about that. Well, anyway, I talked her into getting some breakfast with me, and then I brought her to Urgent Care."

"Why did you bring her to Urgent Care?"

"When we were eating, I noticed some track marks on her

arm...and red spots all over her face. I don't know why I never noticed them before...but anyway...she kept asking me for money, and I finally got her to admit it was for drugs...I told her I can't give her money for that...but get this...she wanted me to ask you if you had any drugs...crazy, right?"

"She wanted you to ask me to buy her drugs? Yeah, I guess that is a little crazy."

"Yeah, she said cops have all the good stuff.... anyway...so, I told her I couldn't give her money, but maybe the doctor at Urgent Care could give her something. She went willingly for a checkup. When I went back to get her to bring her to group, they told me they were going to admit her. She needs IV antibiotics for a bacterial infection she probably got off a dirty needle. I convinced her to stay...at least until she finds someplace to go, and she agreed."

"Wow, great work. You saved her life."

"We'll see if she stays or not...I hope for her sake, she does. Maybe all she needs is just someone to look out for her."

"Yeah, probably. I think that's what we all need."

"True....that's what happened in group today, too. These ladies are really getting close and helping each other out. I'm kinda glad Jeanine made me do it. The ladies are all going out shopping to get Maggie's girls Christmas gifts...and Norma has invited us all to her place for Thanksgiving."

"That sounds a little slippery, doesn't it?"

"What does?"

"Going to a patient's house for dinner. That seems like you're getting a little too close. Doesn't it?"

"Yeah, I guess. I didn't say I was going to go." I picked at the lint on my sock. "It's just so nice to see all these friendships forming and see them looking out for each other. I guess I got sucked up into it all."

"Hey, Val, I didn't mean to upset you. I know you won't cross any boundaries. Maybe it would be good for you to go? You know, to help keep the bound? That's got to be therapeutic, right?"

"I don't know, you're probably right. What are your plans for Thanksgiving?"

"I'm going to my mom's house. I can ask her if she'd be okay with you coming with me if you want."

"Don't you think it's a little soon to be meeting family?"

"Hey, what was last weekend? I got to meet your grandma."

"Good point...but she didn't even know who I was, let alone we're a couple."

"Well, you can think about it. Maybe you'd have more fun with the ladies from your group. It might be good for you."

"Yeah, I'll think about it."

In all of my years as a social worker, I never let myself get too close to a client. I thought it was because I was professional, but it was really to protect myself. I had never wanted to get close to anyone before, but now, it was like I couldn't get close enough. I'm not sure what was happening to me. These women and their stories were the only things I could think about. I wanted to know more. I wanted to help them. I wanted to solve their problems. I wanted them to walk away with perfect lives. I'd do whatever it took to make it happen.

"Hey, so, when you were investigating Carmen's death, did you ever hear about anyone named Ted?"

"I don't think so. I remember Jane and Seth...but I think those were the only people that we were told about. You looked at the file, do you remember seeing anything about Ted?"

"No, it was just Jane and Seth. I mean, if they were living with a guy named Ted, you would have interviewed him, right?"

"Yeah. I'm pretty sure the apartment was in Jane's name. If I remember correctly, it was just Jane and Carmen living there."

"Why would she lie about living with some guy named Ted? And why would she say he kicked her out?"

"You can never trust anything that comes from someone who is actively using. And she just lost her daughter, so I mean, I get it. I don't blame her for wanting to be high."

"Yeah, true. But, isn't that a bizarre thing to make up?"

"It's honestly not the strangest lie I've heard before. I don't know why people do the things they do. I don't think you'll ever know the truth unless she decides to tell you, and even then, who knows."

"Yeah, I guess you're right."

"Why is this case bugging you so much? I know you saw Carmen, but you've seen a lot of dead people. What makes this case so...intriguing?"

I thought about his question before I answered. Why was I so drawn to this case? What made this one different than all of the rest of the deaths I'd worked on? "I'm not sure. Maybe it's because Carmen and Gabriel were the same age. But I think it's more than that. I just had a bad feeling when I walked into that room...and it hasn't left me since."

"I get that. What I saw today will haunt my dreams for the rest of my life." He stared straight ahead as the images from the day replayed in front of his eyes.

"Do you want to find something funny on TV tonight to help clear your mind? I could use something funny to help take my mind off things."

"Yeah, sure. That sounds like a good idea. Would it be cool with you if I stayed here tonight?"

"I think that sounds like a great idea."

CHAPTER TWENTY-SEVEN

J ust a few days before Thanksgiving, I decided the best place for me to be would be with the ladies from group. It wouldn't be crossing boundaries, as long as I was invited. The thought of meeting Tim's mom this early made the idea of crossing boundaries sound like a good idea. I'd never had to meet anyone's family before, let alone the mother of the man I love. Everything was moving way too fast and including other people in it put fear in places I tried to ignore. If his mother didn't like me, he might not want to keep seeing me, and I wasn't ready for that yet.

I called Norma to let her know I planned on coming and asked if there was anything she wanted me to bring. She said she was excited to have a house full of people to cook for and there was nothing she needed. She said the other ladies were going to spend the night after dinner and then leave early the next morning to go shopping. Lucky for me, Gabriel couldn't be left home alone, so I had an easy way out of that invitation. I took her address and entered it into my phone. Only about a fifteen-minute drive from my place, so if I did want to meet up with them to go shopping the next morning, I still could.

"Hey, Tim, I guess I am going to go to Norma's and having Thanksgiving with the ladies this time."

"I asked my mom, and she said she'd love to meet you if you change your mind."

"Ah, thanks for asking. And, tell her I said thank you."

"Sure thing...or you could tell her at Christmas? I mean, if you want to come with me next month."

"Yeah...okay...definitely, something to think about."

"That's the polite way of saying no, isn't it?"

"I didn't say no."

"Okay, I'll remember your answer isn't no. Do you have plans today? Want me to come by for lunch?"

"My day is pretty full since I'm taking the rest of the week off. Tonight would work better for me."

"Oh, that sounds like a nice way to end my day. I hope you have a productive day. I love you, Val."

"I love you, too. See you later."

I wasn't sure if I'd ever get used to saying I love you and meaning it. The idea of saying those words and hearing someone say them back was not something I imagined would be part of my life. Believing I deserved to hear them was something I needed to work on.

Since my talk with Tim, I tried to stay away from Jane, to try to distance myself from her and the whole situation. But, since the holiday was coming up, I wanted to make sure she had what she needed before I left for the next few days, that was my excuse anyway.

Jane was sitting in the recliner in her room, her feet up,

watching TV. An empty tray sat on the bedside table next to her. The color in her face looked good, and she was wearing clean clothes and fluffy pink slippers. I knocked on the edge of the door before entering. "Hey, Jane, you're looking good."

She took her eyes off the TV long enough to look at me, then returned to the show. "I thought you were coming back the other day to take me to group."

"I'm sorry you thought that, Jane. I didn't want to get in the way of your treatment. If you want to come to the next one, I can see if a nurse can bring you down."

"Hmmm...I don't know if I need to come now, or not."

"Well, that sounds good. Are you feeling better?"

"I am now. The first few days, I felt like shit."

"I'm sorry to hear that."

"The good news is I never want to feel like that again. The social worker told me she is going to help me go to rehab once the medication is done."

"Oh, wow, Jane. That's great news. I'm so happy to hear that."

"She showed me some pictures of the place and I think it'll be really good. It'll give me more time to think about stuff. And, get my shit together. I don't have Carmen to take care of anymore, so now I can take care of myself."

"That sounds like a great plan. I'm proud of you. How much longer are you staying here?"

"I'm not sure. I'll get to leave once the treatment is finished and a bed is ready for me. The doctor said he wouldn't release me until he was sure I have someplace to go."

"Smart man."

"Thanks for not just giving me money to get more drugs... and for making me come over here."

"My pleasure. I'm glad you're doing so well. Is there anything I can do for you while you wait for a bed to open up?"

"Stop by and visit? It would help pass the time."

"I'm going to be off the next couple of days, but I'll be sure to stop by when I get back. Have you had any visitors?"

"Nah...no one knows I'm here. There isn't anyone who would notice if I was missing. No real friends or family left."

"I can relate to that."

"Oh, I'm sure your cop boyfriend would miss you."

"Yeah, I think you're right...but I don't have anyone else... I know how lonely it can be."

"I think that's why I started using...to keep my mind off all the shitty stuff."

"I'm amazed I never did...I have no idea how I kept away from it...I'm just glad you're going to find a new way to live."

"Me, too."

"Happy Thanksgiving, Jane. I'll see you next week. Stay out of trouble."

"Not like I have any other choice." She smiled, and as our eyes connected, I felt changes were coming for her. Life was going to start looking up for her. She wanted it. I could tell.

CHAPTER TWENTY-EIGHT

When I arrived at Norma's ranch-style house, there were already three cars in the horseshoe-shaped driveway. My eyes went to the clock on the dash; I wasn't late. I picked up the blueberry pie I picked up at the bakery by the hospital and went to the door. Christmas music was playing and laughter greeted my knock on the door. Sonya, wearing a white apron, opened the door. "Hey, don't you look cute?"

She tugged at the apron and smiled. "There's one waiting inside for you, too. Come on in and join the fun."

When I walked through the door, Norma and Maggie were peeling potatoes, and Maggie's daughters were in the living room sitting on the couch watching the Macy's Thanksgiving Day Parade. "Happy Thanksgiving, everyone." I sat the pie on the counter and looked around the open floor plan. The table was set for six with a beautiful lace tablecloth and a ceramic cornucopia in the center with gourds spilling out of it. "Sorry if I'm late. I thought you said eleven. What can I do to help?"

"Oh, you're not late, dear. Everyone else decided to spend the night last night, too. We watched Christmas movies and had pizza and played cards. I haven't had this much fun in ages."

"That does sound like a lot of fun."

Norma handed a frilly white apron to me. "If you want, you can put this on to keep your sweater clean. Do you want to help get the rolls made?"

I put the apron on, wrapping the straps around my waist and tying it in the front. "Alright, but I haven't made rolls in years. My grandma and I used to make them every year...but it's been ages." Memories of Thanksgivings past took my breath away as a single tear rolled down my cheek.

"It's just like riding a bike, it'll come right back to you." She handed me a recipe and showed me where to find the ingredients.

She was right, it did come back to me, the skill and the pain. I hadn't considered this was the first holiday in sixteen years I hadn't spent alone. Or that it would hurt so much to think about all of the years that I had wasted living my life so closed off so I would never get hurt again. Kneading the dough was just the cure I needed to release the emotions I didn't want to share with a room full of almost strangers. Maybe Tim was right, maybe being here was crossing some boundaries. Or, perhaps this was the first step in my allowing people into my life.

"How are you doing, Val?" Norma's hand rested on my back as she stood next to me.

"I'm doing okay. Thank you for having us today. I don't know the last time I felt so welcome someplace. You have a beautiful home."

"Thank you, it's nothing special. It's been a lot of fun having a house full of company. And Maggie's girls are such sweethearts." The joy oozed off of her, as thick as the smell of the turkey roasting. "Are you sure you're okay, honey? You look sad. Is something bothering you?"

"I'm okay...being here, with all of you, makes me miss my grandma."

"Oh, Val, that can be so hard. When did you lose her?"

"She's not gone...I just can't see her...it's complicated." I brushed tears off of my face with the sleeve of my sweater. "Is there anything else I can help with?"

She took my cue to change the subject and didn't ask any more questions. "No, I think we have everything under control. Now we just wait. Why don't you come meet the girls?" She took my hand and led me into the opening of the living room. "Sammy, Lexi, this is Val. Val, this is Sammy and Lexi."

Both girls turned and looked at me and pushed the same half-smile onto their face. Lexi waved and went back to watching the TV, and Sammy quietly said hello before returning her eyes to the TV. "It's nice to meet you both. How is the parade this year? Has Santa arrived yet?"

"It's alright." Lexi didn't take her eyes off the screen.

"I don't think Santa's in the parade...it's Thanksgiving." Sammy looked behind her in an attempt to locate her mom.

My awkward attempt to make small talk fizzled before my eyes. When I looked at the girls, all I could picture was that evil man hurting them, stealing their innocence from them. I understood completely why they were so reluctant to talk to me or trust me. They didn't know me. I knew exactly how it was living in a world where you didn't know who was safe and who wasn't. I also knew when it was best to walk away and not force myself on them.

Back in the kitchen, Maggie and Sonya were sitting at the table, sipping their cups of coffee and nibbling on the cheese and crackers that were arranged precisely on the white platter. I pulled out a chair next to Maggie and took a Ritz cracker. Norma came over with a small paper plate and handed me a cup of coffee. "It's just so nice to have you all here."

"This is nice," I replied as I added the cream and sugar to my coffee. "This is the first time in a long time that I haven't been alone on a holiday. I used to think I didn't mind, but I really did. I guess it was easier saying I was fine than to think about what I was missing."

With her mug between her hands, Sonya leaned her body into the table to get closer to me. "Why has it been so long? Why were you alone?"

"I'm not even sure anymore. It's a long story."

"Lucky for you, we have all day. Tell us about you...you know about us, but we don't know anything about you." She sat back into her chair and took a sip of coffee.

"I'm more of a listener. I don't really talk about me to..."

"Clients? Jesus Christ, you still think of us as clients? How many clients have you been to Thanksgiving dinner with? Or been at their houses?"

"Well, actually, I used to do home visits, so a lot."

"You know what I mean. I thought we were your friends."

"Sonya, you are...you ladies are the first people from work that I've spent time with outside of work hours. I do think of you as friends...I guess I just don't want to dump my problems on you all. It's not your job to fix me."

"We don't want to fix you...we want to get to know you." Maggie spoke up and then looked away.

With a deep breath in, I pushed the hair behind my ear as I felt my temperature rise. "When I was eighteen, I left home and never looked back. I didn't stay in touch with any friends or family. I moved away, got an apartment with the money I had saved. After I found a job, I enrolled in the community college and started taking night classes."

"Why did you leave?" Sonya asked as I took a drink of coffee.

"My mom was not a good person. She did some messed up stuff to me, and I didn't feel safe around her. I cut off all contact with everyone so she wouldn't be able to find me...but I don't even know if she would have looked for me. I could have just wasted the last sixteen years I could have had with my gram. I thought I was punishing her, but I think I was the only one that paid the price."

"Oh, honey." Norma put her hand on mine. "How awful it must have been to give up your whole life and start a new one so young. You're a brave woman."

"Until I met you all, I never let myself miss my gram. If I didn't think about it, it wouldn't haunt my thoughts. But, seeing how you all are with each other, and the friendships you all have made makes me miss parts of my old life."

"What did your mom do that made you want to run away?"

"Sonya, don't be rude." Maggie scolded her.

"What? I just want to know. It might do her good to talk about it. I know I've heard that from someone before."

"You're probably right, Sonya." I turned to look at the girls in the living room. "I just don't think it's something I should talk about right now." I nodded my head toward the living room.

"Hey, Norma, have you given Val a tour yet?" Sonya winked.

"Not yet. Would you like to see the rest of the house?" Norma stood up, Sonya and Maggie followed. Norma led us down a long hall past the kitchen. She opened the door on the right. The room was set up with a double bed, neatly made with a dusty pink bedspread and matching pillow shams. Sonya was the first to climb onto the bed and she patted the mattress next to her for us to find a spot. "So, you were saying?"

Maggie closed the door behind her before finding her spot next to Norma on the edge of the bed. I pulled out the rocking chair to face them. "I'm not sure where to start...well... when I was fifteen, my counselor raped me, my mom married him, I got pregnant by him, my mom sent me away to a home for pregnant teens, they stole my baby, my mom never left him and I ran away."

Sonya's mouth hung open, and tears were streaming down Maggie's face. Norma sat holding Maggie's hand but didn't say a word. "So, your life sucks as bad as all of ours? No wonder we all like you so much. I won't get after you for giving us the Cliff Notes version...because that was a lot." Sonya shook her head. "We're sisters. All of us."

"So, yeah, I guess I can relate to a lot of what you all have shared in group. I have a hard time trusting people, but I felt like you ladies were different. I guess I was right."

"Thank you so much for sharing that with us. If you ever want to talk, you know we're here for you, right?"

"Thank you, Sonya, that means a lot."

"So, you know what Lexi is going through?" Maggie brushed the tears off her cheeks.

"Well, I can't say I know what she's going through, only what I went through. I know the pain and confusion, but I think we all deal with our stuff differently."

"Does it get easier? I mean, will she ever be able to move on...have a normal life?"

"It does get easier, I think time helps take some of the sting away, but it doesn't fix anything, it just makes it not hurt as bad. I think about my son every day. I wonder what he's doing, where he lives, if he's happy and healthy, what he looks like. I miss him, but I don't focus on the pain my stepfather caused, or that my mom made me give up my baby. The pain just changes over time. I never went to counseling and I think it could have helped me. I think the best thing you can do for her and Sammy would be to make sure they have a good counselor. You already did more for them than my mom ever did for me. They are lucky to have you."

Maggie's quiet sadness filled the room. Tears fell off her cheeks as Norma rubbed her back. "You really think so? You think I'm a good mom?"

"Oh, Maggie, I would have loved to have a mom like you.

You love those girls and it shows. You are there for them. You did some tough stuff to make sure they're safe. You're an amazing mom."

Sonya stood up and stretched her arms above her head. "I think we should get back out there to check on the food...and the girls."

"Oh, dear, I almost forgot what we were doing." Norma walked to the door, Maggie and I following.

"Group hug." Sonya stood in the hall and held her arms out to wrap around us. "I love you, girls."

"I love you all, too." Norma leaned her head onto my shoulder and wrapped her arms around as many of us as she could reach.

After dinner was finished and everything was cleaned up, I excused myself to get home to Gabriel. I opted out of going shopping with them all in the morning. I just needed some time alone, away from everything, snuggling up with Gabriel with a cup of tea on the couch. It had been too long since it was just the two of us, undistracted. "It's just you and me tonight, buddy. I've missed you."

He nuzzled into my chin and rubbed his head on my face. "What do you think of Tim? He's a nice guy, huh? I think I'm in love with him. Crazy, isn't it? I never thought there would be anyone I could trust. He's as close to perfect as it gets. You know what else? I saw my grandma the other day...I never would have done that without him.

"I've got a few friends from work and I feel good about how life is going." I reached up to my necklace and held the broken heart between my fingers and rubbed the metal. "I just need to find Gabriel now. I just have a feeling I'll be able to find him. I just want to make sure he's OK. He's a man now...I wonder where he lives...or even what his name is."

Gabriel's snoring took over the conversation. There was something calming about feeling his chest rise and fall against mine. If only in those moments I knew our love was enough to get us both through the tough times, just like the love I had found in Tim and now in Sonya, Maggie and Norma...who knows...maybe even Jane. The circle I had kept so empty was suddenly filling up with people I wanted to spend my time with. There was so much to make up for in the last sixteen years. I was sure to make every moment count.

CHAPTER TWENTY-NINE

I arrived at the hospital early to have extra time to spend with Jane. As I walked down the hall to her room, I wondered if I would even find her. My thoughts echoed throughout the hallway as I got closer to her room. I should have stopped by over the weekend; she might have been lonely or sad. She might have decided getting clean wasn't worth the work.

As the thoughts kept creeping in, I knocked on the door, hoping to find Jane. No answer came and every thought I had on the way in multiplied into every horrible scenario. I pulled back the yellow curtain to find Jane fast asleep in her bed, the TV on with just a whisper escaping the screen. I turned to walk away to get caught up on work from the long weekend when I heard Jane's voice. "Hey, stranger, don't go."

"Good morning, Jane. I was going to come back so you can get your rest."

"Nah, I don't need to get rest...I'm here all day...there will be plenty of time to sleep."

"I'm glad you're still here. How are you doing?"

"You don't have any faith in me, huh?"

Embarrassed at how my social awkwardness seemed to always turn into judgment, I tried to be careful with the words I used. "No...it's not that...I just mean it's easier to... staying clean is hard work, and I'm proud of you for sticking it out."

"I want to get better...I want Carmen to be proud of her mom. I couldn't do it right for her in life, so I want to do everything I can to make it up to her."

"That sounds like a great reason to get better. I am so glad you are doing so well. What are your plans after your treatment is complete? Are you still going to rehab?"

"Yeah, those plans didn't change in the last four days. I still plan to go, and I plan to beat this crap. I have a lot of time to make up for."

"I'm glad to hear that, Jane. Has Ted tried to contact you?"

"Who? Who's Ted?"

"You said Ted kicked you out of the house."

The color in Jane's face faded away. "Oh, that's right...I guess I've been working so hard at getting better that I forgot about him."

"You forgot about him? Jane, you don't have to lie to me. I want to help you, but I have to be able to trust you."

"Why do you think I'm lying? What makes you think that I would make this up?"

"I don't think you made up what happened to you, I just don't think there is anyone named Ted...I think it's Seth."

"You think I'm living with my dead daughter's boyfriend? What kind of a monster do you think I am?"

"Jane...I don't think you're a monster. I...I just want to help, and I can't without the truth. I don't care who you live with, I just want to make sure you're safe."

"Why do you care?" She crossed her arms and turned her head away.

"I do care...I've cared about you since the first day I met you. The pain you had that day...when you lost Carmen, is a pain no mother should ever have to go through. From that moment, I just wanted to help."

"You don't care. It's your job." Her tone was tinged with anger.

"That's not true. I do care. Probably too much. I do want to help you and I am so happy you are going to get treatment."

"What would it matter if it were Ted or Seth or Jim or whoever? What difference does it make?"

"None, really. I just don't want to be lied to. I want to know if you are safe."

"You know drugs make you do stupid stuff. If I lied to you, it wasn't my fault."

"I know. Of course, it's not your fault. Can we start fresh now? Whatever happened in the past can be left there and we start over?"

"If I tell you the truth, you won't think I'm a piece of shit? You promise you'll still want to help?"

"Yes, of course."

"Fine...there is no Ted." She picked up the TV remote and started flipping through the channels. "Seth...I live with

Seth. He's the one that kicked me out and hurt me. He's a junkie, too."

"Has he come by since you've been here? Are you...dating?"

"What? Are we...dating? What kinda piece of shit do you think I am? What the fuck? I'm not an animal."

"No, of course not. Are you safe? Has he tried to bother you here?"

"Yeah, I'm safe. He hasn't come by. He probably doesn't even know I'm gone...or he doesn't care. He has the place all to himself...that's probably what he wanted all along anyway."

"What do you mean? What he wanted all along?"

"Jesus, what are you writing a book? Enough with the questions, OK? I'm tired." She rolled onto her side and pulled the blanket up over her head.

"I'll let you get some rest. Sorry if I upset you. If you want to talk later, just have them give me a call."

I knew Jane had been lying to me. I just didn't expect her to tell the truth so quickly. Still, I wasn't sure I'd ever know the truth. And, what did she mean it was what Seth wanted all along? Was she talking about Carmen's death? Does she think he killed Carmen? I wondered how long they had been living together...and if there was anything more to their relationship than she was saying. I didn't know if I'd ever know the truth, or why I needed to know it so badly.

At my office door, I could see the piece of paper that was stuck in the door jamb. I pulled it out as I opened the door. As I shut the door behind me, I opened up the paper. A note from Tim: *Call me, I have something you want.* At my desk, I pulled out my cell phone and sent him a text. *Call you? What decade do you think this is?* As I typed my second response, my phone started ringing.

"Are you calling me old?"

"Maybe...who leaves notes anymore? You know you could just send a simple text, right? It does the same thing."

"Ha-ha...yeah...I know, but I wanted to tell you in person. Are you still in your office?"

"Yeah, why? Why can't you tell me now?"

I heard my doorknob jiggle. "Well, are you going to let me in?"

"Were you just hanging around the hospital waiting for me?" I opened the door and hung up my phone.

"Well...I wanted you to see this." He handed me a manila envelope. "Go on, open it."

"What is it?"

"You'll see."

I pulled the paper out and started to read it. Carmen Davidson's name was at the top of the page. My eyes went up to scan his face. "Is this..."

"Yeah, it's the toxicology report. It finally came back. But look at it...look at what it says was in her system."

I scanned the page to see if I could find what he was talking about. High levels of Benzodiazepines were listed on the report. I looked up at Tim to see his reaction. "This is strange, isn't it? I mean, do you think she took this much? That's a lot, right?"

"I think it's bizarre. That *is* a lot. It looks like she tried to overdose, but how would she have been able to cut her wrists like she did? It just doesn't add up. Why would she want to cause physical pain when she could have just taken the pills?"

"That doesn't make sense. I mean, why would she do both? Do you think someone did this to her? Is that what you're thinking?"

"I don't know. If we had these results before the case was closed, I don't think it would have closed so quickly. I think there's a case here, but what can we do now? There's nobody to examine now. There is no evidence. No case."

"So, someone gets away with murder? Carmen gets thrown away...and the baby..." I stopped as I thought about two lives that were stolen. "Their lives didn't matter?"

"Of course, they mattered. They matter. It's just not going to be easy to charge anyone with murder when we don't have proof."

"What if someone confesses? Then would they get in trouble? Would they have to pay for what they did?"

"Well, that's still tricky. They might, but there is also a chance they might not. It's hard to say what would happen. And, how would they get a confession?"

"I don't know. I just don't want to think that it's so easy to kill someone and then walk away like nothing happened." As the words left my lips, my breath left, too. Essentially, that was what I did. The difference was I was ridding the world of a monster, where a monster stole two beautiful babies. I closed my eyes tight and shook my head to get the thoughts out. No. There was no way this was the same.

"Are you okay, Val?" Tim reached over and put his hand on my shoulder.

"Yeah, ...it's just...too much."

"I know. I don't like this either. But don't give up. Justice might be served when you least expect it. I believe in Karma, you know, what goes around comes around."

"You're right. Whoever did this to them will get what's coming to them." My recent conversation with Jane replayed in my head. "It was Seth...I have no doubts...Jane told me he was a drug dealer...he would have had access to the pills...he didn't want to deal with Carmen or the baby...it's the only thing that makes sense."

"I see why you think that, but we have no proof. And, we don't know if Carmen had a prescription...it's a common prescription."

"She was pregnant...she wouldn't have been taking it..."

Tim pulled me into a hug and kissed me. "Val, I know you want Carmen to have justice, but it is out of our hands. We can't bring her or her baby back."

I let my body fall into him. "I know. Life isn't fair. It really sucks sometimes."

"It really does. Sometimes it takes way too long to figure things out, and sometimes they just fall into place. But look at it this way, the energy you have put into Carmen since she died is probably way more than anyone had in a long time. Your interest in her and her death is something I'm sure she would have appreciated. You've got such a big heart, Val. Right now, I think the best thing we can do is keep her memory alive and be there for her mom."

"I love you, Detective Phillips. You're right, as usual." There was so much more to say, but he was right. It didn't change the fact that Carmen needed justice...deserved it, and if no one else was willing to get it for her, I knew what I had to do, even if I had to do it alone.

After Tim left, I had to talk with Jane again. I needed some questions answered that only she would know the answers to. When I entered her room, her bag was packed. "Where are you off to?" My voice took her by surprise.

"What, are you a mind reader, too? I was just going to ask them to call you."

"Well, that is a quality I would love to possess, but no such luck at this time. What's going on, where are you going?"

"That's what I wanted to tell you...they found me a bed at a treatment facility about an

hour away." She picked up a brochure off her bedside table and handed it to me. "Hope Springs Eternal Rehab Center...kind of a cliché name...but I hope it does. I am ready for this. I never thought I'd see the day."

"Wow, Jane, that was fast. I am proud of you. I know you'll do great. I can't wait to see all of the great things you are going to accomplish."

"Whoa...slow down...let's take one step at a time." She laughed. "I mean, that's what I'll be doing there, taking one step at a time towards recovery."

"Ha-ha...cute."

"Ah, the creativity didn't come from me, it's in the pamphlet."

"Well, regardless as to where it came from, I am proud of you for taking the first step."

"What brings you by...if you didn't know of this new, exciting development?"

"I... ah...just had some questions...but they can wait."

"I have some time before my ride gets here. What do you want to know?"

Jane was in such a good mood; I wasn't sure now was a good time to bring up Carmen. The thought of having to wait until she returned from rehab made me antsy. "It's nothing...really. It can wait." Regret filled me as soon as my answer left my lips.

"Come on, help me kill some time. What is it? What do inquiring minds want to know?"

"I just had some questions about Carmen. I've been thinking a lot about her, and I guess I just wanted to try to learn as much about her as I can. Are you up to talking about her today? I don't want to make you..."

"Make me what? Sad? Angry? Pissed off? You're pretty good at all three, but I don't mind. I like talking about her."

"Did Carmen ever take any prescriptions?"

"No, she didn't like pills. I couldn't even get her to take pills for a headache. I guess watching me act like a fool was enough to make her never want to touch anything."

"Do you think anyone else could have gotten her to take something? I know love can make you do funny things."

Jane paused and averted her eyes from mine. "No. I told you she didn't like it. What made you think of this question anyway?"

"I'm not sure. I just want to understand what frame of mind she was in to want to take her own life. You said before she was into drugs."

"What frame of mind do you think she was in? I mean, she killed herself...I don't know what else to say."

"So, you think she did it to herself?"

"What are you talking about? You know she did." A bitterness left with her words.

"I just mean...you had said...well...that you didn't think she could have done this, and she was into drugs. Do you remember that conversation?"

"I wasn't in my right mind. There's no other explanation. I was angry at Seth and I wanted to get him in trouble. That's all that was."

"So, there's no doubt in your mind?"

"No." She crossed her arms tight against her chest. "And you should drop it." She walked over to the window and looked outside. "I'm sorry, but I just want to get on with my life, and if I have to keep wondering what went wrong with Carmen, I'll never get better."

Her explanation didn't sound right; it seemed like she was covering for someone. I also knew she was not going to answer any more of my questions, and now I had more than I did before our talk. "I'm sorry, Jane, I won't ask you any more questions. I don't want to get in the way of your recovery."

My apology softened her. As she uncrossed her arms, she made eye contact. "I just can't let my mind take me to those places...you know?"

The tears in her eyes made my heart hurt for her. Justice for Carmen was all I was after, but not at the cost of destroying Jane. The pain of losing a child was something I was familiar with. My hand went to my neck, where my fingers wrapped around the broken heart. Thoughts of Gabriel weighed down my heart. "Actually, I do know." I couldn't fight the tears back. I adverted my eyes to the window, to try to get my mind off Gabriel and back to Carmen. "And, I'm sorry I upset you."

"Nah, it's nothing. Don't worry about it. My ride should be here soon...I hope." She picked up the white and green plastic bag with the hospital's logo on it and walked to the door.

"Jane, there is one more question that I do need to ask, what is your address? I have some forms to fill out for the group and want to make sure it's complete."

"Like where I was staying before I came here?"

"Yes, your last physical address."

"156 Wildflower Avenue, apartment 3...but I don't know if I'll be going back there or not."

"That's okay, we can change it if we have to. Good luck, Jane. I'm rooting for you, all of us are."

"Thanks. I'm ready for a new life."

CHAPTER THIRTY

I f Jane wasn't going to answer my questions, the only other person I knew who might was Seth. He was the last person I wanted to see, but he was my only hope. Wildflower Avenue was on the other side of town, but only a fifteen-minute drive. When I found 156 on a ramshackle white apartment building, I knew I had arrived at my destination. I put my car in park, took a drink of my iced coffee and opened the car door. A large breath I had been holding expelled from my lungs as I took in my surroundings. There were children's toys spread across the lawn, a gas grill covered in Bud Light cans, a black, mangy looking dog tied to a doghouse and a dumpster overflowing with trash. I scanned the building to see if I could find apartment #3, the second door on the left had a black, upside-down number three to the right of the door. As I got closer to the door, I noticed the flowerpot complete with dead mums. This was the right place.

I knocked on the door. The second my knuckle hit the

door, I regretted my decision. "Just a minute." A male's voice shouted from inside. When the door opened, Seth stood in front of me, wearing a dark blue hoodie and black sweat-pants. He looked like he hadn't showered in days, the odor coming from his apartment confirmed that.

"Hi, Seth, I'm..."

"I don't want any." He went to shut the door.

"No, I'm not selling anything. I just had some...questions." My heart beat against my chest as I tried to come up with a plan to convince him to talk to me. "I'm with the hospital and I'm offering a cash reward for information about Carmen Davidson."

"What kind of information?" He opened the door, leaving only enough space for his head to poke out.

"Well, ...we just want to make sure we did everything for her...you know...to make sure it wasn't our mistake."

"Oh...so, they sent you here to cover their ass?" He cleared his throat with laughter.

"Um...yeah, I guess you could say that."

"What's the reward? How much are we talking about?" He opened the door and motioned for me to come in.

"Well, that depends on the information, but you'll get $50 just for answering some questions."

"Just to answer questions?"

"Yes. It's that easy." Standing in the kitchen, I scanned the apartment. The trash overflowed onto the floor and dirty dishes filled the sink. The cupboard doors were open, exposing the lack of food.

"What do you want to know?"

"Do you know if Carmen was on any kind of medication?"

"No, she didn't like to take anything, not even for a headache."

"So, to your knowledge, she wasn't on any medication for anxiety or depression?"

"No, not Carmen. Her mother...well...she's a different story. She's on all kinds of stuff...she couldn't get enough pills..."

"Do you know what kind of pills her mother was taking?"

He walked into the bedroom and came back with a plastic basket filled with prescription bottles and handed them to me. "These are what she had been on...the last time I saw her."

The bottles still had pills in them. The first bottle I picked up was Xanax, prescribed to Jane. Bottle after bottle of different drugs with Jane's name on the labels. "She just left her pills here? Do you know where she is?"

"No idea...the dumb bitch stole my van and left. I haven't seen her for a few weeks now. She hasn't even called."

"How long had she been living here?"

He scratched his stomach as his eyes looked up at the ceiling. "I'm not sure...a couple years, maybe."

"And Carmen, did she live here the whole time, too?"

"Yeah, she was here until, well, you know."

"Did Carmen have a boyfriend?"

"She never brought anyone here, if that's what you're asking."

"Did you know Carmen was pregnant when she died?"

"What? Are you fucking lying? How the hell could she have been pregnant?"

"I assume you know how that works."

The color drained from his face. "Are you sure? I mean, how do you know?"

"The medical examiner told us she was pregnant, although not that far along, but still enough to get DNA to see who the father was."

"Why does that matter? They're both dead. Why does it matter who the father is?"

"Well, he might want to know. Don't you think? Wouldn't you want to know?"

"What other questions do you want to know? And when do I get my $50?"

"Seth, I know you were the father. Now, can you just tell me about your relationship?"

"Why the fuck does it matter? She was legal, it shouldn't matter."

"I'm not saying it does. I'm just asking questions. Did Jane know you and Carmen were in a relationship?"

"Yeah, it was her idea. You know...when she couldn't pay the rent, she offered Carmen up...I wasn't going to take her up on the offer, but Carmen wanted it...she was in love with me."

"And you? Were you in love with her?"

"What?" He paused. "Well...I guess I did care about her. I miss her so much. I had no clue she was pregnant. I had no idea she was going to kill herself."

"Do you know of anyone who would have wanted to hurt Carmen?"

"No...well, other than her mom. But Jane's all talk."

"What do you mean? All talk?"

"She was always a bitch to Carmen. Telling her she was too ugly to get a man of her own...pissed off that she didn't protest fucking me. I think she was mad that she knew we had better chemistry. I'd rather be with Carmen, but Jane didn't want to hear it." He crossed his arms against his chest and swayed back and forth. "I guess I did love her." A single teardrop made its way down his scruffy cheek.

His words presented a new reality, I just wasn't sure I could believe him. Why would he tell me all this, only for $50? I didn't expect to see him as human. I wanted so badly to keep him as the monster I had thought he was, but now, I didn't even know who the monster was. I took a step closer to Seth and placed my hand on his back. "I'm sorry you lost someone you love. I know how hard that is."

With his right hand, he unfolded his arms and rubbed the tears that had pooled on the tip of his nose. "Yeah, it really does suck, and then with Jane's bullshit, it doesn't help at all. She had this big act of how much she misses her, you know? She just does that shit to get attention."

"I'm sure it's been hard for her, too. She lost her daughter."

"That doesn't matter to her, she wasn't even good to Carmen. All Jane cares about is herself."

"Do you remember the day Carmen died? At the hospital?"

"Yeah, of course, I do."

"Do you remember seeing me in the room? I was there when you and Jane were in the room with Carmen."

"I really can't remember the details, I wasn't in a good space, you know?"

"I understand. I remember you were agitated; you were very rude to me...and it looked like you were high, or something."

"Jesus Christ lady, I just found out the woman I loved was dead, how the fuck was I supposed to act?"

"Yeah, I get that. To me, it looked like you had something to hide."

"I don't like hospitals, or cops, or any of that shit. I probably was high, too...that's never good when you have to talk to the cops."

I replayed that day over in my mind, to try to see it from a different perspective. Jane was so convincing. Seth had guilty written all over him and his actions. It didn't seem like he was the same guy from that day. Can people really change that much? How could I have been such a poor judge of character? Something still didn't feel right. How could I have been so wrong? "Are you still using?"

"What does that even matter? Is that part of the $50 questions?"

"Sorry, no... you just seem so different to me today then you did the last time. I just wanted to know why."

"After Carmen died, I've been trying to get clean...but it's not easy...especially when all Jane wanted to do was get high."

"So, you were high the last time I saw you, but you're not today?"

He hesitated with his response as he ran his fingers

through his greasy hair. "Yeah, I guess. But wouldn't you have been, too?"

"Were you here when it all happened? When Carmen... when she...took the pills and cut herself?"

"Wait a minute...took the pills...Carmen didn't take any pills; she wouldn't do that."

I realized my slip up after it was too late. "Oh, that's right, I must be thinking about a different case."

"Don't fuck with me...it's not the wrong case, is it? Jesus fucken Christ." He shook his head as his eyes closed. "You gotta tell me the truth about this. Carmen would never take pills, never. She hated them. I mean, she slit her wrists, why would she take pills, too? But fucken Jane." His head hung down. "Jane told me once she wanted to kill someone ...she said all she would have to do is make it look like an overdose." His hand covered his mouth.

Could it be true, all that Seth had told me? It was all so hard to believe. How could a mother do that to her own child? Thoughts of my own mother came rushing into my mind. I felt the heat flood my body as rage set in. I didn't even know what to believe anymore. "Jane told you that? That she wanted to kill someone? Did she ever say who?"

"Not exactly...I mean, every time she got pissed off at someone, she talked about killing them. I guess there were a few times she said it about Carmen, but...how could she really do it? You don't think Carmen killed herself, do you? That's why you're really here, isn't it?"

I hadn't expected the conversation to end up here. I wasn't really sure what I expected to come from the visit. I just wanted answers, answers Jane wouldn't give me. "No...I just wanted to ask some questions...to get to know her better. We wanted to make sure we did everything we could to make sure the hospital was not liable for her death. I appreciate your time."

"Am I still going to get the $50? I did answer a lot of questions."

"Of course. Just let me get that for you." Luckily I had cash in my wallet because I didn't want to write a check and give him my information. I pulled out two twenty-dollar bills and a tattered ten from my purse and brought it back to Seth. "Thank you again. And I'm sorry for your loss. Make sure you take care of yourself. Have a nice night."

As I backed out of the driveway, I couldn't help thinking about all he shared with me. I wasn't sure if I was happy to have this new information or if I was better off without it. One thing I did walk away with is even more certainty Carmen's death was not a suicide. But, could I trust Seth? Or Jane? How would I ever get the truth?

CHAPTER THIRTY-ONE

Sitting in my driveway, I called Tim. I had to talk to someone about what Seth had said. He was the only one who would understand. After the third ring, Tim's voice came on the line asking me to leave a voice mail. All the breath I had been holding since I left Seth's filled the car in a heavy sigh. "Hi Tim, it's Val... I need to talk to you. Please call me back. Love you."

I leaned into the car to get my tote bag, banging my head on the way out. I slammed the door shut and tears streamed from my eyes as sobs followed. *Get a hold of yourself, Val.* The thought I needed Tim made me weak in the knees. It had been a long time since I could depend on anyone, and the desperation it brought was not something I missed.

"Well, well, well, look who decided to come home and eat dinner with her boyfriend. It's probably cold by now." Sitting on the steps to my apartment next to a paper bag, Tim stood up when he saw my tears. "Hey, Val, I'm only joking around, what's wrong?"

I fell into his arms and sobbed as his jacket caught my tears like a tissue. "I'm just so happy to see you. I just left you a message. I'm so glad you're here."

"Is everything alright? What happened to you today?"

"It's a long story." I kissed his cheek and then took his hand to bring him inside. Gabriel was waiting for me and meowing for dinner. "Hey, buddy." I scooped him up and kissed his head as he rubbed against my chin. "I'm so glad to have both of my boys with me tonight. You are staying, right?"

"Are you talking to the cat or me?" A laugh followed as he set down our dinner on the table.

"Funny...but it wasn't long ago he was all I had. And, his name is Gabriel, not cat." I kissed Gabe one last time before setting him on the floor so I could fill his dish with kibble. "Isn't that right, Gabriel?"

"Whoa, I'll back off." He held both of his hands by his face and took a step back.

"You're a nut...but I love you anyway."

Tim took out two plates and put the cold Chinese on them. "Do you want to heat this up?"

"No, it's good cold. Thanks for always knowing when I need you. You're a lifesaver, even if you are a smartass."

He winked at me. "See, I know things. Let's go eat while you tell me about your day." We made our way into the living room, both of us found our usual spot on the couch and started our dinner. Tim stood up. "I forgot something." He walked to the refrigerator and took out two Sam Adams and held them up for me to see.

"It's like you can read my mind."

"Scary, isn't it?" A smile spread across his face as he handed me a bottle.

"Nah, I like it."

Silence filled the room as we ate our dinner. I didn't know how to tell him I ended up at Seth's, or better yet, why I went there. The truth was, I didn't even know why. My obsession with Carmen and getting her justice felt like it was taking over my life. Reaching for my necklace, I pulled it away from my chest and held the broken heart in my hand. This was my reason, it was my reason for everything I do.

Tim set his plate on the coffee table and turned to look at me. "You're awfully quiet for someone who has a long story to tell."

"I guess it's not that long... or exciting..."

"Spill it, Val, you can't leave me hanging like that. You were too upset about it to stay inside of your head. You'd tell Gabriel...so just pretend I'm him." He put his hand up to his mouth and pretended to lick it and rubbed it on the side of his head. "Meow."

"Oh my God, you're insane." Laughter helped ease my nerves as I looked for a way to tell him where I had been. After a loud sigh, I started. "Promise not to get upset and I'll tell you."

He raised his eyebrows. "Promise."

"Remember the report you showed me, Carmen's toxicology?"

"Yeah."

"Well, you know me...you know I can't just drop anything...so I went to Jane's room to ask her a few questions.

She got pissed off at me for meddling...so I tricked her into giving me Seth's address."

"I don't think I like where this is heading. Please tell me you didn't go see him."

"I'd be lying if I did. But, before you get mad, just let me finish." I waited a few seconds until he looked like he would listen. "I did go to Seth's and we did talk...but you'll never guess what he told me..."

"Let me try, he's innocent, he didn't beat up Jane, he loved Carmen. Am I close?" He tilted his head to the side as he raised his right eyebrow.

"Not exactly, but close enough, I guess...but just listen for a minute. He did say all that stuff, but he said Carmen would never take pills, he even showed me bottles of Jane's Xanax. And, he said Jane had talked about wanting to kill people...even Carmen a few times."

"So, now you think Jane killed her? Her own daughter?"

"No, I'm not saying that. I just don't know what to think. I hated Seth....but this visit made me see him differently. He's really hurting. He even said he's trying to get clean."

"And you honestly believe him?"

"I know how crazy it sounds. I'm not even sure. I just saw him differently. Last time I despised him, I couldn't wait for him to leave, I knew in my gut that he was the reason Carmen was in that bed. But now, I don't know what to think."

"So, he's either a terrific liar, Jane's a monster, or Carmen really did do it."

"Yeah, that's what I'm left with. I know in my heart Carmen didn't do it herself. What I don't know is who to believe. Jane has issues...lots of them...but she's a mom, moms are supposed to love their kids, no matter what. But I know first-hand that's not always how it works. And then there's Seth, a junkie with anger problems, but that wasn't a fair judgment. I just feel so lost. I knew for sure Seth had something to do with it, but now...I have no idea."

"The sad part is, it really doesn't matter." He paused when he saw my mouth drop open. "I mean...of course it matters, but without a body, we can't charge anyone. So, whoever did this will get away with it. The only punishment they will get is from their own guilt."

"I doubt they will even have that...obviously they didn't care about right and wrong before, I doubt it will even phase them. He didn't even know she was pregnant...but he admitted it was his."

"So, her mom is sleeping with the father of her grandchild? That's just messed up."

"Yeah, it's all just gross." I put the cold amber bottle up to my lips and took a sip. "I think I'm going to need a few of these tonight."

"I'm kind of worried about you, Val. Carmen's case is taking up all of your time. It seems like she's all you think about. I know you want to give her justice, but what if you can't?"

"I know, this case just feels so close to my heart. She was so young and beautiful. Her life was wasted. From all I've heard, it doesn't seem she had much love in her life; I just wanted to give her one last hurrah. I guess it's stupid." With one long chug, my first beer was gone. I didn't think there were enough to help take this off my mind.

"No, you're not stupid. You just have a huge heart and

you want to see the right thing happen. But it seems like that happens less and less these days. I love you; I don't want this to drive you crazy or consume you. There are more people who are living, who need you and your heart." He leaned over and kissed me. I wasn't ready to let go of what he had said. I sure wasn't prepared to give up on Carmen, not yet. Not ever.

CHAPTER THIRTY-TWO

As the ladies arrived for group, I couldn't shake the uneasy feeling of not knowing. I wished I had a shut off for my thoughts at times. Tim was right, I was obsessed with Carmen, but if not me, who? The fire that burned inside me was now so intense the intensity from the flames was heating my flesh. It was more than anger or revenge; now the fire had lit my desire for vengeance.

"Any word on Jane?" Sonya's question took me out of my head and got my focus back to the group.

"I went and saw her after Thanksgiving and she was doing well. She has been discharged and is at rehab, she said she wants to be her best self."

"Oh, that's just lovely. I'm so happy to hear that." The smile on Norma's face gave me the comfort I had been missing and put a smile on mine.

"It doesn't even feel like she's part of this group." Maggie paused. "I don't mean to be disrespectful or anything, but I kind of like it with just the four of us. Jane's kind of a..."

"Drama queen?" Sonya interrupted. "Yeah, I totally agree, she's not like us. I'm glad she's not here."

"Oh, stop it, don't be rude. She's been through a lot. We just have to give her time." Norma looked over at me to chime in, except I wasn't sure they were wrong. This group was so much better without her.

"So, tell me, how was shopping?" I hoped changing the subject would drop the chatter about Jane.

"It was so much fun. We got some great stuff for Maggie's girls." Sonya elbowed Maggie. "We also got some awesome stuff for us big girls, too."

"It was fun, but I don't think I want to go Black Friday shopping for a long time...there were so many people, but I can't remember a time I've had so much fun. It's been a long time since I've been one of the girls." Norma's eyes sparkled as she looked over at Maggie and Sonya.

"The girls stayed at Norma's while we went shopping. It was so nice to feel like they were safe and not worry about them. Norma's right, there were a lot of people, but it was still so much fun. I can't believe these ladies have kind of adopted my girls. It's a nice feeling after being away from my family for so long." Maggie pulled out a tissue and dabbed her eyes.

"It sounds like I missed out on a great time. I'm glad you all had such a good time. We are becoming a nice little family. I've got to say, I agree with Maggie, it's been a while since I've felt this connected to anyone. Thank you, ladies, for being so caring and thoughtful." My heart was full as I thought about our time at Norma's. This group had become something I looked forward to each week. I was so glad Jeanine forced me into it.

"We've already planned Christmas; you should join us." Sonya sat on her hands as she leaned forward to await my response.

"I might have plans, but if not, I'd love to join you. I want to know all the gifts the girls are going to get. Sounds like they'll be surprised."

"Yeah, they sure will. They had just as much fun at Norma's as we did. It's been so long since I've seen them happy and carefree." Maggie pulled up another tissue and pushed it against her nose.

"Do you want to tell her the news, dear? Or should I?" Norma seemed just as antsy as Sonya.

"I'll tell her. Norma invited the girls and me to move in with her. After talking with the girls, they think it's a great idea. It will be such a big help, and the girls just love Norma."

"What's not to love?" I smiled as I thought about the hope this group had brought these ladies, who just a few short weeks ago were strangers.

Norma giggled and her cheeks reddened. "It will be such a relief to have a full house. It gets so lonely in that place. I'm looking forward to cooking dinner and being a family."

"That's so nice. I'm so happy for all of you. Sometimes the families we pick are way better than the ones we are given. This sounds like a great solution for both of you."

"The more you talk about it, the more I think I want to come, too." Sonya's smile made it unclear if she was being honest or just being Sonya.

"You know you're always welcome." Norma put her hand to her heart. "We're family, even if you don't live under the same roof. I'm afraid you're stuck with me."

"I'm just teasing, I need my own space. I love you all, but sometimes I just need to be alone."

"I totally understand that, Sonya. My alone time helps recharge me."

"Yeah, exactly." Sonya nodded her head in agreement.

The more they talked, the more I realized Sonya was right—Jane didn't fit in with the rest of us. Norma, Maggie and Sonya were all capable of loving each other, but I wasn't so sure Jane would ever be capable of loving anyone. It was nice knowing she wasn't going to appear in the middle of the group or come in and take it over. I hoped rehab helped her see how different life could be. If all goes well, it would be a few weeks before Jane would be around. The program she went to was 90 days. That might be enough time for our bond to grow even closer, without the interruptions. These ladies had enough of their own issues to work on, without having the burden of Jane's unpredictability. Her sobriety would be good for all of us.

"I just wanted to thank you again for sharing part of your story with us. It helped me trust you more." Maggie's voice trailed off as she finished speaking.

"I kind of felt bad for unloading that all on you. I'm not usually the one doing the sharing. It was nice to tell people who understand. Most people wouldn't get it, but I know you all know what it's like to be taken advantage of and hurt."

"I've been thinking about what you said about your grandma and I think you should go see her. You know, sometimes we are left with regret when we could have prevented that pain with a simple visit or call." Norma held out her hand for me to hold as I felt the warm tears seep out of my eyes. "Honey, you only get one chance at this life, make sure you aren't filled with regret when it's your time to return home if you know what I mean." She squeezed my hand tight as our eyes connected.

She was right. The minute we left my gram's, I knew I wanted to see her again. Regret replaced the fire inside me. It wasn't fair. I had to give up my life because my mom didn't support me. I shouldn't have been the one punished. The only way to stop the punishment was to spend as much time with my gram as I could before she returned home. I knew what I had to do. I knew where I had to spend Christmas. The fire returned, with a new vengeance this time.

CHAPTER THIRTY-THREE

I picked up my phone as my memory punched in the familiar numbers. As the phone on the other end rang, I froze as I waited to hear her voice. "Hello. You have reached Peter and Hellen; we can't come to the phone right now..."

The phone dropped on my desk as the unfamiliar voice reminded me, she had moved. I returned the phone to the cradle and thought about my options. I didn't want to just arrive as Stephanie Mills again, I wanted to be myself. I wanted a relationship with the only person from my past who showed me love. I searched the computer to see if I could locate her new number, but the only listing that appeared was the number I already knew. A visit might be the only way to gain access to her. My only hope is that her memory was bad enough to have forgotten the visit Tim and I made a few weeks ago.

My mother was not going to hold me prisoner any longer. If I wanted to see my gram, I would. The fear of seeing her or

Chad was no longer strong enough to keep me hidden away. With Norma's encouragement, I knew what I needed to do. It was what I should have done years ago. I was just so grateful I had the opportunity to do it now.

I picked up the phone again, this time dialing an inside extension. "Jeanine, hey, it's Val, I need to leave early today... I...ah...have an urgent matter I need to tend to."

She didn't care that I was leaving, as long as I had my work done. That was all she cared about, and the morgue was slow lately. Not too many deaths had been taking up my time. As much as I loved that part of my job, I was glad I had more time to focus on the group and forming relationships with the ladies. The line between being professional and being human was getting fuzzier every day. Once it became the least bit unclear, there was no turning back. Boundaries had been crossed and I wasn't willing to uncross them. I enjoyed it too much on this side of the ethical code. What would it hurt anyway?

As long as I acted with the best interest of my clients, I didn't see anything wrong with crossing the lines every now and then. It sure made life a lot more interesting. I grabbed my tote bag, shoved my arms through the sleeves of my winter coat and headed for the parking lot.

The drive didn't seem to take as long as it had before. Bluebird Lane appeared after a long car ride driven by thoughts and memories. Not fear. I would never allow fear to dictate my life again. It was time I started living. As I turned off the ignition, I took a long breath before exhaling it. It was only then that I wished I had brought Tim with me. What was there to be scared of? I was not allowing any more of my life to be stolen. Today started a new chapter. Today, I was in control.

Once out of my car, I started down the paved path to her door. They all looked the same, but I remembered which door belonged to her. The last visit was etched into my memory. I had wanted to return since the day we left. One last deep breath before my knuckles hit the wooden door. "Come in." Without hesitation, I opened the door and stepped inside. She was sitting in the same navy recliner with a book in her lap, the TV off. Frozen, I stood as I tried to catch my breath enough to find words. "Do I know you?" Her eyes squinted up at me.

I nodded my head as I tried to speak. "Yes, you do...I'm..." The pressure behind my eyes pushed out tears. "It's me, Gram, it's Valerie."

Her squinted eyes widened. "Valerie? No, that can't be. Valerie? My baby girl?"

I walked over to her chair and dropped to my knees. "Yes, Gram, it's really me. I've missed you so much."

"Valerie? But Elaine told me you died. She told me I'd never see you again." Her hand covered her mouth as tears moistened her glasses. "Valerie?"

"Yes, Gram, it's really me." I placed my hands on her knees and looked up at her. "Elaine was lying to you. She's the reason I've been away, but I've missed you so much."

"I don't know what to think. Oh, honey, I'm so glad to see you. I've missed you, too. I didn't think I'd ever see you again. Oh, my goodness." She put her hands on top of mine. "Oh, Valerie, you're a gift from God."

"So are you, Gram." I tilted my head to kiss the top of her

hand. The warmth from her frail skin brought comfort to me that I had been missing. She wrapped me in her arms, encasing me in enough love to make up for all of the years we had been apart. She was the one person I regretted leaving and now, after all these years, I get to have her back in my life.

"Tell me about your life, Valerie. How have you been?"

I stood up and found a place to sit on the couch across from her. "I've been good. I went to college and I'm a social worker in a hospital. Work keeps me pretty busy, so there's not a lot of time for much of anything else.

"Do you have a husband? Children?"

My hand went to my necklace. "No, Gram. I do have a nice man that I've been dating. You'd like him. He's funny and kind."

"Well, that's nice. I'm glad you're happy." Her eyes drifted across the room to a picture of my mom and Chad. "Why would Elaine tell me you were dead?"

Gram didn't know the evil my mother was capable of; she only knew how unpleasant it could be if she disobeyed her. I never told her about anything; I didn't want to taint the love she had for her daughter. "I don't know, Gram. I don't think she ever really liked me. Maybe she wished I was dead."

"But I don't understand. Why would she do such a thing? Have you talked to her? I'm sure she'd love to see you."

"No, I don't think that would be a good idea. I think we should keep this between us. I don't want to see mom."

"She probably wouldn't believe me anyway. She thinks I'm senile...and to be fair, I do have my moments."

"We all do, Gram. Being forgetful is normal, don't let her

get to you." I felt my body temperature rise as I imagined what she had been telling my gram. "Does Elaine visit you often?"

"Not really. She sends a nurse in to take care of me, but I don't see her very often. Only on holidays. She drops by for a quick visit and then has to leave. I don't know why she bothers."

"How about Chad? Does he come by?"

"No. I'm not sure the last time I saw him. I know he's very busy with work and I don't mind...he's never been a favorite of mine."

"So, can this be our little secret?"

"If that means you keep coming to visit and you don't disappear again." Gram's smile softened. "I don't want to lose you again."

"I never want to lose you, Gram."

"Oh, honey, you do know I'm an old lady, right?"

Her words felt like a weight on my chest. "I know. As long as you're living, I want you in my life. I never stopped needing you, even after all these years. I always dreamed about being with you again."

"What kept you away? What were you running from?"

I forced a fake smile as I searched for a believable answer.

"Did your mom do something to hurt you? I know she's difficult sometimes. Was it her you were trying to escape from?"

I nodded my head, not knowing what else to say. "Yeah, she wasn't very supportive...I didn't want to be hurt anymore. I didn't know what else to do, so I disappeared. There was no other option at the time."

"I understand. She has gotten meaner as every year passes...so talking with her wouldn't be a good idea." Her eyes drifted away from mine. "I'm sorry she hurt you. I would have tried to make it right for you."

"I know Gram. I just didn't know what to do and I didn't want to upset you. I didn't think it through, I just ran. It was the only way I knew to keep myself safe. As the years passed, I wanted to come back, but I wasn't sure how."

"It's okay, Valerie, I'm just glad you're here now."

I was grateful for Norma's push. Without it, fear would have kept me paralyzed until it was too late. I felt a shift inside my body as more of the broken pieces mended from the love in my life. It was near perfect. The only part missing now was Gabriel. I could only hope he would be as understanding as Gram had been.

"What do you have planned for Christmas?"

"I think Elaine is stopping by. She said something about going out to dinner, but I never know what time she will show up."

"When did she stop making Christmas dinner?"

"Oh, I don't know. It's been like this for a while now. Sometimes she brings Chad, sometimes she's alone."

"Hmmm. Do you think they're happy? Mom and Chad?"

"It's hard to say, but they don't seem to spend as much time together."

Hearing there might be troubles in their relationship brought a smile to my face. I had always imagined nothing could come between their love. The bond they had when I was at home was the thing that came between my mother and me. There was nothing I could say to make her listen to me, no matter what he did. And for what? For her to lose me? For me to lose contact with my gram? It was all just a disaster waiting to crumble. I should have known perfect couldn't last forever when it was all based on lies and manipulation. "That's too bad." I managed to spit out.

"Is it?" Her smile brought me back to my childhood.

My smirk said more than I could have managed.

"It's so nice to have you back. Please make sure you come back."

"You couldn't keep me away...not again. I'm glad you won't be alone for Christmas."

"What are your plans?"

"I think I'll be meeting my boyfriend's mom."

"Oh...that sounds exciting." The sparkle in her eyes took away some of my reservations about it.

"Yeah...or terrifying. This is a first for me...I've never dated before, but Tim is worth it."

"All these years and you've never dated anyone? You've been all alone this whole time?" Her smile faded. "Oh, honey, I'm so sorry your life has been so lonely."

"It's okay, Gram. It wasn't that bad. I keep pretty busy at work and I have a cat." Crap. He must be hungry. The urgency of this visit made me forget everything else. I pulled my cell phone out of my jacket pocket to find three missed calls and two texts. I hadn't told anyone where I was going. "Speaking of the little guy, I have to get going, so I can feed him dinner." My mind went to the missed calls and my heart raced as I stood up to put my coat on. A slight tremble in my hands made it impossible to zip it. I snapped the top and bottom buttons to keep it closed before entering the frigid air.

"I love you, Gram. I am so happy to have you back in my life. Oh, before I forget, can I have your phone number? You want to hear something funny? I picked up the phone before I came and dialed your old number...I guess there are some things we never forget."

I punched the numbers into my contacts as she rattled them off. "I'm glad, too. See you soon?"

"I'll be looking forward to it." I closed the door behind me as I dialed my voicemail. All three messages were Tim. I hadn't ever had someone worried enough to leave me so many messages. In my car, I sent him a quick text letting him know I was alright and on my way home. I wished I had given him a key so he could feed Gabriel. He was who I really would have to answer to when I arrived home late. Poor guy.

CHAPTER THIRTY-FOUR

Valentine's Day was never a day I cared for. Being perpetually single does that to a person. This year, though, Tim told me he would change my outlook on the day, forever. The one thing that came to mind was not something I was ready for, or at least it was not something I ever thought would happen. Meeting his mom at Christmas was not nearly as bad as I had imagined. It was easy to see where Tim got his charm. She was eager to please, but not too pushy. Whatever this surprise was, he said his mom approved. That alone was enough to cause my thoughts to spin out of control.

All the commercialism from the day made me as nauseous as the smell of cheap drug store chocolates. We'd only been dating a few months; it was way too soon to go the route my mind was taking me. And if he thought the day a baby flew around with a diaper shooting arrows into schmucks was a good day for it...I already knew my answer. I could hear my gram's voice reminding me it was the thought that counts...but this seemed as though there wasn't any thought at all. I mean, how many people get engaged on Valentine's Day? That can't take that much thought. Years of cynicism took way longer to snap out of than I would have imagined.

I was able to make it through the day without a special flower delivery at work, and now the moment Tim had me prepare for all day was finally here. A quick knock on the door caught Gabriel's attention before I knew where the sound was coming from. The door swung open, with Tim standing with the usual large, white box filled with pizza. No flowers, no candy, no oversized stuffed animal. So far, there didn't seem to be anything to worry about. "Happy Valentine's Day." My voice was as chipper as I could manage.

"Really? I thought you didn't celebrate the day of love."

"But I thought you did. You've had me wondering all day what you have up your sleeve. I thought the least I could do was greet you properly."

"Nope, not today. I changed my plans. Today is just another amazing day with my love. I love you every day, Val, I don't need a special holiday to show you."

"So...no surprise? You had me on my toes all day...for nothing?"

"Not nothing. I am respecting your wishes. Did I do something wrong? Should I have disobeyed you and done something cheesy? Damn it."

"No. Not at all. Pizza and murder shows with you sounds like a perfect day. Thank you for loving me enough to listen."

"I do love you. My goal is to help you see the beauty in

letting me spoil you some Valentine's Day, but I will be patient."

"That could take years."

"That's okay, I have time."

I didn't notice how big the smile on my face had grown until Tim traced it with his index finger. "I guess that's the best gift you could give me; an endless supply of your time."

"Sounds perfect to me." He pulled me into a hug, and the warmth and safety of his arms were just what I had been missing. "I love you, Val."

"Love you back. Want to eat? I'm starving."

"There she is. My awkward little lady." His eyes met mine.

"Ouch. Good thing you're so cute, or you might have just gotten yourself into trouble." His head fell back as his laughter filled the room.

Tim carried the pizza and plates into the living room and flipped the TV on to the Oxygen channel. I brought a six-pack of cold beer in and settled into my spot on the couch. "You know, you had me worried all day that you were going to..."

"Going to what?" His question was muffled by a mouth full of pizza.

"Umm...going to...send me flowers at work."

He raised his eyebrows. "What were you really going to say?" The color of his face matched the sauce on the pizza.

My cheeks matched his as I tried to find my way out of the conversation I started. "Oh, nothing. You just had me nervous about what you had planned, that's all."

"What did you think I had planned?"

"I told you...flowers."

"I don't believe you. Please, just tell me what made you so nervous?"

The heat in my cheeks had spread to my ears and down my neck. "It's dumb...I shouldn't have said anything."

"Well, now, you have to."

"This pizza hits the spot tonight."

"Val."

"Ahh...I thought you were going to propose tonight." My eyes went to the TV to avoid eye contact.

"Hmmm. And that made you nervous? So, you don't want to marry me?"

"I didn't say that. I guess I was just nervous you were going to do it on one of my least favorite days. I guess the real issue wasn't the question, only the timing. And now I've made things super uncomfortable."

"So, if I were to ask you on any other day, you'd say yes?"

"What?"

"If I asked you to marry me any other day, your answer would be yes?"

"You'll have to wait and see. I can't answer a hypothetical question...not that one anyway."

"Noted."

The silence in the room was only masked by the sounds of our chewing. I wished there was a way to rewind the night and take back everything I had said. Tim seemed hurt by what I said or didn't say. "I'm sorry I'm so awkward."

"You're not the awkward one, I'm sorry I made you worry all day for nothing."

"I didn't mean to hurt your feelings. I wasn't thinking."

"You didn't hurt my feelings. I'm good." His expression didn't match his words.

He turned up the TV as an episode of Snapped came on. I nuzzled up next to him and pulled the blanket off the back of the couch and covered up. His arm rested on my hip as I placed my head on his chest. The episode played without conversation, and I wasn't sure how to get the normalcy back. I knew talking wasn't the way to fix it, so I let my mind wander to every what-if possibility.

At midnight Tim turned off the TV. "It's not Valentine's Day anymore. I think it's safe to go to bed now."

I sat up and stretched as a yawn escaped. "Okay, I am pretty tired."

Tim took my hand to keep me from leaving the room. "Umm...can you just wait a minute?"

After another stretch and yawn, when I opened my eyes, Tim was on one knee in front of me. My heart raced, the sound from my heartbeat echoing in my ears. "So, like I said, it's February 15th now, not Valentine's Day, and, umm...I love you, Val, more than I've ever loved anyone. We're the perfect pair. Your sarcasm and my quick wit...or the other way around...but, anyway, Val, will you marry me?"

"Oh, my God. You sneaky little..."

"Hey, I listened, I was patient...so? What's your answer to the not so hypothetical question?"

"Yes...I'd be happy to be your awkward wife." Unable to fully comprehend what just happened, I held out my shaking hand as Tim slipped the ring on. "Oh, it's beautiful."

"It was my gram's ring. My mom gave it to me after she

met you at Christmas. She knew right away you are the one I want to spend the rest of my life with."

"Wow...you've been planning this since then?"

"Val, I love you and I can't imagine my life without you in it. I know how important it is to live in the moment. Why wait when everything is so right?"

"This is why you were so...strange earlier? Because I read your mind?" I held out my hand to help him up off his knee. He leaned over and kissed me.

"Yeah...I was nervous; it was still bad timing. I've been a nervous wreck for months trying to plan something when I just figured you wouldn't want anything fancy. The best bet was to do it in private...but I also knew you hate Valentine's Day...but I just couldn't wait any longer."

"Fair enough. We can celebrate our anniversary on fifty percent off chocolate day. That's a much better day."

"And this is why I love you."

CHAPTER THIRTY-FIVE

A knock on my office door made me jump, causing my elbow to hit my cup of coffee, spilling it all over the files on my desk. *Shit.* I placed tissues on the mess and pushed the files to the floor to save them from any further damage. "Just a minute." *Who the hell could be at the door?* I kicked the files into a pile and did a quick scan of my office. It was in the normal state of chaos, not suitable for company. "Who is it?" My hand went to the door handle as I waited for the response.

"Val? It's Jane."

"Jane?" I opened the door to confirm her identity. "How did you get down here?" I stuck my head out into the hall to look around. She was the only one in the hall. "Hang on, let me get my stuff and we can go upstairs to talk."

"No. I want to talk down here, that's why I'm here." Jane's voice was quiet.

"I don't usually meet with people down here."

"It's okay, I don't mind. Besides, I want some privacy."

I hesitated as long as I could before I held the door open. "Okay, but just this once. When did you get back? Has it been 90 days already?"

"Time flies, huh?" She sat on the edge of the chair in front of my desk to avoid the pile stacked in it.

I walked over behind her and took the books and files out of the chair and placed them on top of the bookshelf next to my desk. "Sorry, Jane, people don't usually come down here." I made my way to my desk and picked up the files I had just tossed on the floor before I sat down. "So... how was it? How did it go?"

"Pretty good. I made it the whole time...and I feel pretty good." She pushed herself back into the chair.

"That's great, Jane. I'm proud of you." Thoughts of the conversation with Seth lingered in my mind.

"Thanks. I learned a lot about myself."

"I'm glad to hear that. I think it's good to take a step back and find ourselves every once in a while."

"Yeah. I know the situations I need to stay out of. I know I don't want to use again...it was hell getting clean...I never want to do that again." She crossed her legs and played with her shoe as it dangled over her knee.

"Where will you be living? I can't imagine you'd want to..."

Her eyes squinted up at me. "Want to what?"

"Oh, nothing. Just being nosey. But, if you need help finding a place to live, I could help."

"I think it'll be okay to go home. I mean, Seth stopped using, too. I just want to start over." She shifted in her chair.

"Have you talked with Seth yet? About coming home?"

"No... I thought it would be better to just surprise him...I'm sure he missed me."

"Sounds like you are all set. So, what can I help you with?" I smiled to mask the frustration in my voice.

"Well, that's why I'm here. You were my first stop. We worked with the twelve-step program...and I'm stuck on the fifth step. I hope you can help me with it."

"Twelve steps, like in AA? What can I do to help?" My guard went up as the conversation I had with Seth came back to me. I wasn't sure I wanted to be alone with her, at least not down here.

"Well, the fifth step is where I have to admit my wrongs to God, myself and another person. When I thought about this thing I need to clear up, I knew you were the one I had to tell."

My mouth went dry as I waited for her to tell me what I didn't want to hear. "Okay...I'm ready." I hoped she couldn't hear the tremor in my voice.

"Well..." She paused as she played with the sleeve of her sweatshirt. "The worst thing I did involves something I did...to Carmen." Her eyes looked up to meet mine.

I took a deep breath in and hesitated before I exhaled it. "Okay."

"And, well...the reason I got so mad at you about asking so many questions...and stuff...is because...I... umm." She paused and closed her eyes. "I did it."

"Did what?" My breathing increased as I held my lips tight together.

"I did it. I killed Carmen."

"But Jane, why? Why would you want to hurt your own child?"

"She just had a way of getting under my skin...and when I found out she was pregnant, I knew I had to get rid of her...before Seth got rid of me. So, in a way, I guess it was self-defense."

"Self-defense? How?"

"Well, if I didn't kill her, he would have killed me." Her eyes stayed wide open as they stared into me.

"How did you do it? I mean, the police thought it looked like a suicide."

"That was my plan. I didn't want anyone to know. I crushed up a bunch of my pills and put it in some ginger ale. She told me she wasn't feeling well, so I knew she would drink it because she always did when she was a little girl. After she passed out it didn't look like it was working fast enough, so I took a razor blade and cut her wrists." Her eyes stared ahead as she waited for my response.

"And the note you showed me?"

"I wrote it and made her sign it before she passed out. Well, I used her hand to sign it. She wasn't able to do it herself."

"Does anyone else know what you did?" I rubbed the bridge of my nose.

"Just you and God." Her affect stayed flat.

"And, you're not telling anyone else?"

"Nope."

There was no way I would ever understand her logic, and the more I questioned her, I knew she would stop talking.

"Okay. I guess I understand. What is it you would like my help with?"

"I don't need any help. I just needed to tell someone the truth. That's how I get to the next step."

The expression left my face as I sat across from her. "Do you want me to help you tell the police?"

"No. I'm not telling anyone else. All it said was I had to tell one person...not the police." She stood up. "I'm done now. I can move on to the sixth step."

"I don't know if it works like that. I think you also have to be held accountable for your actions."

"No. Just tell someone, that's all I needed to do." She walked toward the door. "I'll never repeat it. Not ever."

"Jane...we have group tomorrow; will you be joining us?"

She paused in the doorway. "Maybe. But I'll never admit to what I just told you again. So don't think it's going to be a topic for everyone to lecture me about."

"Of course not. The ladies would love to see you. I know they've been thinking about you." I forced a smile; the sincerity grew as my thoughts raced. The plan started to formulate. I knew what I had to do.

CHAPTER THIRTY-SIX

Tim arrived at my door minutes after I called him. I already knew what he was going to say, but I had to tell someone. I locked the door behind him and stood with my back against the door. "You'll never guess what just happened."

"Hmmm...let me see...Jane is back in town." He raised his right eyebrow as he put his left hand to his chin.

"How..."

"I'm a detective, Val... I just know things...and I saw her leaving the hospital when I got here."

I felt my eyes widened. "She didn't see you, did she?"

"No, I was still in my car when she got on the bus. Why? What's going on?" He rested his back against the corner of the bookshelf.

"She just confessed to killing Carmen. She told me how and why...but she said she won't tell anyone else. What do I do with this? Seth was telling the truth."

"There's nothing we can do, not without a body. I mean,

if she's not willing to make a confession to law enforcement, we can't touch her. The case was closed...without her talking, no one is going to listen to what you have to say." His eyes found mine as I stared back at him. "Val, I want to help, but there really isn't anything we can do."

"I know." Defeat shifted to revenge. "I just had to tell you...I'm not crazy...I knew all along, I just had it a little mixed up."

"I know, Val. I'm sorry. I know how much this case has been weighing on you. I wish it were easier to get people to pay for what they do, but sometimes it doesn't work that way." He walked toward me and took my hand.

"It's such a backward system. You know, if your guys just did their job in the first place, there might still be a body and then there'd be a case." I regretted my choice of words as soon as I heard them. "I'm sorry, Tim...I'm just pissed off. I didn't mean to be such a bitch."

"Hey, I get it. I know they do things half-assed. The easy way, but to be fair, it looked like a suicide. I wished it were different."

"I know." My shoulders rose and fell with a sigh. "I love you. It means a lot that you got here so quickly. It feels nice to know you're there when I need you."

"I love you, too, Val. I really am sorry."

After Tim left, I pulled out the *Village News* from after Carmen's death, where it prematurely ruled her death a suicide. It was like everyone was working together to make it as easy as possible for people to get away with crimes. I tossed the paper back into the drawer and wiggled my mouse to wake up the screen on my computer. I logged on to Facebook under my fake account and searched for Jane's profile. I scrolled through her timeline, looking for a reason she was so evil. Nothing stuck out. I sent a friend request and clicked on her list of friends. As I looked through the list of people she knew, I canceled the request. I didn't want anything to connect me to her, even under a fake account. From Facebook, it didn't appear she had too many close friends. That made sense for the Jane I knew.

After looking at the same content, I knew I needed to get away from the screen. There was no new information I would be able to get from there, and even if I had found something, I didn't know what it would do. What needed to happen next was not something that could happen online.

I picked up my phone and dialed Jeanine's number. As I waited for her to answer, a calm came over me. "Hey, this is Val...I'm not feeling well...I've got a migraine and these lights are killing me."

With her blessing, I picked up my tote bag, put on my jacket and locked the door behind me. Out in the parking lot, I tossed my bag on the front seat and got into my car. After I put it in gear, it started to drive me, as though it was on autopilot on a familiar road. A road I had been on not too long ago. When I parked my car, I was back in the driveway at Seth's. It appeared to be quiet, meaning Jane hadn't made it to her destination yet. Just as I hoped.

I knocked on the door and waited while I heard Seth mumble, "Just a minute."

"Hi, Seth, I wanted to drop off some money from the last time we met."

"You already paid me."

"Yeah, I know, but I have a couple more questions. This time, about something else. Can I come in?"

He scratched his head. "How much?"

"We can talk about that inside."

He held the door open for me and I found my way to his kitchen as I waited for him to follow. "Okay, so what do you want to know...and what's in it for me?"

"I have $200 for you and all I need from you is some pills, maybe fentanyl."

"Are you crazy? That shit will kill you." He crossed his arms tight against his chest.

"Oh, it's not for me. I have a patient that needs some for pain control, but we're not able to write the prescription. You'd be helping an old lady, and you get $200, that sounds like a win-win to me."

"Why do you think I have any of that shit? Why come here?"

"I know you could use the money and I know you know where I could find some."

"I told you last time, I'm trying to get clean." He uncrossed his arms and crossed them again tighter. "Is this a setup? Did you bring the cops?"

"No. I swear. I could get in just as much trouble as you. I just want to...help this client of mine. I hate to see her in pain and no one will listen to her. Can't you just help?"

"I don't know who sells that shit anymore. And you don't need that, there's plenty of other options to kill the pain." He rubbed his nose with the palm of his hand.

"Well, I really need that. Or at least something as strong. Her pain is unbearable."

"Lady, you're playing with fire. What if she takes too much...and, you know...dies?" He shifted his weight from side to side.

"Don't you worry. She's had it before...they just won't give her anymore. She knows what she's doing." I pulled the cash out of my pocket and set it on the counter. "Do we have a deal?"

"It's going to take more than that." His eyes focused on the cash. "Make it...ah...$300, and we have a deal."

"I only brought $200. That's all the cash she had. Do we have a deal?"

Seth scratched his head, his eyes never leaving the cash. "Hang on." He left the kitchen and returned with a small cardboard box. He set it on the table and took pill bottles out and set them on the table, shaking each one before he set them down. He took one of the amber-colored plastic bottles and twisted off the cap and emptied the contents into the palm of his hand. Tiny white pills filled his cupped hand, he closed his fingers around them. "$200 will get you ten of these. That's all. If you want more, it'll cost you more." He counted out ten pills and slipped them into a sandwich bag. "These are potent, I'm not sure what they are, but they're the strongest thing I've got. A buddy brought them here after one of his customers OD'd."

"How many did it take...to OD?" I felt my eyebrow lift as I waited for his answer.

"I don't know. Jesus, I just know these aren't a joke. These can kill if they're in the wrong hands. It's on you if your friend dies, not me. I won't admit anything." He swung the plastic bag between his fingers.

I took a step closer and grabbed the bag on the final swing. "I understand. It's our secret." I winked and nodded my head in the direction of the cash. "So hypothetically speaking...if someone were to take all ten of these, they'd..."

"Be dead. Yeah, and it's on your hands, not mine."

"Got it. Thanks for helping out a friend." I folded up the bag and placed it in my jacket pocket and walked to the door. "Oh, and just so you know, Jane is on her way here. She stopped by to see me today."

"Jesus Christ. I don't have time for her shit today." He ran his fingers through his greasy hair.

"Stay strong." I smiled as I walked to my car.

CHAPTER THIRTY-SEVEN

Maggie and Norma arrived together for group and found seats next to each other. Sonya strolled in a few minutes late and found a seat next to the other ladies. I looked down at my watch, there was still time for Jane to show up. She'd never been on time before; I hoped this time wouldn't be any different. "So, Jane is out of rehab and seems to be doing well. I reminded her about group, so she might show up, but we can start without her."

"Ah, man. I had a lot to talk about today...I'm not sure I want to be interrupted if she decides to show up." Sonya sat back in her chair with her legs crossed and let out a heavy sigh.

"Is everything okay? We have time to listen, right ladies?" I leaned into the circle to check their facial expressions.

"Oh, yes, dear, I've got plenty of time." Norma's smile faded as concern took over her face. "What's wrong, honey?"

"My life is going to shit. I'm probably going to lose my job and Jimmy is trying to get back together...and everything else just sucks." Tears streamed down her cheeks.

I handed her a box of tissues. "That is a lot to deal with all at once."

"Yeah." She sniffled into the tissue. "Jimmy is the reason I started coming here. He punched me in the stomach when he thought I was pregnant. I knew I didn't want him in my life, but I didn't go through with the protection order...I just didn't have time to deal with it. So, I can't even do anything about it."

"It's not too late to get the protection order. I can help you if you'd like. Just stay after and we can go to the courthouse to get the paperwork." I looked down at my watch to check the time. Maybe Jane wasn't coming after all.

"No, I don't want to deal with it. I don't want to deal with any of it. He doesn't scare me; I just don't want to deal with his bullshit. Like, leave me the fuck alone already. It's my job that's really stressing me out. I can't afford to lose it...I've been there too long. I don't want to learn something new."

"Why do you think you're going to lose your job?" Maggie tilted her head to the side.

"Because my fucken boss said if I don't fuck him, he's going to find someone who will."

"You can't be serious. That's against the law." Maggie looked over at me. "How can he do that?"

"Well, you are right, it is against the law. He can't fire you for that. Have you told anyone else about this yet? HR?"

Sonya shook her head. "I haven't told anyone. Honestly, I was considering it...but then with Jimmy back in the picture...it's just too much."

"Considering sleeping with your boss?" Judgment slipped out with my question.

"Yeah." Sonya blew her nose. "He's cute and I thought, why not? I might get a promotion. It seemed like a win-win."

"So, Jimmy is the real problem?" Maggie took over for me.

Sonya nodded her head. "I guess, yeah."

"What if you tell your boss about Jimmy? Tell him you need him to take care of Jimmy and you'll take care of him." Maggie winked at her.

"Hmm. That just might work." Sonya's eyes lit up. "Best of both worlds."

I felt my eyes roll and bit my bottom lip. Something felt off with Sonya, more than what she was saying. The sound of the door opening pulled me from my thoughts. Jane entered the room and took a seat next to Norma. "Hi, Jane. I'm glad you could make it."

"Sorry I'm late, I missed the first bus."

"That's alright, we were just helping Sonya out with a dilemma." Norma turned and patted Jane's knee. "It's so good to see you."

"Thanks. I'm glad to be back. I learned a lot while I was away."

"I'm so happy, dear." Norma looked around the circle. "We're all happy for you."

"Yeah, it's great." Sonya picked up her phone and looked at the screen. "Oh, it looks like I got to get going. I've got some things to take care of at work."

Maggie giggled and coughed to hide it. "Have fun, Sonya."

"Oh, I plan on it." Sonya winked at Maggie and left the room.

Norma and Maggie looked at each other and had a silent conversation. "We've got to get going, too." Maggie stood up and held out her hand for Norma. "It was nice seeing you again, Jane."

After the women left, it was just Jane and me. "I'm glad you came, Jane."

"Doesn't look like anyone else was. I thought you said they missed me."

"Oh, they did, they were just busy today. I'm sure it's nothing personal. What are your plans for lunch?"

"I don't know, I hadn't thought that far ahead. I don't have any plans for the next few days. I was going to go stop by and say hi to the nurses that took care of me, but that's it."

"Want to go get lunch? My treat?"

Jane looked up at me. "Lunch, not lecture?"

"Of course." I smiled to help convince her. "I'm going to grab a drink at the cafeteria before we leave, do you want something?"

"Yeah, sure. I'll take an orange juice."

"Alright, I'll meet you in the lobby in fifteen minutes? Is that enough time for your reunion?" I looked down at my watch.

"Yeah, that should be enough time." She stood up and walked down the hall to the med-surg unit.

When she turned the corner down the long hall, I went to my office and got my tote bag and jacket. I put my hand in my pocket and felt the crinkling of the plastic bag under my fingers. My heart raced as I inhaled a deep breath and exhaled it slowly to remain calm. I locked my door behind me and walked up the stairs to the cafeteria. At the cooler, I grabbed two bottles of orange juice and a water and swiped my badge to pay. Before I left the room, I pulled a spoon out of the basket by the napkins and tucked it into my jacket pocket.

I looked around the room, it felt like everyone was watching me. I closed my eyes and shook my head. I made my way to the single-stall bathroom down the hall from the conference room and locked the door behind me. I pushed up my jacket's sleeves and took out the plastic bag and spoon from my pocket. I pulled a pair of purple latex gloves out of the box on the wall by the mirror and put them on. I put a paper towel on the counter and dumped out a few of the pills. With the remaining pills in the bag, I took the spoon and started to crush them.

In just a few presses of the spoon against the pills, they turned to powder. I opened one of the bottles of orange juice and poured some out into the sink and carefully guided the powder into the drink. I returned the cap and gave it a shake and watched as the powder dissolved. I placed the remaining pills back into the bag and repeated the steps. Once the lid was back on, I gave it another shake and held the bottle up to the light. The particles slowly blended into the liquid.

I took a damp paper towel and washed the outside of the bottle and then dried it and placed it in my tote bag. A knock on the door made my heart leap into my throat. "Just a minute." I pulled out a few more paper towels and washed down the counter and wrapped the spoon and plastic bag into the lump of soggy white paper. I took a few more paper towels out and placed them on top of the trash, pressing it down with my gloves still on. I took the gloves off and wrapped them up in more paper towels and tossed them into the trash can. I flushed the toilet, pulled down my sleeves, put my tote bag on my shoulder and picked up the two drinks off the counter, and exited the bathroom. There was no one waiting on the other side of the door. I must have taken too much time.

Jane was waiting for me when I arrived in the lobby. "I thought you stood me up." She stood up and walked toward me.

A nervous laugh escaped. "No, sorry, just had to make a quick phone call." I handed her the orange juice. "I'm starving, how about you?"

"Yeah, I haven't eaten yet today." She rubbed her stomach over her coat. She opened the orange juice and took a drink.

"Want to grab a pizza? Lawrenceville pizza is always pretty good."

"Yeah, that sounds good. I haven't had pizza in a while."

The pizza place was only a five-minute ride from the hospital. I turned the radio on to discourage small talk. Jane sang along with Adele and then OneRepublic, only stopping when the radio shut off with the car. "What kind of pizza do you like? We can get whatever you want." When I got out of the car, I looked back at my tote bag on the floor of the back seat, where I had placed it before we left.

"I love Hawaiian, no one else does, though." She shut the door and walked with me into the restaurant.

"I like it. I order that every once in a while." I held the

door open for Jane. Once inside, I ordered a large Hawaiian. No drinks. We found a booth in the back, away from the window facing the parking lot, and waited for our pizza.

"Oh, look at that rock." Jane grabbed my hand and held it up. "When did that happen?"

"Just a few days ago." I pulled my hand out of her grip.

"That hot cop? Or some other guy?"

"The hot cop."

"Well, that escalated quickly." She laughed. "I'm happy for you. He seems like a nice guy...but I don't think you can ever really trust a cop. At least that's been my experience."

"Thanks. He's pretty great." It was easier to ignore than to engage. "So, tell me, how was it going home?"

"It's a little rocky. Seth said he doesn't want me there, but it's my place, too. I think it'll just take a little time." She picked up a napkin and twisted the end into a point.

I picked up my jacket off the seat next to me and felt the pocket. "I left my phone out in the car. I'm expecting a call from work. I'll be right back." When I got out to my car, I put on my thin, black driving gloves and picked up my tote bag. I pulled out the orange juice, gave it a quick shake, and replaced it with the one Jane took a drink out of. I took my phone out of my bag and brought the other juice with me. Before entering the restaurant, I tossed the bottle into the trash.

The pizza was on the table when I returned and Jane was already eating a piece. "Didn't think you'd mind if I dug in."

"No, not at all. There's nothing as good as hot pizza." I placed the phone on the table and put a slice onto my plate. The conversations stopped while we ate. I looked up at the

TV on the wall playing the recap of the weekend sports. I had no idea what I was looking at, but it gave me an excuse to not make eye contact. I felt like a farmer getting ready to take my cow to slaughter. The less chance I had at getting attached, or sensing her emotions, the more likely I was to finish the *job*.

Jane took the last slice off the tray and took a bite. "You didn't want this, did you?"

"No, it's all yours." I pushed my plate away from me and refocused my attention on the TV. When she was finished, I picked up our plates and the pizza pan and we walked out together. I picked up my phone and looked down at the screen. "Oh, no, it looks like I have to get back to work. I won't be able to bring you home. Do you want me to drop you off at the bus stop down the road?"

"Yeah, sure." She got into the car and took a drink out of the orange juice. I held my breath as her sip turned to a gulp. "I guess I was thirsty."

I pulled out of the parking lot and drove down the road to the bus stop. "Sorry I can't take you home."

"It's alright, it's not that cold out today." She opened her door and started to get out of the car.

"Jane. Don't forget your juice." I pointed at the bottle, careful not to touch it.

"Oops, I almost forgot. Thanks for the pizza." She shut the door behind her and made her way to the bench at the bus stop. As I drove away, I saw her take another long drink from the bottle. I wanted to watch and make sure it was enough, but I didn't want to be there in case it was.

CHAPTER THIRTY-EIGHT

My office phone rang. When I looked at the number, I saw it was Tim. "Hey, Tim."

"Val, I, ah...I have to tell you something."

"What's wrong? Are you okay?"

"Yeah, I'm fine. I have some bad news, I'm afraid."

"Oh, no."

"Val, I was just called to the bus stop by Lawrenceville Pizza...and...it was for an unresponsive female."

"Okay." My heart was turning upside down in my chest.

"It was Jane. She was pronounced dead at the scene."

"Oh, my God. That's awful."

"Yeah, I know. It's such a shame. It looks like an overdose, but we won't know until the autopsy."

"Wow. I thought she was clean."

"You just never know when a bad day will hit."

"No, I guess you don't."

ACKNOWLEDGMENTS

I want to thank my family for their patience and support during my writing process. For listening to me talk through different characters and scenes and encouraging me along the way. To my children; every dream I achieve, I do it for you. To my husband; I am forever grateful for your unconditional love and for believing in me, even when I can't.

I want to thank the ladies from the senior center that encouraged me along the way. You helped keep me focused. To the ladies from the writing group; I have enjoyed traveling alongside you in your writing journey. Your enthusiasm and love helped keep me motivated. We are lucky ducks.

Many thanks to the people who helped Boundaries come to life:

Victoria Cooper for the amazing cover. Her work can be found at Facebook.com/VictoriaCooperArt.

Proofreading by the Page: Samantha Wiley, Rachel Pugh, and Anne Dailey for editing and proofreading.

Diane Abesse for the first round of edits and beta reading. Jill Nichols, Robin Locke, and Sarah Hart for beta reading.

To the victims of child abuse and domestic violence who become survivors; I believe you. You are stronger than you think. You are not alone. Never stop believing in yourself. You are worth so much more. Take time to love yourself first; you won't regret it.

Thank you to the readers. Without you, my characters would never have any fun! Your honest feedback is always appreciated and helps improve my craft. Reviews help other readers as much as they help me. Please consider leaving one.

RESOURCES

If you or someone you know is struggling, please know there is help.

Domestic Violence Hotline
www.thehotline.org
1-800-799-7233
National Suicide Prevention Lifeline
www.suicidepreventionlifeline.org
1-800-273-8255
Child Abuse Hotline
1-800-4-A-CHILD
National Alliance on Mental Illness (NAMI)
www.nami.org
1-800-950-NAMI (6264)

ABOUT THE AUTHOR

Jessica Aiken-Hall, author of her award-winning memoir, *The Monster That Ate My Mommy* lives in New Hampshire with her husband, three children, and three dogs. She is a survivor of child abuse and domestic violence and is a fierce advocate. Her mission is to help others share their story.

She has a master's degree in Mental Health Counseling, with over a decade of experience as a social worker. She is also a Reiki Master and focuses her attention on healing.

When she is not writing, she enjoys listening to Tom Petty, walking along the beach, looking at the moon, and watching murder shows.

To follow what she's doing next check out http://www.jessicaaikenhall.com.